THE BEGINNING OF FOREVER

THE BEAUMONT SERIES - NEXT GENERATION

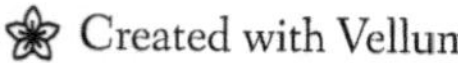 Created with Vellum

THE BEAUMONT SERIES

THE BEAUMONT SERIES READING ORDER

Prequels:

Forever Mason

Finding My Way

Forever My Girl

My Everything

My Unexpected Forever

Finding My Forever

12 Days of Forever

My Kind of Forever

Forever Our Boys

Holding Onto Forever

My Unexpected Love

Chasing My Forever

Peyton & Noah

Fighting For Our Forever

A Beaumont Family Christmas

Fourth Down

Give Me Forever

Everything For Love
The Beginning of Forever

PEYTON

The four of us enter the fertility clinic. Noah holds the door open for Elle and me, and Ben brings up the rear. Everyone in the waiting room stares, and I can only imagine what they're thinking—here come the swingers. It would be laughable if I hadn't read a book about swingers and how one ended up pregnant, which was a major no-no according to the pact or contract each person signed. As much as I hate to admit it, the story was a page turner. Mostly in the sense I had to know what the hell was going to happen, and the sex scenes were hot. I made Noah try a few of them out. He was game at first until shit turned a bit freaky and he asked if I wasn't happy in our relationship. Talk about hurting his feelings and embarrassing myself in one fell swoop. Noah apologized and offered to read it with me, but I declined and deleted the book. I didn't need to know how it ended.

Still, I can't help but wonder what the people in this room are thinking when they see the four of us walk in. The guys take a seat while Elle and I go to check in. What we're doing is unconventional, but on par with how our lives are.

"Hello," I say when we get to the counter. "I'm Peyton Westbury and this is my sister, Elle Miller. We have a consultation today."

The receptionist smiles, types, and then hands us each a clipboard to fill out. "Are Noah and Ben here as well?"

We nod.

"Great. We'll call them back shortly."

"For what?" Elle asks.

"A sample," she says.

"Ben shoots blanks," Elle says. I have to cover my mouth to stifle a laugh. What Ben went through isn't funny, and I don't mean to laugh, except he and Elle crack jokes about it all the time. They're comfortable with the comedic relief and they need to see we're laughing with them. "His spunk is already on reserve."

"Elle . . ." I grit my teeth as I say her name. She looks at me and shrugs. She doesn't like the "words" as she calls them. They're clinical and too scientific for her.

The receptionist probably wishes she stayed home instead of dealing with the likes of us. She goes back to her computer and presses a few more keys and then nods. "Yes, I see that now. Okay, we'll call Noah back shortly."

I thank her and drag my sister away.

Elle sits down next to Ben. It's nice to see them on the same page, finally. They've both struggled with acceptance —Elle having a famous father and Ben being an outsider, their careers, and finding their footing when one has felt unequal in their relationship. Their break—as Elle calls it— thankfully was short-lived, and now we're planning their wedding. Actually, it's a vow renewal since these two got hitched in a hospital room and then paid the nurse off to allow them some "alone time" in the room. I don't even want to know how many health code violations my sister and her husband broke that day.

"The receptionist said they're going to call you back for a sample," I tell Noah.

"You're going to jack off to porn and dump your seed into a cup," Ben says, as if the room isn't filled with other people.

"Jesus Christ," Noah mutters, while I try to hide behind my clipboard. "A little tact."

Ben laughs and man slaps Noah on his shoulder. Maybe this wasn't the best idea I've ever had, but I thought in some odd way, it would be fun for us to do this together. Well, mostly Elle and me. I know the last thing Noah wants is to have to make another deposit into a cup, among other things. He's already gone for testing once to see where the issue of infertility is. He's definitely not the issue. It's all me and all a result of the car accident. The eggs are there, but the scarring I have is too much work for the egg and sperm to meet.

And then there's the question of whether I can even carry a baby.

Sigh.

We've done all the research on IVF, the side effects, the pain and agony, the hope and despair. I've gone back to counseling to help with what I'm feeling—the hopelessness and failures as a woman and a wife—the burden I've put on my shoulders and on Noah. He doesn't like to see me hurt or in pain, and yet that's what I'm going to be in, no matter what.

I want to carry our baby in my womb. I know it may not be possible, but I have to try. If this fails . . . if my body betrays me, we'll look for a surrogate. It's not what I want though, especially since it won't be my sister, and I'm having a hard time accepting it may be my only option.

A nurse comes out, stares at the clipboard in her hand, and calls Noah's name without even looking up. It's easy to see she's done this a time or two and could be tired of the redundancy. Or maybe I'm looking too deeply. For all I know, she's having a bad day and wants to go back to the comfort of her home. Like me.

Noah groans. I squeeze his hand in a silent thank you. Men look at us. At him. They recognize Noah and my heart sinks. Someone will undoubtedly Tweet or X this and everyone will know we're struggling. Except it's me; Noah isn't. His swimmers are strong and ready for the job. Today, we'll find out if my eggs are willing to party with his sperm. It's the best way I can describe it because like Elle, the scientific words annoy me.

If it wasn't for the crash . . .

"Peyton?"

My sister's voice pulls me from a memory I don't want to look back on. I glance at her. "Yeah?"

"You good?"

I nod and offer her a kind smile. She was there when I had the surgery to repair some of the damage to my pelvic area. My sister held my hand throughout my recovery and never left my side. At times, I felt bad for Noah because he wanted to be my constant presence, but Elle was steadfast in her support. I see a side of Elle no one else does. Many think she's selfish and only cares about herself. Those people are wrong. My sister will walk through fire for those she loves. She just has a hard time showing it to outsiders.

For as long as I can remember, I've dreamed of us having babies at the same time, but it won't happen. Sure, they'll be close in age. Maybe weeks apart if we're lucky.

If I'm lucky.

Elle's process is going to be the same, yet we both suspect she won't have an issue getting pregnant. Ben had his sperm harvested prior to his surgery and chemotherapy, which was smart of him to do. The doctors will extract her eggs much like they will with mine. We'll both have implantation and then wait.

Still, aside from Noah, this isn't how I pictured becoming a mother. Not sitting in a waiting room with strangers who casually look up from their phones and then at us. I don't need to be a genius to know they're searching the web to confirm their suspicions. Our dad is famous. It's not like we stayed out of the spotlight. My husband is famous in the sports world.

It dawns on me as I look at Elle and Ben, that we could very well have a mix-up. My heart races as imaginary scenes play out in my mind. What if the clinic gives me her eggs or puts Ben's sperm with my eggs?

Lord help me.

I look at the people across from us, and then the others along the walls. I take in the posters of pregnant mothers, with the expectant fathers, and partners, trying to get all the wrong thoughts out of my mind. The people here are professionals. It's their job to pay attention to detail. Unfortunately, I catch the gazes of a few people and while everyone in here has the same goal, I feel like I'm being scrutinized.

Elle stands and goes to the counter. I push off the arms of the chair to follow, but Ben puts his hand on my arm and shakes his head slightly. I don't question him. Elle's protective of me and, by default, Ben is as well.

When my sister returns, she reaches for my hand. "Come on," she says. I stand and allow her to tug me behind her, with Ben following. We're shown into a room . . . *the* room!

"Um—" The walls are painted a muted pink or what could've been mauve when it was the fad of the late eighties and early nineties. The paint desperately needs to be refreshed. On the coffee table, stacks of magazines, some are open showing naked women, while the television displays a pornographic movie.

"It's private," Elle says. "We don't have to watch porn."

I can't believe she's cracking another joke.

"You were feeling a bit uneasy out there," she says. I nod. "So, we're going to wait here until our appointment."

"I'm not sure I want to sit down," I tell her. Ben steps around me and picks up a magazine off the table. I expect Elle to smack him, but she doesn't. My eyes widen at her in a gesture that's meant to ask her what the hell is he doing, yet she ignores me. I'm about to say something, even though he's not my husband. Except when I open my mouth, words fail me. Ben's not looking through the photos. He's turning the magazines over so we don't have to see the covers.

"You're the best," Elle says as she gives him a kiss.

I grab a handful of paper towels and set them on the seat. Elle and Ben do the same. "My mind is going places it shouldn't. Is this the type of room Noah's in? I didn't ask him last time because deep down I don't think I wanted to know about him touching . . ." Nope, not going there. Honestly, they should let wives in with the men, then the process can be enjoyable for both.

Ben nods. "Yep. If I turn the TV on, you're going to see things you wish you hadn't."

"Yeah, let's not. Peyton's having enough of a crisis right now."

She's not wrong. Although is it much different from

reading about it in books? Maybe Noah should read something with me and then we can talk about it, maybe even experiment.

"It's the people," I say. "The stares and then their faces when they realize who we are."

"I'm surprised it bothers you," Elle says.

I shrug. "It normally doesn't, but this is private. I suppose we should've made better arrangements."

"That's on me," Elle says. "I'm sorry, I wasn't thinking. This is the doctor Ben used before his surgery and it made sense for us to come here. I should've asked for something after hours."

"It's fine," I tell her.

The door opens and Noah walks in. His cheeks are red. It's his . . . *face* though, the expression on it, and I immediately regret having my sister and her husband at this meeting. "Hey, did everything—" I cut myself off, unable to ask him if everything went okay. This isn't the first time he's had to leave a sample. This is just the important one.

Noah comes to me and leans down. "Everything went fine." He kisses the spot where my ear and cheek meet, then stands and clears his throat. "Uh, why are you in this room?"

"It's very peopley out there," Elle says.

I'm surprised Ben didn't shout that we wanted to watch porn or something.

"Ah," Noah says. He reaches for my hand and holds it while standing next to me. "The nurse said she'd be in to get us shortly."

"Do you want to sit?" I stand and offer him my seat. He takes it and then pulls me down onto his lap. I nestle into his chest and breathe him in. His familiar scent is a natural aphrodisiac for me. From the time I knew what it was like to feel something for someone, it's always been Noah. Anytime he was near me, his cedarwood after-shave has caused my lady bits to sing, dance, and beg for his attention. I've been attracted to one other person, but it was nothing like this. Noah gives me butterflies. He always has, and I suspect he always will. It's in his eyes and the way he looks at me. It's in his touch, even the subtle ones like when he reaches for my hand at night or grips my hips mid-thrust. Even his voice, when he says my name or calls me babe, can turn me into a wanton woman, willing to stop what I'm doing just to be in his embrace.

Noah rests his hand on my stomach, protecting what's there and not there, yet. There isn't a doubt in my mind he's going to be the most amazing father. It's me who I worry about. The irrational fear I have about the world, life, and society. My therapist assures me I'll be a good mother, but words and actions are different. I already feel like a letdown.

The door opens, and the nurse comes in. She sits down without reservation, making me question her sanity. She knows what goes on in this room and if she thinks for one second men are cleaning up after themselves, she's sorely mistaken.

"I'm Dakota, as I understand it you want to have your consultation together?"

"Yes," Elle says. "We figured we'd save time. Obviously, my sister and I don't need to be on the table at the same time."

"Right, your sister?" The nurse looks at her file. Noah and Ben stifle a hard laugh while I look at Elle, knowing my eyes are bugging out.

"Yeah, she's my twin. Don't you think we look alike?" Elle asks.

Noah can't contain his laughter.

Dakota looks up from her file. She eyes Elle, then me. "I can tell you apart," she says with so much enthusiasm I want to believe her. Teachers we had for years had trouble telling us a part, which Elle used to her advantage. A lot.

"No, you can't," Ben chimes in. "You don't even know them."

Dakota's cheeks redden and briefly I feel sorry for her, but it's obvious—Elle and I are identical twins. Over the years, we've tried to change our looks and have failed. She cut six inches off her hair once and called me while I was at the salon, sitting in the chair, getting six inches cut off mine. We figured, what's the point? The important people in our lives know the difference, and with us living in different states, it's really not an issue.

Until now.

"Well, let's go meet the doctor."

2

NOAH

Nurse Dakota shows us into the office. Dr. Hilda Rock stands and greets us and asks Ben how's he doing. They chat for a bit while Peyton, Elle, and I sit down. The desk in front of us is large and ornate, and I find myself looking at the carvings, knowing in the back of my mind, they aren't what I think they are, but can't help but wonder if I'm staring at wooden vaginas.

"Are those what I think they are?" I whisper into Peyton's ear. She nods. "What the fuck?"

"I know. Elle said she's a good doctor though and . . ." She stops talking when she sits down.

"Elle and Ben, we've already discussed the process, so I'm going to focus on Peyton and Noah," she says. She explains in detail the process my wife is about to go through. Each time I hear the word shot, I want to pick her up and carry her out of the room. Something as natural as carrying a child shouldn't be this painful or heartbreaking. Ever since we started this journey, it's been so hard seeing the boxes of pregnancy tests only for them to be negative, hearing her cry at night when she thinks I'm asleep—my wife shouldn't have to go through this. No woman should.

I'm thankful doctors like Dr. Rock exists, even though the costs are abhorrent and not covered by health insurance, which is another bone of contention with me. Medical assistance that supports a woman's right to have a child should be covered. Right down to the last penny.

She opens a chart but doesn't look at anything in there. "Peyton, I've gone over the records sent from the specialist you saw in Portland. I don't see anything about Clomid. Did you want to try this route first?"

Peyton shakes her head. "I tried, but the side effects made me ill," she tells her. "To the point where we couldn't have sex when needed."

Fun times for Noah.

I lost count of how many nights we spent sleeping in the bathroom, so she was near the toilet. I've come to learn if there's a horrible side effect, Peyton will have it.

Dr. Rock sighs. "All right, well first, let me say I'm sorry you're having difficulties conceiving. I take my job very seriously and have a high success rate. Two, I've looked over your chart and, barring any unforeseen circumstances, the scan of your uterus shows healthy. Three, Noah's initial sample results showed very strong and eager swimmers, ready to impregnate. I'm expecting the same results today and expect fertilization almost instantly once we get your eggs out. She closes the file and lays her hands over it.

What in the actual fuck did we just sign up for? I glance at Elle, who stares forward because she knows I'm about to wring her neck. There is no way in hell this woman is the leading specialist in infertility. She's a quack, and that's putting it mildly.

"Do you have any questions?"

"Yes," I blurt out. "Where did you go to school?"

"Harvard," she says proudly.

I make a mental note, and plan to call the school to verify.

"I suspect you don't appreciate my humor when it comes to making a list, Mr. Westbury. I like to lighten the mood sometimes." She pauses and looks at Peyton. "When would you like to get started?"

"The sooner the better," Peyton says before I can whisk her out of the room. "Noah's currently off work, and I've taken some vacation time."

She opens the chart again and huffs. "I see here it says you're a professional athlete?"

"Let me guess, you don't watch football?"

She shakes her head. "You any good?"

Peyton squeezes my hand hard, holding me in place.

"So, scheduling," Elle says, interjecting before I can say something sarcastic. "Ideally, soon. We're both excited and eager to start our journey into motherhood."

When did Elle become the voice of reason?

"Like I said, we're on vacation and I'd really like to start the process as soon as possible," Peyton says.

"I understand. Will you continue having treatment here?"

Peyton nodded. "We have a home here."

"Perfect," she says as she picks her iPad up. "We need to start by getting your blood drawn and tests run. I know you did a few in Portland, but levels change. This will tell us how many eggs are available in your body. We'll also schedule you for an ultrasound, which will help us predict how your ovaries will respond to fertility medicines. As I understand it, you both want to come in on the same day?"

Peyton and Elle say yes.

"Okay, we'll draw blood today and schedule the ultrasound for the end of the week," she tells us. "Ben, we don't need to do anything with your semen at this moment, and Noah, yours is being analyzed now."

Nothing like making someone feel small. While I know my semen is good, I still feel like I'm being set up to fail a major test.

"Ben and Noah, we'll have your blood drawn as well."

"For what?" Ben asks.

"We need to run a battery of tests, mostly for diseases. We want to give the egg and sperm the best possible chance of survival."

"I see." Nothing like the implication you're being deceitful. Peyton squeezes my hand again. I'm so thankful for her and her trust in me.

"Peyton and Elle, I'm going to schedule you for a practice embryo transfer," she says. "We do this to figure out the depth of your uterus. This will also help determine which technique we'll use for implantation. We'll also test the lining of your uterine wall."

"How do you do that?" Elle asks.

"We use a test called sonohysterography. It's where fluid is sent through the cervix into the uterus using a thin plastic tube. The fluid helps make a more detailed ultrasound image of the uterine lining. Sometimes we can skip this step if the uterine test gives us everything we need to know."

All of this is so my wife and I can have a child. Clinical, and not the way things are meant to be for anyone.

"Now, when it comes to sex," the doctor sets the tablet aside. "Now that we have your sample, you don't need to abstain from ejaculation. Moving forward, once your wives start the ovarian stimulations, we ask that you wear condoms. Your wife also might experience swollen ovaries, so listen to her if she says things are painful."

I lean toward my wife and whisper, "Guess we better stop at the store." It's been five days and the longest we've gone without some form of sex since we've been together. Peyton smirks and says nothing. You better believe when I'm about to blow my load tonight, I'm going to yell, I'm ejaculating.

Damn, I hate this shit.

ON THE WAY HOME, we do, indeed stop at the local pharmacy and I buy not one, but two jumbo boxes of condoms. Peyton eyes me warily but says nothing. I can't tell if she thinks I'm going overboard or if I'm not purchasing enough. Regardless, I carry the boxes to the self-checkout machine only to find it out of order. Dread creeps in as I walk to the counter. The lady behind the register reminds me of my Grandma Preston and I can't help but feel judged. Much like the time when I was sixteen or seventeen and stopped for a three-count box of rubbers at the store before heading to the water tower. Without fail, the cashier then got on the intercom and asked for a price check. Talk about humiliation. I think they do that especially when teens are buying, to try to teach us a lesson. The only lesson it taught me was to either force Quinn to go buy them for me or drive over to Allenville, where hopefully no one recognized me as QB1 from Beaumont High or Liam Page's son.

The woman behind the counter slowly scans the boxes. She has her technique down and never takes her eyes off me. I'm half tempted to tell Peyton to show her the rock on her finger, but I don't. Let her think whatever. The fact is, I'm going home to fuck my wife and I'm going to enjoy it, even though I haven't worn a rubber in . . . I don't even remember. It wasn't long after Peyton and I started dating that we did away with them. I wasn't going anywhere, and neither was she. Getting pregnant then didn't matter to us.

It matters to us now.

I pay in cash. No need for her to be a football fan and realize I was in her store. Honestly, unless you see your favorite player without a helmet on or they are all over television doing commercials, people have no idea what we look like when we're off the field. Granted, the cameras are on me, especially if I'm on the sidelines after a major fuck up. Unfortunately for me, I had a few of those this past season. I'd like to chalk it up to luck. It wasn't. It was all stress. Peyton may have to go through the hard part, the testing, injections, and eventually carrying our child. Sure, all I had to do was put my shit into a cup and I'm good to go. I get to sit back, right?

Nope.

No one considers the emotional toll men go through when their wives find out they're not pregnant. Again and again. We feel it too. We're not just there to pump, dump, and run. No one thinks about the demand we have to perform to make sure we're getting the job done.

Peyton has done the ovulation charts, and at first, I was game. Hell yeah, call me out of a workout to have sex with my wife in her office. It was sneaky, daring, and the thrill of it was exhilarating. Until it wasn't. I never thought I'd groan when a text would come in that she was ovulating. Talk about performance anxiety. I never told her, and I never will. She doesn't need my bullshit on top of the pile she already deals with.

I take her hand and lead her out of the store and to the Escalade. Before I let her get in, I pull her into my arms and hold her. Sometimes, I need this.

"I love you."

"I love you more," she says into my neck.

When we part, I cup her face with my hands and kiss her lightly. "When we get home, I'm going to make love to you."

Peyton laughs lightly. "And this differs from other days?"

"Lately, it's been sex. Which I love. But we've been so focused on getting you pregnant that I feel like some of the passion was pushed to the side. I want that back." I close the gap between us. Not that there was much.

"I want to kiss you." I follow my words with actions and leave a trail of kisses from her ear to her lips. When there, they part, allowing my tongue to enter her mouth. Pulling away and resting my forehead against hers, I inhale deeply. I'm already hard, ready, and wishing we were at home.

"Then what?" My minx asks.

I chuckle. "Then I'm going to touch you, tease you, make you come with my fingers, my mouth and then finally on my cock."

"Noah?" she says my name headily.

"Yeah, baby?"

"We're in the parking lot, out in public," she says, stating the obvious. "Unless you calm down, the car next to you that just pulled in, is going to see your erection and the two boxes of condoms we just bought."

"Fuck me," I say as I look down at my pants. Slacks do nothing to hide what you're packing.

"Oh, I plan to, if you ever get us home." Peyton winks.

I shake my head slightly. "Get in the car, Peyton." She

does, and I shut the door. With courage and muster, I walk around the back, hoping the people in the other car go toward the front. Only, they stop when they see me and my tented pants coming toward them.

"Hey, you're Noah Westbury," the young kid says as loudly as possible. "Can I get your autograph?"

Fuck my life.

As much as I want to say no, I don't. I clear my throat, set the boxes of condoms on the roof of my Escalade that I should've given to Peyton, and think about the last time I got hit in a game where I thought I'd lose my manhood. It's not quite the deflation I need, but it helps. I sign a piece of paper, a T-shirt, and pose for an ungodly number of photos before heading to my car.

"Don't forget your prophylactics," the father says as they walk toward the store.

"Dad, what's a propowatic?"

I stand there, shaking my head. Could this day get any worse?

Actually, it could.

I grab the boxes and slip in behind the steering wheel and start the car. Peyton's laughing and has clearly been living it up while I've been in misery for the last handful of minutes. She reaches across the console and palms my flaccid dick, which jumps to attention. I swear it's saying, "Hey, yeah, I know this hand."

"Rude," I mutter as I shift into reverse, pull out and then into drive. "You left me hanging."

"There was no way I was getting out of the car. Besides, they want to see you, not me."

While she's not wrong, I enjoy having her with me for these random fan encounters. Everyone who meets her loves her.

"I don't care," I tell her. "I want you next to me, always."

Her fingers brush through my hair on the drive home. It's strange how her touch can calm me most days. A mile out, I turn on the radio. It's a sports talk channel, which I usually avoid when she's in the car. I'm man enough to admit my wife knows more about sports than I do, and during the off season I take full advantage of her knowledge during trivia night.

"The free agency market is bananas right now," the commentator says. Peyton reaches to turn the radio off, but I tell her to leave it.

"I want to hear what they have to say."

"Teams are going to spend some money tying down those who haven't signed."

"You know who's out there that hasn't signed?"

"Noah Westbury."

My hands grip the steering wheel, a bit too tightly causing pain to radiate up my arm. My foot slips from the gas with a noticeable thud. I don't want to be a topic of conversation. No athlete ever does.

"What's up with that?"

"Don't know, but Portland is stupid for not having him under contract, and these other teams?" The commentator whistles. "If the rumors are true, they're throwing money at him. He needs to come to L.A."

"Dude already lives here. Might as well stay."

"Maybe it's better for us if Portland sleeps on it. Then we'll get a decent QB. I'd love to have Westbury on any one of our teams here."

I pull into the driveway and shut the car off, but don't move. It's nice to be wanted. Mega shitty when the team you've dedicated the beginning of your career to doesn't act like they want you. My head spins with this knowledge, wondering what the fuck I'm doing.

"They'll make an offer," Peyton says, breaking the silence.

"Do you know something I don't?" My voice catches. I hate asking her this. Mixing our marriage and work was something we swore we'd never do.

She shakes her head.

"Will you quit your job if I go somewhere else?"

Peyton's quiet for a moment and I know I've put her on the spot. Any decision I make, we make together. "We have time, Noah. Let everyone get settled and out of vacation mode." Her fingers trail down the side of my face. "Let's go inside. I'm hungry."

"For lunch?"

She shakes her head and palms my crotch again. "You promised."

Damn straight, I did.

3

PEYTON

Tomorrow, Elle and I have our appointments for our ultrasounds. We plan to go together to save the guys from having to drive into downtown. Mostly, it saves our sanity. It never fails, some other driver will piss either Ben or Noah off, and then a mood is set. I'm trying to remain positive and think only happy thoughts. I figure if I tell myself this is going to work on the first try, then it *will* work, and I won't have to continue going back. I'd be happy with one round of shots. I know Noah would be.

I caught him reading about IVF and the process even though we know everything there is to know about it. Thanks to social media and vlogging, mothers and even some fathers detail their journeys. The highs and lows, the good and the bad. Even the ugly, which I appreciate. I know it's going to be ugly. I hate being poked and prodded and as much as I'm looking forward to morning sickness, I'm really not. No one enjoys puking, even if there's a good outcome at the end of the duration. That shit hurts and since the accident, my bones ache.

I grip the railing of our balcony, tip my head back, and

close my eyes to let the sun beat down on me. I love being in California, with the warmth, the ocean, and of course the sun. But I miss home. By home, I mean Beaumont. I never thought I'd miss it as much as I do, but ever since Elle moved back and I've gone back and forth a few times to see her, I've realized that's where I want to raise my family. Deep down, one part of me hopes Noah takes an offer from a different team, maybe one closer to Beaumont. But then, there's a part of me who wants to be here, near my parents so my mom will be there when I need her. Because I'm going to need her. The football analyst in me wants him to stay in Portland. We've made a good home there and have a lot of friends. Friends I'd miss, but who could come visit wherever we are. I'm not foolish enough to think those friends won't be traded, although I imagine Julius would retire if that was the case.

Behind me, Noah's on the phone. I glance over my shoulder and see him pacing. His hand is in his hair, tugging at the ends. He's frustrated and rightly so. The Pioneers are taking their sweet time making him an offer. Honestly, all of this should be a no-brainer. He's the face of their franchise and has a Super Bowl under his belt. Not many teams or quarterbacks can say they've done that with an expansion team in the time he's been there. Yet, they're dicking him around. Which makes me wonder about my job. Is it worth staying if my husband isn't there? I've had other offers before, from teams here and on the east coast. Noah has options, as do I. We're definitely not a packaged deal, but it is nice. And now I wonder if I am the cause of their delay. Do they want me gone? If they do, they just need to say so.

I pull my phone out and press the contact for Liam. Normally, I'd video chat, but I don't want Noah to hear his dad's voice and come out here.

"Hey," Liam says when he answers. "Everything okay?"

"Hi and yes. Can't a girl call her father-in-law?"

Liam chuckles. "No, but she can call her uncle. What's up?"

When he refers to himself as my uncle, I smile. My memories from childhood are fuzzy, like everyone's. The older you get the less you remember. I remember Liam and the day he walked up to the pew. At five, I knew he was going to change my life. Be someone I could count on no matter what. With him, I still got to be Mason's little girl, his football loving daughter.

"I'm worried about Noah," I tell him. "Between this baby stuff and the Pioneers dragging their feet, he's stressed. I think he can use some dad time."

"That can be arranged," he says. "I'll be there tomorrow. Does that work?"

"Yes. I'll make sure your room is ready."

Liam laughs again. "As if it isn't immaculate already."

"Hey, I can't help it."

"Sure, you can't. Anything else? Are you okay?"

"I'm nervous," I tell him. It's not like any of our matriarchs have been through this and I'm not naïve enough to think Elle's struggles will be like mine. I face an uphill battle without an ax, but with all the support in the world. The problem with the support is they can't get me pregnant or make sure I stay pregnant. They can hold and care for me. Be there when I tell them I don't need anyone. The hurdle is me and I can't fix me. "And scared."

"We have to believe everything is going to work out the way we want," he says. "Is your mom going with you?"

"No, tomorrow is just an ultrasound. It won't take long. Elle and I didn't think she'd want to sit in the waiting room."

"Makes sense. All right, I'll see you tomorrow. Love you, P."

"Love you too, Uncle Liam."

We hang up and I find my husband is still pacing. I wish there was something I could do, but his contract is out of the scope of my responsibilities. It's my job to show him and the others where they need to attack, move better with and without the ball, and how to move ten steps ahead instead of waiting for the obvious.

When I walk into the house, Noah looks at me and sighs heavily.

"I gotta go," he says into the receiver and then hangs up. Most people would slip their phone back into their pocket or set it down. Not Noah. Not today. His phone flies into the couch, bouncing off the cushion and tumbling to the floor. "Fuck!"

What do I do? I can't offer help because there isn't anything I can do on my end. This is the line we can't cross. We may work for the same company, but we aren't anywhere near the same. I can negotiate my own employment, he can't.

Maybe it's Allen.

Maybe Noah needs a new agent.

Because I'm at a loss, I stand there, waiting for my husband to say something. He doesn't. He picks up his phone and walks down the hall toward our bedroom. I choose not to follow. He's in a mood and sometimes we're better off apart when he's like this.

Instead, I sit down on the couch, pull my legs underneath me, and read the book about this one woman's journey through IVF. For the most part, it's inspiring. Except when she writes about miscarrying, and then losing her husband to an accident. What ensued was a battle over her eggs because she and his parents weren't on speaking terms. I can't imagine what she went through, but then again, my life situation is very different from others.

There was a time, back in elementary or middle school, where a group of classmates were convinced Noah and I were related and would tell anyone who cared to listen. It didn't matter what I said, no one believed me. They never let up on their theory, no matter how many people disproved it. The fact that he went to prom with me really sent those kids into a tailspin. I wish I could've seen their faces when they found out we got married.

Well, maybe not.

Noah returns. He stands there, still somewhat in the hall and partially in the family room. He looks angry, pissed off at the world. I say nothing and go back to reading.

"What are you reading?"

I show him the cover and he makes a face of disgust.

"Why are you reading that shit?"

"Excuse me?"

"You heard me," he says. "Why put yourself through that? Those issues she wrote about are hers. Not yours."

"No, I certainly have my own, don't I?"

"I didn't say that."

"You literally just did." I go back to reading, not wanting to engage with him when he's like this.

"I'm going out."

"Okay."

"That's it? Just, okay?" He huffs.

This time, I set the book down and stare at my sour-faced husband. I love him with all my being but he's a pain in my ass. "Yes, just okay. Okay, you're going out. Okay, you're being a pissant. Okay, you're throwing an adult size temper tantrum."

"You don't get it."

"You're right, I don't. You have teams willing to offer you millions and you're holding out for a team that isn't even returning Allen's calls. Why? What's so damn important about the Pioneers?"

"You," he says matter-of-factly.

His one word gives me pause. I blink back a rush of tears and shake my head. "Don't stay there because of me," I tell him.

Noah drops his head and sighs, then walks toward me and surprises me when he drops to his knees and hugs my legs. "I'm sorry, baby." He kisses my legs, torso and finally my lips. "I'm so damn mad."

I thread my fingers through his locks. Now that he's not playing, he's let his hair grow. The ends curl and they make me hope our child will be lucky enough to inherit his curls.

"I know you are, but please don't base your decision on me."

"How can I not?"

He's right.

I trail my fingers along his hairline and down his cheek bone. "I love you for thinking of me, but don't let that drive you, Noah. We'll figure it out."

"How?"

"It'd be no different if I took a sideline reporting job. I'd have a home base and I'd travel."

"You know that doesn't work with your type of job, right?"

I nod. It also won't work if we have a child and we're not living together. The thing is, I'm not ready to give up on my career just yet. I lean forward and kiss him.

"I love you, Noah. No matter what you decide, things will work out."

He climbs onto the couch and pulls my legs over the top of his. He takes my book, looks at the cover, shakes his head, and then sets it down, making sure to save my spot. "I'm sorry I said what I did about the book, it's just that her story isn't yours and I don't want those thoughts in your head."

"I know."

Noah leans his head back, over the edge of the couch. "When did life become so complicated?"

"It's not complicated, we're evolving."

He half chuckles, half sighs. "My career's a mess. I thought re-signing would be a no-brainer."

"I can't help but wonder if it's me. Maybe they want to let me go but figure if they re-sign you, I come back."

Noah looks at me. "Do you think about quitting?"

I shrug. "At times. There are a lot of sports analysts who work and have children. I certainly wouldn't be the first, but I also don't want a nanny raising our child. Since you asked the other day, I've given it some thought. I just don't know."

"Well, I want to be wherever you are."

"What if that means not playing football or only seeing each other one day a week?"

Noah shakes his head. "The one day a week thing won't work for me, and I'm not sure if not playing works either."

"Then it looks like we're in a wait and see holding pattern. Maybe we need to take some trips to these other teams and document everything on social media. That might make the Pioneers get off their asses."

"I'll have Allen set some things up."

"Just wait six weeks."

Noah looks from me to my stomach. His hand rests there. "I wish it were me putting our baby in there."

"Me, too."

4

—

NOAH

After Elle picks up Peyton, I slip into some running shorts, sneakers, grab my ear buds, and head for the door. I pause in the hallway and look at myself. It seems I've forgotten a shirt. I think about heading out without one. The likelihood that I need to go into a store or something is nil, but you never know. On closer inspection, I spot a love bite from my wife.

"Yep, definitely putting a shirt on," I say to our empty house. She wouldn't let me make love to her this morning, no matter how hard I tried. As much as the rejection stings, I accepted her reasoning. Some medical professional will be doing uncomfortable things to her today and the last thing she wanted was for some tech to ask her if she had sex this morning. I really didn't buy her excuse but didn't push further. I respect her boundaries, just as much as I respect the fact that she wanted to take care of me and satisfy my needs. The damn hickey is another story.

With a T-shirt on, I head back toward the front door, open it, and find my father standing there, poised to knock. I slip one of the ear buds out and say, "What are you doing

31

here?" My question is snotty and not meant to be rude or insulting. My parents can visit whenever they want. But they normally give us a heads up.

"Hi, son." My dad smirks. "May I come in?"

I shake my head, clearing the instant fog, and step back to let him in. He has an overnight bag, which he sets down near this table Peyton found at some desert antique shop last summer. The person who sold it to us gave my wife some song and dance about its history and then instantly charged us a hundred less than the price shown on the tag. *History my ass.*

"Not to sound like a broken record, but seriously what are you doing here?" It's not that I don't want to see my dad, it's that he's incredibly busy buying up dilapidated buildings in Beaumont and turning them into either affordable housing or office space so businesses can come to town. Most of us in the family think he's gearing up to run for mayor. Which is a bit comical. Sure, the prodigal son returned home, but he's a musician. Even though 4225 West hasn't toured in a few years, every album they've released has gone platinum. I think Liam Page would have a hard time sitting behind a desk every day, stamping his name on documents.

"Can't a father visit his son?"

I scoff and eye him suspiciously. "Sure, he can. Where's Mom?"

"With your sister. She's on vacation for another month."

Ah yes, no more traveling without Miss Betty Paige. At least not since Mack asked my dad permission to take her on a date. Mack confided in me that he kissed Paige. I had a hard time not wanting to wring the boy's neck and hers. The problem is, I can't be in the middle of this relationship. I love them both but will always side with my sister. I was a teenager once. I'm not even playing stupid when it comes to those two. Which reminds me, I want Peyton to talk to Paige about protecting herself. I can't do it because . . . hello, embarrassing. And I'm not mentioning it to my parents.

"Anyway," my dad sighs. "I thought we'd hang for the weekend."

"Okay," I say, still suspicious. "Want something to drink? Eat?"

Liam shakes his head. "Were you about to leave when I got here?"

I nod. "I was going to head out for a run. Peyton went to an appointment with Elle. I need to clear my head or keep it clear. I hate this entire process."

"Let me change and I'll go with you."

Before I can protest, he's grabbed his bag and disappeared down the hall to the room he and my mom stay in when they're here. I sigh. The last thing the streets of Malibu need to see is Liam Page running.

"Fuck my life," I mutter as I head into the kitchen for a glass of water. My dad joins me minutes later and helps himself. He drinks heartily from the glass and then sets it in the sink.

"Ready?"

"Yes, but don't be embarrassed when I kick your ass," I tell him.

The ever-charismatic Liam Page grips my shoulder and bends over in laughter. He heaves, feigns being out of breath, and fans his imaginary tears away. "Son, you slay me."

"Who taught you that word?"

"Your sister."

I shake my head. "Come on, old man."

"Who are you calling old?"

We get outside and begin to stretch.

"Hi, Noah," one of my neighbors from down the road waves as she power walks by wearing those incredibly tiny workout shorts. I have no idea what her name is though. I wave, being a friendly neighbor and all.

"Who's that?"

"Dunno," I say, shrugging. "They all say hi when they go by. It's not like I'm standing out there introducing myself."

"Who else lives around here?"

I look around at the houses. Some you can see because they're perilously perched on cliffs. Others you can only see gates or driveways. "Uh, Cyrus, Streisand, Leo, the Hiltons, and that tequila maker, what's his name . . ."

"Mr. Crawford," Liam says, fanning his face.

"No, that's not it."

My dad rolls his eyes. "Randy Gerber. He's married to Cindy Crawford." He lets out a low whistle.

"Does Mom know?"

He shrugs. "She has her freebie list."

"What the fuck is a freebie list?"

"You know a list of people you can sleep with and can't get into trouble for."

I stare at my dad as rage boils. "You fucking kidding me with this bullshit?"

"What?" He shrugs as if he didn't just admit he has a list of people he wants to sleep with.

"I'm going to kick your ass, old man."

He holds his hands up. "Your mom has a list, son. Not me. I did all that shit a long time ago, found the error of my ways and haven't looked back. Your mother is the only woman I want to be with."

"Then I'm going to have words with her."

He shakes his head. "It's just a thing. No one actually acts on it. It'd be like you finding another celebrity attractive."

"Never gonna happen," I tell him as we head toward the street. "And if Peyton thinks like you do, we'll have words." We start with a slow jog. "Is this really a thing?"

"It was back in my father's time. Must have died out."

"Thank god for that. I can't imagine my wife having a list of people she wants to be with, and if she does, I better never learn of it. No, I take that back. The list better contain ten Noah Westburys."

"Jealous much?"

I shake my head. "It's not about being jealous, Dad. I love her far too much to let another woman touch me, and if another man touched her . . ." I trail off. I honestly don't know what I'd do, but I'd likely end up in jail.

We run in silence for a mile, both of us huffing and puffing thanks to the heat and air quality. While I like being in California where the sun shines almost every day, there is something to be said about cozying up on a gloomy day by the fire with the love of your life nestled next to you. Those are the days in Portland that I don't want to give up. My thoughts on the job aren't always about football, but about the life Peyton and I have built there. While I know my friends can travel to wherever and vice versa, relationships change when people move away, just as priorities change when a couple has children. Once Julius and Autumn welcomed their third child, Autumn considered quitting her job. Julius instead, took over more of the parental duties, except during the season, so Autumn could continue to do the job she loved. This all meant the time Julius and I spent together lessened. Honestly, I sort of look forward to hitting up the park with our kids.

We hit a two-mile mark and slow down to a jog. "Want to sit for a minute?" Dad asks. I'm breathing just as hard as he is, otherwise I'd call him old. For his age, he's in damn good shape and I can only hope I look the same. We walk until we find an empty bench and sit down facing the water, which surfers have taken over. I bet that if I squint, I'll find Quinn out there or even Ben. They seem to spend a lot of time together when Ben's here. I don't mind that I'm not included, surfing really isn't my thing.

"Wanna talk about what's going on with Peyton?"

"Not really," I tell him. I doubt he'll understand. I know my mom struggled getting pregnant after she and my dad married, and at one point were adopting a baby until the mother changed her mind. As a family, we never discussed this or how I felt. One day I think I'm about to get a sibling and the next I'm not. For a young kid that's a tough pill to swallow. But then, Paige comes along, and everyone is happy, and all is right in the Westbury house.

"I figured, but I thought I'd give it a try."

"It sucks," I tell him. "I didn't imagine things to be this way, even though I knew the accident did a number on her body. She's so strong though and never lets anyone see when she's in pain. You know, she keeps her office at eighty degrees because the cold affects her. She rarely stays on the sideline, which I get, but still. Peyton wants a baby, one she gives birth to, and I'm doing my best to support this decision. I want it too, but at what cost to my wife?" I look off into the horizon, fighting back a wave of emotion. I can never say these things to her, not in a million years. It's not about communication. These are my fears, and mine alone. I refuse to burden her, she has enough to worry about.

"As a father, there's a lot about a woman and her desire for motherhood that we'll never understand. Women have a time limit on their bodies, where men can produce children into their seventies and eighties. None of it will ever make sense. What Peyton's going through . . ." He trails off and then sighs. "All you can do is be her support and let her know when you're hurting too. Bottling it up and combining it with this contract shit isn't good for either of you."

"I do support her," I tell him. "I hate that I'm not getting the job done for her, giving her the one thing she wants most right now. It destroys me to know our child will be created in a dish and maybe her body will reject carrying it. I also know, if I had come clean about how I felt about her from the jump, none of this would be happening. If I hadn't cared about what our families would say about me wanting to be with her, she wouldn't have been in that car."

My dad sits there, knowing he can't deny my logic. I will forever regret that I didn't have the balls to tell Peyton how I felt and act on my feelings. She should've been mine from the night of her prom. Hell, even before that, but I was scared. Scared of what my parents would think, what Katelyn would think, and how I'd look to the NFL. The headlines would've done me in, and I'd forever be known as the quarterback dating an eighteen-year-old. My agent would've canned my ass. And because of my ego, the love of my life almost died in a car accident.

Dad and I walk back to the house. The old man finally admitted he had a cramp and then jokingly said the cramp was me. Once we enter my neighborhood, he brings up the contract.

"I can't tell you what to do because I bailed on this part of my life, but if Portland is where you want to be, push for it. If it's not, leave. Don't wait for them to show you they care. If they did, you wouldn't be going through this right now."

I nod. He's not wrong. Neither is Peyton. Deep down, I know the reason I want Portland is because of her. I don't want to be away from her. Right now, I have the best of both worlds. When we travel, she goes with us. If I'm with another team, she'll be home, taking care of our baby. Sure, she can go to the away games, but will she? It's hard to say.

We're standing at the edge of my driveway when I blurt out, "What if I quit?"

Dad's eyes bug out. "What?"

Shrugging, I look down at the ground and toe a loose pebble. "The Stars want me," I tell him. "They've asked me to come in, throw a few."

"You know you can do both," he tells me. "Bo Jackson and Deion Sanders played football and baseball successfully."

"I've researched them. Game film, that sort of thing. I'm interested," I say. "I miss baseball. I never thought I would, and I think I only pursued football because there was an opening at Notre Dame, and I could walk on. I never gave baseball a second look."

Dad rests his hand on my shoulder and gives it a squeeze. "Maybe we should hit the batting cages and see if you still have some heat before you go out there, embarrassing yourself. Some of these kids these days are smoking the ball in."

"Like Mack."

My dad laughs. "Definitely like Mack. That boy is going places."

"He's fun to watch."

We go inside and find Peyton sitting on the couch, reading the book I'd suggested she stop. She works herself up over things that may or may not happen to her. When she hears us, she looks up, closes her book, and comes toward us. I hold my arms out for her, but my wife goes to my dad first. I don't even bother to try and stop my eyes from rolling.

"Ouch," I say to them as they hug like long lost friends. "You guys suck."

Dad snickers.

They follow me into the kitchen. I go to the sink, turn the water on and let it run for a second under the filter before filling my glass. My wife's arms wrap around my waist. My free hand instantly finds hers. Once I finish drinking, I turn in her arms, glide the back of my fingers under her cheek to lift her face to mine and kiss her.

"How did it go?"

"Okay," she tells me. "Preliminary results say I'm a good candidate, but I'll know more once the scans are read."

"Shots next then?"

She nods. "Then extraction."

I lean down and kiss her again. "Then a baby."

She nods and I kiss her again, not caring that my dad is in the room. He can deal. I need my wife to know I am with her, her constant support. I'll be her cheerleader no matter what, even when I know there could be a time when I'll want to beg her to stop. She'll never know the fear I have deep within, or how I feel about the things her body puts her through because of me.

Those secrets will go with me to the grave.

5

———

PEYTON

"Hey, P."

I turn at the sound of Elle's voice. She finds me on the lower portion of our patio, where Noah has built a fire pit, curled under a blanket. There's a fire burning, but I'm still chilly. In my hand, a glass of wine. I poured it, thinking this would be my last for a while and yet I haven't touched it. I can't seem to lift the glass to my lips to taste the sweet, berried drink.

"Hey." I uncurl and move so my sister can sit next to me. "What are you doing here?"

Elle sighs. Something's on her mind. She leans into me, wrapping her arm around mine. "Do you ever wonder how we got so lucky?"

A small chuckle escapes me. "Is that what you call this?"

She nods against my shoulder. "Our lives could've been vastly different . . ."

Elle doesn't need to finish her thought. She's right. Our lives could've been different. Hers at least. I feel in my heart I would've married Noah regardless. Would we be as well off as we are? Possibly not. But he could've still gone to the NFL or even Major League Baseball. He had options.

Who or what we wouldn't have is Harrison, the man who stepped up and brought two five-year-old's into his life and treated us as his own from the beginning. He's never once let anyone believe we weren't his daughters. And he's never been jealous of our father. He took his last name so we'd all match. It doesn't matter how many times I tell him, in all those mushy Father's Day cards that he means the world to me, he truly does.

"Things happen for a reason, Elle."

"They do. The world works in mysterious ways."

"So do you," I say as I nudge her. "What's up?"

Elle sits up and faces me. "Don't be mad. Okay?"

"Okay." I'll be mad no matter what because she told me not to, which means she's about to say something to piss me off.

"I want you to hear me out before you interject."

"Okay."

She sits up a bit straighter. "Tomorrow, we start our shots," she says. "And in two weeks, they're going to take our eggs and make some embryos. Then implantation and if all goes according to plan, we'll be pregnant. Together."

I nod since she asked me not to say anything.

"I've been thinking that maybe I don't do the procedure at the same time you do."

"What? Why not? Isn't that the whole point of doing this together?"

"It is, P. But I'm worried."

She lets her statement hang in the air.

"I don't think I could enjoy my pregnancy as much if I were to be pregnant and you weren't," she says as tears spill over. "You asked me to carry your baby for you and I told you no because Ben and I want to start a family. That weighs heavily on me. Me telling you no was the worst thing I've ever had to do. I want nothing more than to see you become a mom, but it would destroy me if in twenty days you don't find out you're pregnant and I am."

"Please don't cry." I wipe my own tears and then pull my sister into my arms. "I know I'll be sad, but I'll be so happy for you and Ben. You guys deserve to have the baby you want."

"And we will, but we're waiting until after your procedure. Once we know it's been successful and you have a baby growing in your belly, I'll go in. Until then, my focus needs to be on you." Elle lifts her shoulder slightly. "And the wedding I'm supposed to be planning."

My eyes widen. "Shit, we forgot to go to the venue last weekend."

"I blame Liam and his surprise trip. Why was he here, anyway?"

I glance toward the house, looking for Noah, even though I know he can't hear me. "He's struggling so I thought if his dad came, they could do the man-to-man thing. It seemed to work."

"Don't worry, Ben's up there with him. What's up with Noah, anyway? He seemed off at the appointment?"

"Football and this baby stuff. He hasn't told me, but I think he feels like he's letting me down. He's not but you tell a stubborn man he's wrong and see how well that goes."

"Ben bought us a book on pregnancy. He's reading it. I'm not. It has pictures and nope." She shakes her head. "Anyway, he's reading and fist pumps, so I'm like what are you doing? He tells me that women who breastfeed are more susceptible to getting pregnant again after childbirth because of all the hormones and shit—I don't know I wasn't listening—anyway, my husband says we don't have to worry about that since he's shooting blanks."

"He's pretty proud of himself, I see."

Elle rolls her eyes. "He's something else. I love him and the positive attitude he has about everything. His last check-up was great. He's not out of the woods yet, but each visit brings us closer."

"I'm happy everything worked out, Elle. I truly am."

She sits back. "You know the chances of having multiple babies is high with IVF, right?"

I nod. "I'll be happy with one."

"What if you drop twenty eggs?"

My eyes bug out. "I supposed I'd have to change my name to fertile Myrtle."

Elle laughs so hard she snorts.

"What's so funny?"

Ben's voice has Elle turning toward him.

Before she can adjust and welcome her husband, Beau jumps on mine and Elle's laps and proceeds to show us how much he's missed us. "Okay, down," Elle says, and he jumps to the ground and sits. Elle gives him some love and holds her hand out so Ben can give her a treat for him. There are times when I want a dog, but then I remember how much I work and think of how unfair it would be for the doggie to be home all day by himself.

Noah isn't far behind Ben. He smiles and I know it's just for me. As much as I like my alone time, I love being with my husband. I hold out my hand for him, to let him know I want him near me. Elle moves over to the other seat and Noah sits next to me. He kisses me, holding his lips to mine for a second. While I know my sister is out here with us, Noah's the only one in my orbit.

"They're coming," Ben says out of the blue.

Noah turns as my mouth drops open.

"Context, Ben!" Elle hollers at him. "You know I've been down here talking babies and shit with P and you blurt out they're coming. Who's coming? The Redcoats? Your imaginary swimmers? Geez!"

Noah snorts. I cover my mouth with my hand. Elle's clearly tired of his shit. God, I love them together.

"My bad," Ben says all sassy like. "I texted Quinn and Nola. They're on their way over."

"Oh good," Elle says. "We can talk about wedding plans."

I shake my head. "What are they waiting for?"

"Her," Elle says. "Quinny says she won't pick a date or there is always something going on at her parent's house. You know they host weddings there and Nola wants to get married there but her mom never puts her on the list."

"I wonder if she doesn't like Quinn," Ben says. Elle and I throw daggers at him.

"That's our brother you're speaking about," Elle says.

"How can someone not like Quinn?" I ask.

Ben holds his hand up. "We . . ." he points to all of us, "love him. Everything about him. Nola's family isn't like your family. They're not famous musicians who raised their kids on a tour bus. They're a southern family who go to church on Wednesdays and twice on Sundays," he says. "They're a big family, lots of grandbabies, and have that mysterious generational wealth. I'm sure when Quinn showed up, all emo rocker like, they were probably a bit taken back by him."

"Ben has a point," Noah says.

"Hush," I tell him. "Do you really think it's her family dragging their feet?"

"Makes sense," Elle says. "Think about it, they never

come out here and Quinn rarely goes there. Huh." Elle trails off.

"If they don't like him then they suck dirty pond water," I say with a huff. "Like, how can you not like Quinn? He's perfect!"

"You're biased," Noah says to her. "I can tell you right now, from experience, my grandparents aren't that fond of my dad. They tolerate him, but given a choice, they'd choose Nick every day of the week for my mom."

My mouth drops open. "What?"

Noah shrugs. "My dad knows this. Despite everything, there's a lot of animosity. Sure, they're cordial but my grandfather isn't rolling out the red carpet for my dad anytime soon."

"Wow, I'm shocked. I never knew."

"Why do you think they're never at any functions? They never come to my games. Christmas. Birthdays. My mom goes over to their house. I love them but they're bitter old people who need to get over what happened when my mom was eighteen. My dad is forever paying for his mistakes. Honestly, it's not fair."

"Noah, that's really sad," I tell him. "They're missing out on so much."

He nods. "Mom invites them to everything. They chose to go on cruises and vacations with their friends. You can't force people to like you," he says.

"Wow, all this talking sucks."

"What sucks?" Quinn comes into view and my smile widens. I stand and go to him. I haven't seen him in weeks. Not my choice. His manager is a royal pain in the ass who makes him and his band practice.

"Hugs," I say when I reach him. He hugs me tightly.

"We really need to find you a new manager. One that lets you come up for air every now and again."

"Hey, I resemble that statement," Elle says, much to everyone's chagrin.

I push Quinn out of the way and hug Nola, working hard to put what Ben said out of my mind. I don't believe it for one second. I refuse to.

"If Ben had told us he invited you over, I would've had some food ready or something," I say as I sit back down.

"You didn't have any for us," Elle points out.

"I didn't invite you over," I retort.

"Touché," she says.

"Done."

All eyes are on Ben, again.

"Context Benjamin!" Elle throws her hands in the air.

"Sorry. I ordered food."

"Thank you, Ben," I say to him. Elle leans into him and kisses him. She mouths "I love you" and it brings a smile to my face.

We chat for a bit about nothing of importance. Quinn knows what tomorrow brings for me, and maybe Elle if I can convince her to change her mind. I pray my egg retrieval is a success, that Noah's sperm does its job, and in two weeks the doctor is putting an embryo where it needs to go. Those are my thoughts though and I don't want to share them with anyone but my husband.

Noah's phone chimes, letting us know there's someone at our front door. He, Ben, and Quinn run off to get the food and bring back drinks for everyone. What a perfect way to spend the evening before my stress levels increase. Before the paranoia sets in.

"How are things?" Elle asks Nola.

What Ben said weighs heavily on my mind. I'm tempted to ask Nola, but it's not my place.

"They're good. Did you make it up to the winery yet?"

Elle shakes her head. "Liam was here last week. We'll go this week. Want to come?" Elle asks. "Maybe that spot will work for you and Quinn."

Subtle, sister. Very subtle.

"Yeah, sure. Although I'm pretty set on getting married at my parents."

"Do two weddings," I suggest. "Elle is. It's totally the thing right now too. A lot of people are doing a destination wedding and then one in their hometown."

"That's not a bad idea," Nola says. "I'll talk to Quinn."

"Talk to Quinn about what?" he says as he comes back with his arms full. He sits next to Nola, and I notice that when Noah returns, he kisses me, and Ben kisses Elle. Although she demanded it.

Now I can't stop thinking about Nola's family and how they may or may not like my brother. This is going to bug the shit out of me.

"Your sisters suggested we have two weddings. One here or some destination and then at my house."

"Fab idea. What do you think?" he asks her.

She shrugs and picks at a French fry.

"Hell, we can go to the courthouse," he tells her. She says nothing, and Quinn doesn't notice.

I stuff my face to keep my mouth occupied. I hate thinking Quinn isn't welcome because of his music. Which would mean our dad wouldn't be welcome. Quinn would never go for that. Ever. Or Liam. As odd as it is, Liam's known Quinn longer than he's known his own son. There's no way Quinn would get married without his family there.

"Ugh." I push my food away, unable to eat another bite.

I eye my sister, but she's making googly faces at Ben and not paying attention to me.

"You good?" Noah asks.

I shrug.

He slips his hand under my blanket and caresses my thigh, and just like that I'm calm. Noah leans back and whispers, "Stop worrying about Quinn. He's a big boy. If what Ben says is right, Quinn will deal with it. He doesn't need his firecracker little sister fighting his battles."

"I know, it just makes me sad."

Noah kisses his favorite spot . . . well, one of them. "You can't be sad," he tells me. "In the morning we're going to start our journey toward parenthood. Happy thoughts."

I lean into him. "How do you do it?"

He shrugs, knowing exactly what I'm asking him. "I've had you wrapped around my finger from day one, Peyton."

6

NOAH

This morning, of all mornings, I have a slight hangover. What's going to exacerbate my shitty mood is the fact that Peyton starts her shots today. To add to my mea culpa stemming from last night's unplanned gathering, is the fact my sister-in-law, who I love dearly, isn't starting her shots today because of some twin sisterly bond I will never understand. I get what Elle's doing, but I'm not sure if I'm on the same page as her or not. Peyton wants to be pregnant at the same time as her sister. I get it. Under the circumstances, it's highly unlikely. IVF isn't a guarantee for anyone. Especially us. Regardless of the doctor being overly positive, both women might not be successful. Elle's never tried to get pregnant, and Peyton's never been able to get pregnant. I've read the pamphlets and done the research. I know how all of this could turn out.

I drag my sorry ass out of bed and hit the shower before facing my wife. Knowing her as well as I do, she'll be downstairs in her yoga room, meditating. When we bought the house, the room was used for storage and didn't have a purpose. In Portland, she started taking yoga classes, but here she has the space to have her own room. We hired a contractor to knock out the wall and replace it with glass doors which open to a recently renovated garden for her. I have my man cave and she has hers. I actually love going into her room. As soon as you walk in, it's like nothing else matters in the world.

Her room is very calming. She followed the Feng Shui guide and created an area that was inviting. Where she'd feel content. She has a laughing Buddha in the corner to help her with fertility.

After my shower, I dress in gray joggers, a blue Portland Pioneers sweatshirt and slip my feet into a pair of runners I'm paid to wear. I'm not trying to hide who I am, at least not today. It's already hit social media that Peyton and I were in the clinic, and I figure this is a good thing. People will see that we're normal, just like them. We struggle too.

Indeed, I find my wife in her studio. The door to her studio is open and I stand there, resting against the door jamb. This morning, her long brunette hair is down, the length almost reaching her waist. She never talks about cutting it, even when it annoys her. Peyton keeps her eyes closed, but her lips form into a smile. She knows I'm watching.

In this instance, I'm glad she doesn't open her eyes to look at me. It gives me a moment to stare at her, to take her all in. To remind myself how fucking lucky I am that she chose me to be her partner. Everyone's a fool if they think I chose her. She was destined to be mine from the moment I met her. I was the idiot who waited too long to realize it.

While she sits there, crossed legs and absorbing the energy in the room, I picture her with a growing belly. With my child growing inside of her, knowing my wife is nurturing and caring for the little human that we so desperately want. I don't even care how many children we have. Hell, if she wants a football team, I'll happily do everything I can to give her one. If we're graced with one, then that'll be enough, too. I just want to see her blossom as a mother. To have the moments she sees in magazines and on TV or with our friends. The longing in her eyes when she sees an expectant mother rubbing her belly. Hell, I want that too. I want to feel my son or daughter kick. I want to read bedtime stories to her stomach and tell my little guy or gal how fucking awesome their mother is. Aside from this, I'm at a loss on how to get my wife pregnant. To give her the one thing she wants.

I inhale deeply to stop an impending wave of tears. Being strong for her is my job and one I take very seriously. The alarm on my phone chimes and I pull it out of my pocket to shut it off. "We gotta go," I tell her.

Peyton finally opens her baby blues. They sparkle as she looks at me. Another smile, a wider one this time, spreads across her face. "You can't wear those sweatpants to the clinic."

I look down at them, looking for any stains or holes. "Why not?"

She laughs, stands, and stretches. Doing so highlights her figure. She used to be tiny, sometimes too thin, and she read that eating a balanced diet of whole grains, healthy fats, and proteins would help her body get ready for pregnancy. Honestly, I like not seeing her hip bones or her ribs showing.

Peyton turns, bends over, and looks at me through the space between her legs. The sight of her plump ass in those tight ass pants does something to me. I feel the stirring, the beginning throb of my growing erection. I clear my throat and change my stance.

She smirks and giggles. "That's why," she says. Peyton rights herself and comes toward me. "No one in the office needs to see what my husband's packing." To emphasize, she cups my dick and gives it a squeeze.

"Not fair." I don't bother to move. "You're touching me and yet as of today I'll be banished from being inside of you."

Peyton shivers. "It's for the greater good."

I refuse to disagree with her. "Mhm." Learning toward her, I kiss her. "We need to go."

"You need to change."

"Humor me."

She rolls her eyes. "Fine."

WHEN WE WALK into the clinic, people look. It's a natural reaction. The door opens, you look to see who's coming through. Thankfully, today isn't as packed as it was when we first came. There are fewer men, which I sort of understand. They're probably working or aren't needed for whatever their wife is having done today. One woman is crying in the corner, and I try not to stare, but end up looking in her direction more than once, wondering why.

We aren't sitting but a few minutes when Peyton's name is called. With my hand on the small of her back, I follow one step behind. The nurse, who didn't introduce herself, takes us into a procedure room. She tells Peyton to have a seat in the chair. I sit next to her and clasp my hands in my lap, and then unclasp them and reach for Peyton's. Even though we are here to learn how to administer her shots, I'm nervous. There's no way Peyton can give herself shots, even if she tells the nurse otherwise. I know her. She hates needles, and the sight sometimes results in her hyperventilating.

"You're going to administer two shots a day for one week, and then you'll come in everyday for your last week of shots," the nurse says. "Over the course of your daily in-person monitoring visits, we'll do bloodwork, pelvic ultrasounds, and we'll track your cycle. This is the time where we'll make any necessary adjustments to your medication. If everything is where we want things to be, we'll do the trigger shot. You'll go home and the anesthesiologist will call you, walk you through what to expect at your appointment. You'll come in, and we'll retrieve your eggs."

"When will Peyton come in for the retrieval?"

"Within thirty-six hours after the trigger shot."

I glance at my wife and smile. "Then our baby is made in a dish?" I say this mostly to her, but the nurse answers.

"Yes. In less clinical terms, we take the eggs and let the sperm have their fun."

Peyton snorts. "I definitely like your version better."

The nurse, who still hasn't told us her name, laughs. "Sperm know what they're supposed to do, so we let them have some fun. Now, for the shots."

"Uh, if you can show me, that'd be great," I tell her. "Peyton's squeamish around needles."

"No problem. Can you lift your shirt?"

I stand and give Peyton my best how you doin' smirk as I lift my shirt. The nurse looks at my torso, then me, and huffs. "Yeah, this won't work. Hold on. You can put your shirt down." She stands, goes to the door, and hollers for someone named Ethel to come into the room.

Ethel does. She says hi and listens to our nurse.

"I'm going to demonstrate on Ethel," she says.

"Turn away," I tell Peyton as I lean forward and watch

our nurse grab poor Ethel's stomach. If it hurts, Ethel says nothing. Maybe she's used to it.

"You try," the nurse says. "You're going to grab a chunk of skin here and slide this in." I appreciate that she didn't say needle.

"How far?"

She shows me on the needle where to stop.

"Okay. So, I'm going to rub the spot with an alcohol wipe and then . . ." I show her what I remember. "Will Peyton need a bandage?"

"Nah," says Ethel. "You can dab the spot for a couple of seconds."

I nod. "Got it. Her uncle is a physical trainer. If I don't feel confident doing it, I'll have him come over."

"Or she can come back here."

"Right, yes."

The nurse has me practice a few more times on an orange and then tells Peyton she's going to administer her first shot. She has Peyton stand, which I know isn't going to go very well, so I stand with her.

"Put your hands on my shoulders and your face in my chest."

My fingers grip the edge of her shirt and pull it up, watching the nurse's every move. She catches my gaze and smiles.

"You're one of the good ones, aren't you?"

"She's my wife," I tell her. "There isn't anything I wouldn't do for her." I hate thinking there are shit men out there, not helping their wives with this stuff.

When the nurse touches Peyton's skin, she tightens her hold on me. I lean toward her ear. "Do you know how excited I am to watch your belly expand with our baby?"

"No," she says quietly.

"This morning when you were in the yoga room, I imagined you all plump, nurturing our son or daughter, giving them the best start to life. You're going to be even more beautiful than you are now."

"All done," the nurse says.

Peyton looks up. "That was it?"

The nurse smiles. "You didn't even flinch."

Peyton looks at me. "Maybe we should talk to Xander because that was really easy."

"Sounds good to me. If we head to his gym, I can get a workout in."

We take our supplies and thank the nurse. On the way out, she taps me on the shoulder. "You really are cut from a different cloth," she says.

I don't take compliments well, not when it comes to people saying I'm a good husband. It's not something I practice. "Like I said, there isn't anything I wouldn't do for her."

"You should teach a class or something," she says and walks away.

In the elevator, I pull Peyton into my side. "Am I different from other husbands?"

She shrugs. "I've only had you. I suppose I could test a few others out and get back to you."

I tickle her side. "Absolutely not. Oh, and this reminds me. Do you have a freebie list?"

Peyton's brow lifts. "Do you?"

"Do you know what a freebie list is?"

"Yes, we all made one in high school."

"Really?" Now I'm worried. I mean, I get it. She dated others but what if Kyle Zimmerman is on it. Or someone I know? What if she put someone like Adam Levine or Lenny Kravitz on there? How am I supposed to compete with Kravitz?

She nods. The elevator door opens, we exit, and then walk right out through the open door. It's overcast but warm out today.

"Who's on your list?" I ask as I open the car door for her, and she gets in.

"You."

"Ah, babe." I kiss her. "Who else?"

"Just you, Noah."

"What, really?"

Peyton nods and pulls the seatbelt over her lap and buckles it. "Yes. The idea of a freebie list is to put celebrities down. I think I was a senior when I did mine at some party or something. Anyway, you were going to be drafted, which meant you rated as a celebrity. I put you down."

"So, in theory, your list is complete."

She cups my cheek. "Yes, Noah. You completed my list for me the night of my senior prom."

I take her hand and kiss her palm. "That night, I should've told you how I felt."

"Well, I know now."

I close the door and hustle to the other side. Once I'm in and have started the car, Peyton says, "Do you have one?"

"No. I didn't even know what it was until my dad talked about Cindy someone being on his list, and then he said my mom has one."

Peyton shakes her head.

"Did you know?"

"No, but it doesn't surprise me."

"I swear, I don't even know my own parents."

Peyton laughs. "Come on, let's go get some lunch. And we'll make you a list."

"No need," I say as I pick up her hand and kiss the back

of it. "You'd be the only name on it, so why waste the ink and paper."

"Ah, you love me."

At the red light, I lean over and kiss her. "Eh, you're all right."

The slap across my chest echoed, and it stings, but it was so worth it.

7

PEYTON

Since we were already in town, as Noah likes to call Los Angeles, we trekked over to Xander's gym. Deep down, I sort of liked the idea of Xander being the one to give me my shots, mostly because I know how much Noah stresses about things that hurt me. This one time, I had a knot in my back, and I needed him to press the Theragun against my skin. He did and I flinched. It hurt, but so did the knot and it prevented me from sitting at my desk. After fifteen minutes, we stopped and when I looked at my husband, he had tears in his eyes. Noah's sensitive when it comes to me, and I don't know if it's because of our history or because of the accident. Maybe it's because I'm his wife. I really don't know.

What I do know is Xander's more than capable of jabbing my stomach with a needle. The problem is going to be time and distance. I'm certainly not driving to L.A. twice a day and I don't expect him to drive out to Malibu. Best case scenario, it's an hour drive. That's with zero traffic. This area hasn't been traffic free since the seventies. I wasn't alive then, so I'm speculating.

Noah pulls into the parking lot, shuts the car off and comes around to let me out. I'll never tire of him being this gentleman, and hope our son follows in his footsteps or our daughter sees how she should be treated. Instead of walking into the gym, Noah retreats to the rear of our car, opens the back and then closes it. When he comes back to where I'm standing, I see the bag in his hand and roll my eyes.

Hard.

"Really? You just happened to have your gym bag in the car?"

Noah looks at me sheepishly and runs his hand through his hair. "I . . . uh . . ."

I shake my head and walk away. This was probably his plan all along, offer up Xander to stick me so Noah can get a workout in, when all he had to do was say he wanted to work out with my uncle.

We head inside. The gym's bustling. Weights clank, music plays from the speakers overhead, and almost every machine has someone on it, getting their cardio workout in. After my accident, my uncle managed my rehabilitation once I was out of the hospital. I knew he'd push me to levels other professionals wouldn't and he'd know when to stop. He had me walking ahead of schedule, which I'm thankful for.

"Hi, welcome. Are you here for a tour?" A peppy tall blonde comes toward us, dressed in workout gear. She doesn't look at me, only Noah. "I'm Clover."

Clover? If that isn't a California name, I don't know what is.

"Hi, I'm Peyton Westbury." I stick my hand out, forcing her to shake it. "This is my husband, Noah." I emphasize "my" because she needs to know I see her looking at him. "We're here to see Xander."

"Oh, I'm sorry. Mr. Knight is with a client. I'll happily show you around though."

"Xander's my uncle," I tell her. "Can you please let him know his niece is here."

Clover smiles, but it's a very meh smile. She apprises me and then she twinkles her eyes at Noah.

"Ugh."

"Stop, feisty." Noah quietly reprimands me.

"She twinkled her eyes at you."

Noah laughs. "How does that even work?"

I roll my eyes, hoping he knows I'm not impressed with Clover.

Minutes later, Xander comes out of the backroom. He claps his hands once when he sees us. We meet him halfway, exchange hugs and then follow him to the back where his office is. "To what do I owe the pleasure and does Yvie know you're here?"

"We need a favor and no. This is a very last-minute trip, and we were sort of in the area," I tell him. Instead of going to his office, he takes us to the break room, where surprise, Clover is making herself a smoothie.

"Did you guys meet Clover?" Xander asks.

"Sure did," I say and give her a little finger wave.

Noah leans close to my ear. "Down, kitty."

I should elbow him, but I don't because my elbow is lined up with a part of his body that I love very, very much. When Clover leaves the room, I turn to him.

"I told you to change those damn sweatpants." My eyes travel south, and while my husband isn't hard or even sporting a semi, the outline of his penis is there and extremely noticeable.

"Sorry," he mutters while Xander quietly chuckles to himself.

Noah and I sit at the table in the breakroom. Xander offers us water to drink and sits across from us. "I just texted Yvie, she'll be over in a minute."

"Doesn't she have class?"

Xander looks at his watch. "Yeah, but she's probably not teaching. She has so many teachers on staff now, I think she only teaches the elite classes."

My Aunt Yvie is a dancer, who thanks to my dad and the early success of 4225 West, was able to go to dance school. After my Uncle Jimmy got shot and had to have rehab, my dad hired Xander to come to Beaumont, where he fell in love with Yvie.

"So, what's up?" Xander asks.

Noah gets up and shuts the door, giving us some privacy. As much as I'd like to do this in his office, I don't want to ask him to move us over there. "As you know, the accident did a lot of damage to my pelvis. I had and still have some scarring but most of it was removed back in December, in hopes I can carry a child. Up until now I haven't been able to get pregnant and today I got my first IVF shot."

"Congratulations." Xander gives Noah a high-five, as if he got the shot or something.

"Anyway," I say, getting their attention. "I'm afraid of needles, so Noah has to give me the shot, twice a day."

"And I hate seeing her in pain," Noah added. "Earlier, when we were in the doctor's office, I held her and talked her through it, and she didn't feel a thing. But I'm afraid of hurting her."

"That's where you come in," I say to Xander. "We're wondering if you wouldn't mind coming to the house in the morning or evening to give me my shot? I would only need you to come out for one week."

"Sure," he said without hesitation. "Gives me an excuse to go surfing with Quinn. Count me in."

If there wasn't a table between us, I'd hug my uncle. "Thank you."

"Who's going to do the second one?"

"I'm going to beg my mother," I tell him.

Xander laughs. "Your dad won't do it," he says matter-of-factly. The thing is, Xander's not wrong. Dad's very much like Noah and won't do anything to hurt any of us.

"My mom's sadistic though," I say. "She'll love sticking me with a needle."

This time, Noah rolls his eyes. "Are you kidding me? Your mom wants a grandchild. She'll do whatever she can to help you. My mom as well."

"I know, but I still think she'll like causing me pain. She'll drudge up some agony I caused her back when I was a kid. I'm telling you, she's sadistic. Mark my words."

Noah and Xander laugh.

The door opens and in walks my pixie loving aunt, who I swear doesn't age and always looks like she's about to take the stage. She flutters over to us as if she has fairy wings, and gives us both a hug.

"This is a happy surprise," she says as she sits next to Xander.

"We were in the area," I tell her. "At our fertility appointment."

Yvie's eyes widen. "Am I going to be an auntie again?"

I nod, even though I'm not pregnant. "That's the plan. Elle too."

She covers her mouth and squeals. "This is the best news ever. Yay, thank you for sharing."

"Well, we're not there yet." I tell her why we stopped by.

"Fabulous, idea. You should call Quinn and tell him you're going to need a regular surf buddy."

Xander holds his phone up. "Already texted him."

"Wow," she says, sighing. "Babies. I remember when Quinn was a newborn. Your dad didn't know anything about a baby. He had no idea how to hold him, or feed or change him. Our mom took over, taught him everything and now he's going to be a grandpa."

The room went quiet and then Yvie's mouth drops open. "Oh my, God. Your dad!" she points at Noah. "The sexy rock god grandfather."

Noah groans.

"Oh yes, the women are going to lose their ever-loving minds when they see him holding a baby. You must make him and my brother do a calendar or something. Shirtless. Show off all their tattoos. You know JD would be up for it, too. Holy shit, that would sell like hot cakes. Imagine if we sold them here. All those women would snatch them up. As is, you can only have Harrison come in after hours to work out."

"As much as I wish you were joking, I think this is a brilliant idea," I tell my aunt.

"No," Noah says. "My dad's ego is already large enough. We don't need to feed it with this sexy grandpa shit. Besides, he'd never go for it."

"He would if I asked him." I bat my eyelashes at my husband. "Maybe, you, Quinn, and Xander should do it as well. Pose with your shirt off, holding a baby. Oh, Ben too!"

"No," he says just as Yvie yells, "Yes!"

"I can see it now; Portland Pioneers quarterback poses with his son or daughter. It's a nice headline."

"It's garbage and you know it."

"And yet, you'll do it because you know we'd donate the proceeds to some worthy charity."

Noah gives up the fight. He knows I've won.

Xander offers to work Noah out and he gladly accepts the offer. They leave Yvie and I in the breakroom.

"Did you meet Clover?"

I nod. "She had a hard time keeping eye contact with me though."

"She has amazing credentials, but I'm not a fan. I trust my husband, but I don't trust her. I asked Xander to make sure she's always gone when he locks up. I don't want her here when the doors are locked and they're alone. I can't stomach it."

"It's weird. I know Noah loves me and he'd never do anything to hurt me, but I worry, all the time. More so now because my body is going to change and once we have a child, things will be different. I'll be different. He'll still be him."

"Does he know how you feel?"

I shake my head. "I'm afraid if I say something, he'll think I don't trust him. It's society I don't trust. It's not like I can keep my husband locked in the basement or be with him twenty-four-seven. We do need our own space."

"Peyton, it's time to accept we married hotness."

I cackle and cover my mouth. "I can't believe you said that."

Yvie shrugs. "It's true. You know, it's funny, your dad didn't reach any level of hot until after he became a drummer, and then all the women wanted him. Yet, he never dated anyone. No exes in the closet or anything."

"Well, there's Alicia."

"What she did to my brother." Yvie pauses and shakes her head. "I love my nephew more than anything, but that woman deserved jail time. Still to this day, I see nothing but rage. And then to pull that shit with Quinn a few years ago. I swear, if I ever meet her . . ." She trails off.

What my dad and Quinn went through is still fresh in my mind. Sometimes, I look at Nola and wonder how he stayed with her. I guess when you've met the one you're supposed to be with, it doesn't matter how they ended up in your life.

8

NOAH

Every morning when Xander arrives, it's like a reprieve because the night before was like a nightmare. I love my mother-in-law—I've loved her my entire life —but I need to find a way to keep her away from my wife. Yes, I know they have some mother-daughter bond, but the daughter in this situation—my wife—is fucking miserable and her mother makes things worse when she's here. I know Katelyn means well, but she's nitpicking about shit that's completely out of Peyton's control. Peyton can't help that she was in an accident that nearly killed her and can't change the damage done to her. It is what it is and there isn't anything any of us can do about it. Katelyn telling Peyton the shots don't hurt and to just relax only make things worse.

Is it my place to say something to Katelyn?

Should Peyton?

She's already an emotional wreck. She's tired, mad at her body, and herself. She's irritable and uses me as her punching bag. But when we go to bed, things are good. Peyton's in my arms where she belongs.

Peyton comes out of the bathroom, her long hair in wet clumped sections after her shower. I beckon her to me and take the hairbrush from her. "Want me to brush your hair?" Her eyes well up with tears instantly. I've done this before and she hasn't cried, but ever since she started these damn shots, even if I stand next to her and brush my teeth at the same time she is, we've got tears.

Never mind walking into a store or near some baby shit. I know I will never fully comprehend how she feels about being a mother. Guys have it fucking easy. And if I could take away the agony and heartache she feels on a daily basis or each time pees on a stick and it's negative, I would do it in a heartbeat. There isn't anything I wouldn't do for her.

My wife sits on our bed with her back to me. I love having a height advantage over her, it's perfect for times like this. She can sit here, where she's comfortable and not on the floor or in a chair. When Katelyn or Elle do this with her or vice versa, they're always getting up on their tip toes or standing on a step stool to reach. It's cute and sometimes comical.

I missed my third calling as a beautician or whatever they're called these days. Brushing Peyton's hair has become like an art for me. I start at the bottom, work through the tangles, and then work my way up. I go slow, so I don't tug on her scalp. Doing this makes me want to have a daughter, and if we do, I hope she looks like her mother. She'd be one lucky little girl, that's for sure.

Regardless, we'll take whoever science graces us with. A boy or girl. I don't even care. I just want my wife to become a mother to our child. We just need one, even though I know she wants three or four. One to spoil rotten will be plenty.

"What do you think of Noah Jr.?"

"Who's that?" I realize after I ask that I'm literally the densest husband on the planet right now. I don't try to correct myself because Peyton has absolutely earned the right to make me look like the idiot I am.

"Oh gee, I don't know, Noah!"

"Yeah, yeah." I continue running the brush through her hair. "Honestly, babe. I'm not a fan."

"Really? I love your name."

"That's because you love my d."

"No, I'm pretty sure your dick isn't named Noah."

"Don't say naughty words out loud."

Peyton cracks up. "Why do you think the eggs can hear you? What are you going to do when there's a baby in there?"

"What do you mean?"

She turns and looks at me, as if I should know the answer. Maybe I do. Maybe I don't. "You are a dirty talker, Noah Westbury. I hope you know this about yourself."

Again, I say nothing.

"And yes, we will have sex when I'm pregnant."

"I don't want my thing poking the baby."

"Your thing?" Peyton laughs hard, and I love every second of it.

I nod.

"First of all, your 'thing' won't reach."

"Are you saying I'm small?"

"Are you fishing for a compliment?"

I shrug.

Peyton takes her hairbrush and continues with her hair while facing me. "I can't believe we are even having this conversation right now. Why did you buy the condoms?"

"Uh, because we've been using them! Or am I too small for you now?"

I flinch before the hairbrush hits me. It's okay, I deserve it. When I start laughing, her mouth drops open. She tackles me. I let her. I can't win all our battles. She has to show her dominance over me. Besides, I love losing to her.

I hold her to me and slip my hand into her robe, my hand ghosting up her side until it cups her breast. She's complained about how tender they've been since she started the shots, so that's at the forefront of my mind. My other hand grabs hold of her ass, pulling her forward. I'm hard and she gasps when she rocks against me. My eyes meet her gaze as my tongue darts out, licking her nipple.

"Noah." I could come just by the way she says my name or the way she's palming my cock right now.

"I'll be fast," I tell her, knowing her uncle is on his way over. Maybe if he rings the bell and we don't answer right away, he'll take it as a clue. I doubt it though. He has a standing surf date with Quinn now.

Peyton maneuvers my joggers enough that my cock springs free. My lovely wife leans toward the nightstand and grabs a whole sleeve of condoms, ripping one off the pack. We have to be careful, especially now. It's never fun going from feeling your wife to having a barrier between you. Although, the clean-up is nice.

I switch to her other breast, paying it some equal attention while Peyton rolls the condom over my cock. She straddles me, taking all of me in.

"Fuck me, babe," I say it to mean, holy fucking shit this is hot, but she takes as me telling her to literally fuck me because my wife with her glorious fucking tits starts bouncing on my dick. Honestly, I'm feeling sort of left out of all this. I can't keep playing with her breasts and she's doing all the work. I did, however, promise her I'll be fast, and I intend to keep that promise.

"You're fucking sexy," I tell her as I let her tits slap me in the face. "God, I fucking love you."

She says nothing. It's probably time for me to shut up and do my part. I lean back slightly, giving myself a beautiful view of where we're connected. Just watching her take my dick inside of her should be enough to make me blow my load, but it's not. Mostly because I need her to come first. It's always been my rule with her.

"Lean back, baby."

She does, giving me the access I need. My thumb presses against her clit, soft and slow at first until Peyton sets the pace. The first quiver makes me smile.

"That's my girl." I'm mindful of what she said about talking dirty and filter all my words to G-rated things. Parenting is going to be tough.

"Noah . . ."

"Do you need me to finish you off?" She's on the cusp, but the orgasm she's hungry for is holding itself at bay.

"I . . . I . . ."

"I'm your man." I pull her to my chest, widen my legs and thrust into her until she's screaming my name and milking my cock in the process.

She stays on my chest, panting. The smell of sex, lust, and spermicide fill the air. It's a good thing Xander isn't coming into our bedroom. There's just something about a family member knowing you just got laid. It's not as cool as it might seem.

After Peyton rolls off me, I get up and hobble my way to the bathroom. Honestly, I should've taken my pants off, but this was a quickie with quickie type effort. Besides, I blame Peyton. She follows me and uses the toilet while I wash my hands. Ah, the joys of being married.

As soon as I leave the bathroom the doorbell rings. Perfect timing.

"Hey," I say as I open the door. Xander has his wetsuit suit on up to his waist. I'm tempted to go surfing with him and Quinn and say fuck it to the Pioneers for dragging their feet on my renewal. I took them to the Super Bowl and won. It's not my fault our team had so many injuries this past season that we didn't make it out of round one. I'm good, but I can't hike the ball to myself, run, pass, tackle, and kick the pigskin through the goal posts. Bud should've listened to me during preseason when I told him the kicker he just had to have, can't kick a decent twenty-yard field goal. If the guy can't kick twenty, he's no use to us.

"Good morning."

It is indeed a good morning. "Peyton will be out in a second. She's running a bit late this morning."

"No worries. Quinn always says he'll wait for me but doesn't."

I laugh and nod. "I think he missed his calling as a surfer. Had Harrison never moved him to Beaumont, he'd probably be a professional."

"Can you imagine?"

I pause and let the magnitude of what I said sink in. No, I can't imagine. Honestly, it's something I think about all the time. Where would I be if my dad hadn't come back? Would I be who I am today? Someone different like a doctor because of Nick? What if my uncle Mason doesn't die all those years ago?

"You okay?"

"Yeah," I say, shaking my head to clear the unmentionable thoughts from my mind. I can't think that way. Not now. Not ever.

"Morning, Xander," Peyton says as she comes into the

hallway. For some odd reason we're still standing there, like Xander is about to start selling us encyclopedias.

"Morning. Ready to do this?"

Peyton nods and leads him into the guest bathroom. I go with them, waiting while he swabs a spot on her stomach, which will inevitably bruise in a few hours. I'll be happy when those go away. I try not to notice them, especially when we're having sex. They're enough to make me want to coddle her and beg her not to do this anymore. But I'll never ask her to stop trying for a baby. At least, not now.

She turns to me and puts her hands on my shoulders, her fingers already digging into my flesh. My lips are near her ear and when Xander nods, I start talking. "This morning, watching you ride my . . ."

"All done."

Peyton sighs. "I wish my mom could do this as easily as you," she says to Xander.

"She has more at stake. Plus, she's your mother and you're her baby. Add in everything you've been through, she's overprotective and probably stressed. If I had to guess, she's probably afraid she's going to hurt you."

"Well, she does," Peyton says as we walk Xander to the door. "But I only have a few more left, so whatever."

"I could always give them to you," I tell her, but she shakes her head.

"You holding me is what gets me through these."

Xander tells us we'll see him tomorrow. Once the door closes, I pull Peyton into my arms. "What do you want to do today?"

"I don't know, but it seems like you want to have sex."

I scoff and then nod my head like a kid heading to the candy store. "What on earth give you that idea?"

Peyton rolls her eyes. "Everything this morning has

been about your . . ." She looks down at my crotch. If he could blush, he'd blush right now.

"You wound my ego."

"Suuuure, I do. Anyway, I think we should sit down and look at some of the offers Alan has sent over, map out a plan and see where we want to go."

Sex sounds much better. "Babe, I'm not going anywhere if you're still in Portland."

"I know, but maybe I'm not staying in Portland if you're not there."

"Are you saying you'd quit?"

Peyton takes my hand and drags me to our home office. "I'm saying that maybe after the baby is born, whenever that may be, I dabble in sideline reporting. It's what I wanted to do and what I went to school for."

"Ah, you just want to interview me after the game."

"Noah, not everything is about you."

I waggle my eyebrows at her. "You're right." I pull her to me and place my hand on her stomach where our baby will grow someday. "It's about this."

9

—————

PEYTON

Finally, it's egg day. That's what I've called it on the calendar, circled in orange. I know most people circle important dates in red, but to me red means something a little more drastic, like danger or stop. I look over my calendar at the array of colors. Yellow indicates the days Noah and I tried conceiving according to the ovulation chart. Sex was a chore then. It wasn't passionate or filled with the love we have for one another. It was two people having sex with a purpose. Granted, the purpose was a child we desperately want, but I missed connecting with my husband. Purple is for our sexy time and ever since we decided IVF was our next step, I've happily marked a lot of days with some purple ink.

I stand on the patio, taking in the very early morning breeze. We have an hour drive to L.A. this morning, although it shouldn't take us that long with no traffic. It's too dark to see the ocean but I can hear the waves. The tide is in, pushing onto shore. In about thirty minutes, surfers will be out there, catching waves while the sun rises over the horizon. I love my time in California. But I miss Beaumont.

I miss the comfort a small town brings. The feel of being in a tight-knit community. I never thought I'd miss it as much as I do, and I think most of those feelings stem from Elle and Ben moving back there. They kept their house here and are only here for their IVF sessions. Then they'll go back, and Noah and I will eventually head to Portland.

I'm not sure how I feel about raising our baby in a city like Portland. While I love the outskirts, the traffic is just as bad as it is here, but it seems people have stopped caring about their city. Although, raising our child there gives me a support group of other mommies, as long as their husbands don't get traded.

I groan at the thought, hating that Noah's in limbo with the Pioneers. Their stalling has put me in a precarious situation. Not only with them, but Noah as well. While I'd like to think I'd keep my job, I don't know if I would. Noah will support me in anything I do, and I mentioned sideline reporting, but I also wonder if staying home once I have a baby should be my thing. I don't have to work, thanks to my dad and husband, and if I really wanted to, I could probably work for myself. Enough of Noah's friends ask me for advice anyway. Maybe I can turn what I do into a freelance job.

Noah comes up behind me and wraps me in his arms. We sway slightly and then he kisses the top of my head. "Are you ready?"

"I am."

"Let's go do this," he says as he takes my hand and leads me toward the front door.

The entire drive into the city, he holds my hand. As much as he does it for me, I know he's doing it for himself as well. This process has been daunting but I know it'll be rewarding.

Noah and I walk hand-in-hand to the clinic. I'm tired and didn't sleep well last night. Once the anesthesiologist called to confirm my appointment time all I could do was pace. Noah begged me to come to bed with him so he could hold me. I know he wanted the comfort as much as I did. After a few hours, I relented but stared at the wall imagining how everything could go wrong.

Even now, as I sit and wait for my name to be called, I think the worse. What if Noah's out of sperm or this process didn't work? What if his sperm are shy and don't want anything to do with my eggs? That's possible, right?

Noah gives me a kiss before he follows the nurse to the porno room. Today, his donation will be used to help make our embryos. The door opens and I look over my shoulder at my reflection. My sister comes toward me, her arms outstretched. I didn't realize how badly I needed to see her until now.

"What are you doing here?"

"Noah called," she tells me. "Mom's parking the car."

"I have to go in alone."

Elle holds my hand. "I know, but we'll be here, waiting."

"Okay." A tear forms in the corner of my eye. I dab at it and then sniff. "What if I fail?"

My sister squeezes my hand. "We're Powells," she says. "We don't fail. Sometimes there are obstacles in our way, but we figure out how to move them out of our way so we can forge on."

The door opens again and my mom walks in. I go to her, and we hug. The week she gave me my shots was hard for her and me.

"I'm sorry for being a brat these past couple of weeks."

"I didn't even notice," she says as she rubs her hand

down my arm. Mom looks around the room and then at me. "Where's Noah?"

"Jacking off," Elle blurts out as she's flipping through a magazine.

"I swear you are not my child," our mom mutters.

I'm used to her outbursts. I think she does it for shock factor. Our mom on the other hand—I think she wants to smack her youngest daughter upside her head and I'm not sure I'd step in the way. Besides, Elle's tougher than me. I'd never say something like that in a public place.

Sometimes I wonder if my sister pushed me out first so she could be the baby and the protector at the same time. I should be the one protecting her, but it's never been that way. Our roles reversed when our father died. We definitely had our favorites with mine being Mason and Elle's being Katelyn's. Then everything changed and I leaned on Liam and mostly Noah. I became his shadow, and he let me, never pushing me away.

We sit down, with me in the middle. Mom keeps a hold of my hand. It's comforting knowing she's here. I do wish Noah, her, or my sister could come into the appointment room with me, but they won't allow that. I wonder if I tell them I'm afraid of needles and have anxiety, they'll make an exception. Or drop my dad's name. Every now and again I want to say, "Don't you know who I am?" Just to see their reaction. Elle's done it and people cave to her.

I should try it.

When Noah comes out of his room looking pleased with himself—I really want to strangle him right now—he kisses my mom on her cheek and kicks Elle's foot as he passes by her.

"Jerk," she says to him.

Noah sits on my sister and then reaches for my hand.

The sly grin on his face makes me laugh. Elle squirms under him. She pinches his sides and tries to push him off her. But Noah's muscular. He's used to being tackled, although far too much this past season for my liking. However, defense isn't my responsibility and it's not like I can show some two hundred pound plus line man how to block.

"Noah." I say his name in that mom tone our mothers have used so many times throughout our lives. I suppose this is good practice for when our little one comes. Or if we have a second. One would think by now, between Noah and Elle's antics, I have the "mom" voice down pat.

"What?" He puts his hands up.

"You're hurting her."

He sighs and turns to look at her. "Am I hurting you?"

"Yes, now get off me you big lug." Elle gives him one good push that I know wouldn't do anything if Noah didn't help her. He stands and faces her.

"Can you move one seat down?" he points in the direction he wants her to move. "I'd like to sit next to my wife and be with her before she goes in for the procedure."

Elle, being Elle, sticks her tongue out at my husband, but does move. Noah sits and wraps his arm around my shoulder, kissing the top of my head. "My guys are ready," he tells me. "They've been waiting for this moment for a loooong time. This is their time to shine. They won't let you down."

"I know they won't."

It's not his sperm I worry about.

Dakota, the nurse we met before, comes out and all of us women hold our breath, waiting to hear if it's our turn. The only ones here this early are either having eggs retrieved or they're getting their embryos. I hope and pray I'm back here in five days.

"Peyton," she says my name. We all stand as if we are all Peyton. At least I know they're Team Baby Westbury.

Noah walks me. "Is there any chance I can go back with her? She's deathly afraid of needles and I don't want her under more pressure than she's already under."

"Yes, but you can't stay during the procedure."

"That's fine."

As soon as Dakota turns around, I look at my husband. "Thank you."

He leans down and kisses the tip of my nose. "Anything for you."

While I know he would do anything for me, it makes me wonder if he promised this clinic something. Honestly, I wouldn't put it past him to have offered a donation or promised them his dad would do a concert for a fundraiser. He loves putting his dad on the spot.

Dakota shows me to a room where I can change. I make Noah turn around because I don't need to see his come fuck me eyes while we're in here. He opens the door, leaving it ajar, to let them know we're ready. Dakota returns and takes me into the room where everything will happen.

The anesthesiologist greets me while Noah helps me get situated on the bed. I hold his hand tightly, while staring around the room.

"Look at me," he says, and I do. He caresses my face, and I flinch. "It's okay, just keep looking at me."

Tears well in my eyes and my heart starts to race.

"Hey, we're good, right? We have to trust the process."

I nod and squeeze my eyes shut.

"Tell me you love me."

"I love you."

"Yeah, you do, babe."

I can't help but smile.

"You're all done," he says. "I'll see you in thirty minutes and then we'll know how many eggs my guys get to play with." Noah winks. "I love you more than this world, Peyton Westbury."

"I love you more."

"Not even possible."

He gives me another kiss and then walks toward the door.

"You have a good support system," the anesthesiologist says.

"I do. I'm lucky."

"Hey, Peyton. How are we feeling this morning?" Dr. Rock walks in and sits at the end of the bed.

"I'm good. Nervous."

"No need, but I get it."

Dakota instructs me to put my feet in the stir-ups. While I'm tempted to watch what everyone is doing, I'm focused on the monitor. There's a Petrie dish on the screen with my name on it.

"Peyton, can you read the name on the screen for me?" Dr. Rock asks.

"Westbury, Peyton."

"Is that you?"

"Yes," I tell her.

"Very good." She nods at the anesthesiologist.

"How do you feel about taking a little nap?" he asks.

"Is this where I count backwards?"

He chuckles. "Sure. Or you can tell me a story, something about your life. Whatever you want."

"Oh."

"How about you tell me about your husband."

Easy.

"I've been in love with him since before I knew what love was . . ."

10

NOAH

I'm not a pacer. At least, I never thought I was until now. I hate that I can't be in there with Peyton. I know she's technically asleep, but I'm not and right now my mind is racing with every scenario possible. Mostly, what if something happens to her? What if she doesn't wake up from the anesthetic? I almost lost her once and I never want to experience something like that again. It damn near killed me.

But it also brought her to me or me to her. Doesn't matter which way you look at it. Her accident was eye opening. And I still hate Kyle Zimmerman. Even though the accident wasn't his fault, he should never have been in a car ten times too small for him and driving it in Chicago when road conditions are always questionable during the season. Stupid motherfucker.

"Noah, come sit." Katelyn pats the seat next to her, but I can't, and I don't understand why the other husbands aren't pacing like me. Maybe it's because I'm obsessed with my wife. That's what my friends tell me. I get it. They're jealous because Peyton's fucking awesome. But shouldn't these guys at least care if their wives are back there by themselves? It's then that I vow to be at every single appointment she has. She shouldn't have to do this alone.

"Do you want me to call Quinny?" Elle asks.

I roll my eyes at the nickname she's given him. He doesn't seem to mind. I guess I wouldn't care if Paige gave me some ridiculous nickname. But Quinny just doesn't fit him. Not in my eyes at least.

"No. She'll be out of there in . . ." I pause and look at my watch. "Ten minutes."

"Then come sit," my mother-in-law says and pats the seat again. I give in and sit next to her and instantly my legs start bouncing. I don't know how I'm going to make it through labor and delivery at this rate. It's not knowing that is going to give me anxiety.

"Everything is fine," Elle says. I know this, but knowing and recognizing are two different things.

"We'll see how Ben feels when it's your turn," I remind her.

"When is your appointment?" Katelyn asks Elle.

"Once we know Peyton's pregnant. We want to have the babies as close together as possible."

"Have you thought about the chance of multiples?"

"No, I'm just having one egg at a time deposited. I don't want twins. They're freaky," she says as she cocks her eyebrow at her mom.

"Well, one's a freak," I mutter, and she throws her magazine at me.

"I'll tell Peyton you went back to the porno room."

I shake my head. "She'd never believe you. Besides we—"

"Stop!" Katelyn demands. She looks at Elle, "You're . . . I don't even know but I'm telling your dad so he can talk to you because I can't. And you," she looks at me. "I've known you since before you even took a breath. Don't talk about the things you do with my daughter." Katelyn lets out a huff.

"Geez, Mom," Elle says as she sulks.

I stifle a laugh. "You know your daughter and I are married, right?"

"Yep, I was there," Katelyn says.

"And you know how babies are made?"

"Noah Michael Westbury . . ."

"Oh, you got your full name." Elle continues with the childish antics by sticking her tongue out.

When my name's called, it dawns on me that Elle did all of this to keep my mind off Peyton. I stand and take two steps before turning and going to my sister-in-law. I pull her to me and wrap my arms around her. "Thank you."

"Don't mention it. Now go see our girl and come back with some damn good news."

"I will."

I follow the nurse down the hall to the recovery room. Each "room" is separated by a partition, giving the women some privacy. As soon as I see Peyton lying there, I'm by her side instantly.

"Hey," I say as I brush my fingers through her hair.

"Hi." Her voice is groggy, but nothing like it was after she woke up from the accident. My wife—the love of my life—had surgery while I was out of town for a game to remove scar tissue and only told her mom and sister because she didn't want me to worry. While I appreciate her efforts, I wanted to shake the shit out of her, and I told her under no certain terms is she allowed to do that again. Something could've happened and I wouldn't have been there.

"How do you feel?"

"I'm okay," she says. They warned us she could have cramps or be queasy for the rest of the day. Such a bummer that we'll go home, and I'll have to spend the rest of the day pampering her.

"Do you have any cramps?"

"No, not at the moment."

"Okay, well that's good."

The nurse comes in and hands me a paper bag. "Peyton has to stay for an hour and then she can leave. We've given her some Tylenol #3 with codeine for pain. Tonight, she needs to start taking Medrol and Progesterone, and then in five days we'll do the transfer."

Peyton smiles. "How many eggs did you get?"

"We got five," she says. "The embryologists will prepare Noah's sperm to fertilize your eggs. Tomorrow, we'll call you and let you know how many of your eggs were mature and how many fertilized. Then on day three, we'll give you an update on their progress. Day five is transfer day."

"All right, seems easy enough."

The nurse nodded. "Noah, you should know progesterone is a shot and we don't recommend self-administration because it needs to be injected intramuscularly."

"No problem," I tell her. "Her uncle is a physical therapist and can do it for her."

"Great. I'll be back to check on you in a bit. Noah, if she needs anything to eat or drink, there's a small cafeteria across the hall; help yourself."

As soon as she leaves, Peyton sits up and grimaces a bit. I sit next to her, rubbing my hand up and down her back. "Five eggs. That's good."

She nods. "I wanted more."

"I know, but we have five. That's more than we had yesterday."

Peyton nods again. "We haven't talked about what to do if multiple eggs fertilize."

"Well, we can definitely save them. Assuming this round is successful, we can do it again in two or three years."

"What would you say if I told you I'd want to transfer all five?"

"I think you're overthinking things here, babe. You're only allowed to transfer two. So, if all five fertilize, we'll freeze them and do this again. We don't know how your body is going to react or if you'll be able to carry. We haven't made it that far yet. Trial and error, remember."

"What if I can't?"

"Then we have the eggs for a surrogate."

Her eyes fill instantly with tears. I pull her to me and remind myself it's the hormones. She's hopped on all these drugs to make the eggs. She knows the ins and outs, probably better than the staff.

"Tomorrow, we'll know. Believe me, my guys are ready. This is their time to shine."

Peyton laughs.

"And then in five days, they'll put that little embryo in you, and it'll do its thing. Nine months from now, you'll scream at me, tell me you hate me, and blame me for all the pain you're in. So, I'd like to point out now, technically I didn't get you pregnant." I hold my hands up in surrender.

"You're such an ass."

"I know." I kiss her. "But I'm your ass and you can't ever get rid of me."

"I can't even if I tried."

"Rude. Your words wound me."

She leans into me. "I need it to be tomorrow already."

"I know. Me too."

❧

THE CALL finally comes in around noon with the news that we have two fertilized eggs. Just enough for a transfer of two or we can try with one. This wasn't the news Peyton wanted. Honestly, I'm not sure how I feel. The nurse told her the next few days would determine whether we come in on day five. The embryo needed to be blastocysts and if not, they'd have one extra day before all of this was for naught.

I stop paying attention to the call when Peyton breaks down in tears. She leaves her phone on the counter.

"Hey, sorry," I say toward the speaker. "We'll wait to hear from you in a couple of days." I hang up figuring if it's important they'll call back. "Peyton." I call her name throughout the house, and finally find her locked in our bathroom. "Babe."

"Go away."

"C'mon, that's not fair, Peyton."

"Life's not fair, Noah."

"You're right. It's not. And you've been dealt a shitty hand. We're trying to make the best of it. We're doing our best. Shutting me out isn't going to help."

"You don't get it."

"To some extent, I do, Peyton. Wanting a child is natural. It's the natural progression in our relationship. Hell, I want you to carry my baby and it kills me inside that I haven't been able to do the one thing you need me to do." My throat tightens. I swallow the sob threatening to escape. I press my back into the door, I slide down and bring my knees up. "I see the tears when you think you're hiding them. I see the calendar, the highlighted dates, and know when you're sneaking out of bed to take a test. These things aren't going unnoticed no matter how hard you try to hide them. Peyton, if I could, I'd go back and change things. I truly would. Not acting on my feelings when you turned eighteen has been my biggest regret. I let perception cloud my judgment and I feared what people would think. What the NFL and our parents would think, and I was wrong."

My wife says nothing.

I don't know how long we stay like this, with me sitting against the door and her hiding in the bathroom. When she finally opens the door, I fall backward and let myself hit the floor. Looking up at her, she's bent forward slightly with her long, dark hair cascading toward me like a waterfall.

"Hey."

"Hey," she says.

I extend my hand out for her to take, hoping she thinks she's helping me up. When she clasps mine, I pull her down to me. Her breath escapes her lungs. I chuckle at the sound she makes when she lands on me.

My arm wraps around her, and I hold her there. She begins to cry, breaking my already splintering heart even more. All I can do is hold her because anything else is out of my control. Right now, all I want to do is make love to my wife, show her how much of a woman she is to me, that she's perfect with or without a child. But I can't. Because hopefully in four days, they'll be able to transfer two embryos, and they can't take the chance I have a swimmer in there, looking for some fun.

Instead, I hold her and let her cry. I encourage her to let it all out, reminding her that I can take it. I do this while staring at the ceiling and fighting back my own emotions, my own tears. Later, when I'm in the shower or she is, I'll break down. That's when I'll let my emotions take over. She doesn't need to see me like that, not when she's dealing with this.

Later, when she's asleep, I'll go to her yoga room and sit in front of her Buddha altar. Maybe he has the answers to help us. That's when it hits me. I may have the answer.

"Come with me," I say as I tap her shoulder. We get up and I take her hand, pulling her to our bedroom. "Sit on the bed," I tell her as I go to my dresser. Inside, I go through my socks until I find the silk pouch I'd been given in Portland from Madame Kiesha.

Inside the bag is the bracelet she gave me. She said this would help Peyton. I don't know why I didn't give it to her before.

"Here," I say as I slip it on her wrist. "I don't know if I believe this or not, but Julius had taken me to this guru once. He needed something from her, and she knew right away we were trying to have a baby. She sensed things and then gave this to me. She said you're supposed to wear this until after the babies come."

"Babies?"

I nod as I look into her eyes. "She definitely said babies."

Peyton lifts her arm and looks at the bracelet.

"I'm sorry I didn't give it to you earlier. I don't know why."

"Because I'm meant to have it now."

I kneel in front of her and rest my head on her lap. She runs her fingers through my hair, comforting me, when I should be the one comforting her.

"It's going to be okay, Peyton."

She nods. "I know. Because I have you."

11

PEYTON

We have, or do I say had, two viable embryos. I suppose, in the grand scheme of things, two is better than none. I'm grateful for those two. I'm not trying to be selfish or entitled. I know there are women out there who desperately want a child and can't have one. It's such a feeling of emptiness, knowing you can't do the one thing your body is meant to do. I can't even imagine how others must feel—those of whom can't afford to go through the process.

On the fifth day, our two embryos were transferred into me. Now we wait. As much as I'd love to be Phoebe from *F.R.I.E.N.D.S.* and run to the bathroom to pee on a stick, seeing a negative line would probably do me in right now. I'll wait, even though waiting is not going to be easy. I want to thank the likes of Amazon and the internet for the instant gratification I get from clicking on something I want and having it arrive at my house two hours later. Why can't all parts of life work this way?

When we get home, Noah makes me lunch and brings it

to me on the patio, which overlooks the ocean. It's funny, we have a view and access to the water, but don't have frontage. Unlike my parents where you walk out the sliding glass door and you're in the sand, here, you have to take a couple dozen steps or so, walk down a path and possibly wrestle some overgrown plants. Maybe if you're lucky, you'll run into some wildlife. Noah has a sign at the bottom of the path that says, Enter at Your Risk, mostly to deter people from coming up. I can't recall a time when a beachgoer decided to take the path and the stairs to the property, which is probably a good thing.

Noah sits beside me. We're sad, relieved, and angry. The barrage of emotions is overwhelming and I suspect they will be for some time. Of course, it doesn't help that I have so many hormones pumping through my system right now I could cry, jump for joy, and beat the crap out of something.

I take a bit of the shredded chicken sandwich and hum in satisfaction. I'm not hungry, but I have to eat. The last thing the doctor said was to lay low and keep things as normal as possible. The normal part is near impossible. Noah and I are active, rarely sitting around doing nothing. If we're not visiting my parents, we're in the water, hiking, or having sex. The no having sex thing is going to unalive my husband. He'll be a whiny brat for a week. Me too. Noah's the best part of my day. My life. Being with him is like finding the answer to everything I question. It's hard to explain.

Halfway through my sandwich, I look over at my husband. He's relaxed with his head tipped back and his feet resting on the firepit. His plate rests in his lap. Noah's already practicing the "I'm just resting my eyes" line the rest of the men in the family use.

"Hey," I say, getting his attention.

He hums in response.

"I think we should start a foundation or something."

"For what?" he asks without opening his eyes.

"For women who can't afford to go through IVF. I'm sitting here thinking, if this round doesn't work, it's nothing for us to do it again. But for some . . ." I take a deep breath. "For many, the cost is out of reach, and they may only get one try. That's not fair. It's not their fault."

"It's funny you're bringing this up. The day we had the consultation, I thought about making a donation, but then I wondered if we made it there, who would it actually help. I think your idea of starting a foundation or even a fund is smart. I bet we can ask your mom to manage it. With her still being a volunteer at the hospital she might know who could spread the word."

"That's a good idea. We'll have to meet with a lawyer, make sure we're not liable for anything and establish the regulations on how we disperse funds."

Noah scoots his chair next to mine and takes my hand. "This could be a big undertaking, Peyton. Are you sure it's something you want to take on right now?"

I nod. "It's hard for me to work if you and the others aren't working. Obviously, I'll have to be at organized team activities, and then go back when you do. But I still have time to help get things set up."

"Ugh," he leans his head back and groans. "Don't remind me about OTAs."

"Sorry."

Noah shakes his head. "It's not you. It's the fact I don't have a contract so I'm going into this last year in limbo because I don't know if they're working on a trade."

"Maybe a trade isn't so bad."

He squints his eyes at me. "What?"

"The more I think about it, maybe I don't want to work after I have this baby." I place my hand below my stomach, in hopes that at least one of the embryos wants to attach, grow, and become our child. I know there's two in there but I'm not considered pregnant yet and it's going to drive me mad.

Noah's hand rests on top of mine. "Honestly, babe. I'd love nothing more than to look out and see you with this little guy or gal in the stands, rooting me on."

"As long as we have baby headphones."

Noah laughs. "Of course. His or her grandpas will demand it. But seriously, Peyton. If you don't want to work, then don't. I don't want you to stress about a job or about my career. I could quit tomorrow, and we'd be fine. We've invested well."

I cup his cheek. "I love you and thank you for taking care of us."

He kisses my palm. "There isn't a place in this world I'd rather be."

My husband's sweet. That is until his eyes drift south of where our hands rest.

"Seriously, Noah?"

"What? I can't help it. I look at you, horny. I think about you, horny. I'm a walking talking erection when it comes to you."

"We can't, so don't even think about it."

Noah leans toward me and rests his forehead against mine. "It'll be worth the wait."

"Even if I'm not?"

"You are," he tells me. "There isn't a doubt in my mind."

For dinner, we head to my parents. When I walk into their condo, my eyes widen as my grandparents surprise me. "What are you guys doing here?" Seeing them together makes me wonder what they're up to. I don't want to think about them dating—not because I don't think everyone needs to find love—but because it feels awkward. Grandpa Powell dating Grandma James.

"Michael and I are going on a cruise," Grandma Tess says.

"I'm going too or am I chopped liver?" The sound of Bianca's voice echoes from the other room. I glance at Noah, who looks as surprised as I am.

Tess rolls her eyes. "Yes, we're all going."

"That sounds fun," I say after hugging her and my grandpa. "How are you?" I ask him.

"Doing great. Things are good. Clean bill of health."

Okay, why did he say that?

"Did you not have one before?"

He kisses me on the cheek. "I'm good. I promise."

I worry about him. About everyone. Life's too short and fragile, and this family of mine has known too much heartache. I'm not naïve in thinking my grandparents are going to live forever, but I'd like them to be around when Elle, Quinn, and I become parents.

Noah and I follow my grandparents into the family room, where Bianca is kicked back and enjoying a mocktail. From what I've been told, she's changed a lot since Liam came back. I don't remember much of her when I was younger, and Noah doesn't talk about the time Bianca wasn't around. My mom always says, it was a different time back then, but I also know she's referring to her parents, who she pretty much disowned after my father died.

After greeting my parents and Bianca, I look at my mom. "Where's Oliver?"

"He's napping."

I groan.

"He'll be up soon. Come sit, tell us how today went."

Noah sits next to his grandma, and we recount everything that happened this morning. "So, now we wait."

"And how do you feel?" Bianca asks Noah.

He looks at her and smiles. "Pretty damn good. I'm confident."

"What are the odds you end up with twins?" my dad asks.

I shrug. "Both embryos could become a fetus."

"Or they could split," my mom adds.

"Could you end up with four?" Dad's eyes are wide. He holds his arms out and then shakes his head. "I don't know if I can hold four at once."

My laugh falls short. I can't imagine four babies. I'd love and welcome them, but lord help me. "No one says you'd have to hold all four at the same time."

"Equal love for all," he says.

"Twins would be fun," Noah says. "We'll be happy with one, two, it doesn't matter, just as long as our little guy or girl is healthy." Noah winks at me.

I know he says one, but he wants eleven, so he has a full offensive line. Years ago, maybe. If things had been different for us. I don't even want to think what it will be like to have eleven children. I marvel and bow down to the women who do.

While everyone is talking and drinking fruity cocktails, I excuse myself and head toward the beach. There's a nice breeze and the tide is out. I walk until the sand becomes hard and then sit down. The sun will set soon. It's one of my favorite times of the day, especially when we are here. Watching it disappear, only to be replaced by the moon is one of the most magical sights to behold. The promise of a new day to come.

I don't know how long I'm out there for when my grandpa sits down next to me. I lean my head on his shoulder as he wraps his arm around me. He's another reason I think about moving back to Beaumont. Aside from Elle, he's all I have left of my father. When I look at him, I like to pretend I'm seeing my father in him.

"It's beautiful here," he says. "I'm surprised Elle wanted to move back to Beaumont."

"Beaumont's family," I tell him. "There's a sense of peace and calm there. And you."

He chuckles lightly.

"A cruise, huh?"

"Yep. Bianca's idea," he says. "I never thought I'd go on a cruise, let alone with Bianca Westbury. She's changed though and apologized for all those times when she wasn't a good mother to Liam."

"That was kind of her."

"She loves you and Noah, that's for sure. Ever since Harrison picked us up at the airport, she's yammered on and on about how today was so important for you and how we need to shower you with love so the egg or whatever it's called knows how loved they'll be when they get here."

"Thanks, Grandpa. I really appreciate it."

He clears his throat. "The reason I came out here, other than to sit with my beautiful granddaughter, is to talk to you about your father."

"Oh?"

"I know you don't remember much of Mason. You and Elle were so young when he passed away, but I know your mom has made sure you girls have always known him. Even Harrison. He's a good guy and I'm happy your mom found him. He's raised you girls as his own and that's all a man like me can ask for. Now, I plan to say this to your sister when I get back from this vacation those ladies are taking me on, but since I may be who knows where, in the middle of the ocean when you find out if you're pregnant or not, I want you to know that you don't have to name your son Mason. I think a lot of people expect you or Elle to do this. When you and Noah sit down to think about names, remember he or she is their own person, and they need their own name."

I absorb his words. Truth is, I hadn't thought about names other than Noah Jr. which my husband has vetoed. "Thank you," I say to my grandpa knowing it took him a lot of courage to say those words to him. I wrap my arms around him, feeling his bones. He's lost weight, which I know happens with age, but I don't like it.

"Promise me."

"I promise to consider the name wisely," I tell him. "Mason's a great name, regardless. Noah might want to honor my father that way. He lost him too and I think sometimes people forget that. Sure, I was his daughter, but Noah had him for ten years. They were close. I think if Noah and I were to have a boy, Mason's probably on the list of names."

Grandpa nods. "Well promise me this—" He takes my hand and holds it. "Never let him think he has someone else's shoes to fill."

"We won't, Grandpa. But he will know what a great man he was. Just like you."

We turn at the sound of cackling coming our way.

"Lord help me," he says when his travel companions come into view.

I can't help but laugh as my grandma and Bianca maneuver through the sand with cocktails in their hands.

"You're going to have the time of your life, Grandpa. I can't wait to hear all about it."

"When you read about the man who went overboard, just know I loved you with all my heart," he says laughing.

12

NOAH

This has been the longest week of my life. I don't know if I'm coming or going or if I'm supposed to sit still. If it's not waiting for the week to pass so Peyton can take her pregnancy test, it's me spending hours on the phone with Alan trying to figure out the next steps in my career.

"I think, regardless, this is my last year in Portland."

"You don't want to wait and see what they come back with?"

I shake my head and then mutter, "No. They've had their time. If I'm their guy, their future, they'd have made an offer by now. Clearly, I'm not. With the draft coming up . . ." I trail off. It's never a bad thing for a team to draft multiple players for the same spot. But when they're not communicating with their captain, who happens to lead the offense, that becomes a problem. "I don't want to be caught off guard."

"I agree. There is interest from other teams. One being there."

I run my hand through my hair. "Here, or near Beaumont. Peyton wants to move home."

"What about her job?"

"She's upset with the situation and is seriously considering staying home after the baby is born. Neither of us want to hire a nanny, and honestly, she doesn't need to work. Or she could open her own business and become a freelance analyst doing what she does for the Pioneers for anyone in the league. Peyton isn't worried about finding work."

"I didn't know congratulations were in order," he says.

"They're not. Yet. We'll know tomorrow."

"All right, let me get to work on some stuff. Do you want to leak this to the media?"

"Nah. If they draft the way I expect them to, the media will run with it."

"Roger that." Alan hangs up and I stand there looking out the window. I hear Peyton behind me before I feel her wrapping her arms around my waist. Her head rests on the middle of my back. Well lower back because she's so damn short compared to me. I wouldn't want her any other way.

I rest my hand over the top of hers and sigh.

"It's going to be okay," she says as she squeezes me tightly. "No matter what, everything will work out."

"You have a lot of faith in people."

"Just you," she says as she maneuvers her way under my arm. I look down at her and close my eyes as her fingers trail lightly over my face and through my hair. "They don't deserve you."

"Or you." I pull her to me, cradling her against my chest and resting my chin on top of her head.

"Can I be real for a moment?" She leans back as much

as she can without me letting go. We look into each other's eyes for a moment before either of us speak again.

"I wouldn't expect anything less."

"What if you finish out your contract and retire?"

My eyes widen.

"Hear me out," she says as she once again traces her fingertips over my face, staying near my forehead. "Each time you get tackled or sacked I fear the worst. Sometimes, you stay down longer than I expect, and the team docs have to go out and see you. Yes, I know sometimes you do it because you're giving your O-line a break, but other times, I worry. What if something happens to you or this?" She runs her hand over my hair, her nails dragging against my scalp. I know she's talking about my brain. "You have a lot to live for especially once we get pregnant. I know I speak for our future children here, but we'd really like for you to stick around for a long time."

"I hear you, Peyton."

"That's all I ask."

"Tell me this. What would I do in retirement?" I'm not yet thirty and she wants me to retire. It's not unheard of, but not necessarily the standard. Although, by thirty-five I could see it.

"Coach with Nick. He's back to coaching baseball and he'll be the head coach for football. You know he'd bring you on as an assistant without hesitation and then turn it over to you. Train Mack. Get him ready for college. There are endless opportunities. Hell, most retired athletes open gyms and run clinics. If we go back to Beaumont, you could open a facility. Give the kids of Beaumont a place to play basketball, add batting cages, artificial turf, and a roller rink."

"A roller rink?"

Peyton shrugs. "I've always wanted to learn how to roller skate or even ice skate. We didn't have a place like that growing up. If we did, maybe you would've stayed out of trouble."

My eyes widen at her statement. "I was never in trouble."

"And I'm still a virgin," she says sarcastically.

"Well, we both know that's not true," Noah says with a smirk.

She pinches me, then laughs. "Whatever you decide, I'll support you."

"And you? What are you thinking?"

Peyton shrugs. "Depending on the test, we'll see. I know I'm young, but being married to you and possibly being pregnant with our first and maybe only child . . ." She pauses and places her hand over her lower stomach. "Right now, I can't imagine leaving him or her for hours on end. I know our moms will be there to help, but I really want to be a hands-on mother."

I kiss her forehead and pull her into my arms. "Like you, I'm in your corner. Whatever you want to do, we'll do."

"Like get a dog?"

I lean back and look at her warily. "A dog?"

She nods and bites her lower lip. "I really like Beau and I think I'd like to get one. We didn't have a pet growing up and I've always wanted one."

"All right. Want to go to the shelter?"

"Wow, if I knew it would be that easy, I'd have asked ages ago."

Noah kisses my forehead. "How many times do I have to tell you, babe, anything for you."

Both of us realize, once we get into the car, we have no idea where the shelter is. I drive aimlessly until Peyton finds one on her phone. After parking, I leave the SUV on for a moment and look at my wife, bouncing in her seat, eager for a dog.

"No one says we have to bring home the first one we see."

"I know. There are things I want."

"Like?"

"Well, obviously baby friendly, especially with Ollie. He yanks on Beau's ears. Not that Beau seems to care. House trained. Not afraid of water, traveling or people. With the amount of people we're around, a skittish pup wouldn't work for us. And I'd like one a little smaller than Beau. He's a big boy."

"I want an Irish Wolfhound," I tell her. She has no idea what one looks like and looks it up on her phone.

"That's a mini horse and we live in an apartment. They're pretty though, but something tells me we won't find one in the shelter."

"Probably not. Are you ready to go in?"

Peyton nods, opens her door, and slips out of the car. I meet her around the front, and we go in. We tell the young man at the front that we'd like to look at available dogs. He seems enthused and says we can go in and let him know if we want to meet one. As soon as we open the door, barking erupts.

"I hate it here."

"Yeah, me too," I say. "All these poor dogs looking for a home."

"Maybe that's something else we can do in Beaumont, if you decide to retire."

"What's that? Work at a dog shelter?"

"No, open one or foster dogs until they can be adopted."

I sigh heavily. "That would be a huge undertaking. Let's start with one first and see how we do as dog parents."

Peyton huffs. "If Elle can do it, so can I."

No doubt.

We walk by each cage, reading the information the shelter has on the sheet attached to the kennel. I'm on one side, Peyton on the other. We follow the rules of no petting even though some of the dogs look at us, desperately seeking attention. At the end, we meet, and both shake our heads. Each one had something that didn't meet our requirements.

"They're either not good with babies or other dogs. The other things on my list we can work with, but not those."

"Definitely not."

I thank the young man for his time, and we head back to the car. Peyton finds another shelter, and then another. Each one yields similar results as the first.

"I want to adopt," she says. "I think that's important. We have the ability to give a dog a good home."

"While I agree with you on adoption, we may want to consider going to one of the stores like Ben did or finding a breeder. With a breeder, we'll know more about the temperament of the parents and such. The store, well those are overpriced and I'm not a fan of them. Although, the one in Beaumont is like the others."

"Adopting gives a lonely pup a home."

"Yes, but you can't adopt them all."

She eyes me, as if I'm challenging her. Peyton will need to buy a new house if she wants to adopt multiple dogs. As I already stated, we live in an apartment in Portland and our house in California doesn't have a yard. As is, we'd have to find a space or clear one for a dog to go to the bathroom.

"Maybe this is my way of putting off the inevitable."

"Which is?" I ask her.

"The pregnancy test."

"You have until tomorrow morning."

"True. But I'm antsy and eager. And I do want a dog because we could never have one because we were either on tour with the band and by the time we stopped doing going, Elle was deep into cheering and went to a lot of competitions. And I was . . ." She pauses and looked at me. "Following you around. I don't know if I would've given up my obsession with you for a dog."

I start laughing and she sighs. "You're something else."

"Eh." Peyton shrugs. "There's one more not far from here. Let's see what they have."

We drive for a bit and then pull into another parking lot. This shelter is bigger than the others we've been to. We go inside and for the first time, they ask what we're looking for in our forever friend.

Peyton gives the woman the list and explains our lifestyles, stressing how a skittish pup wouldn't be best due to extensive traveling.

"What breed?"

Peyton shakes her head. "It doesn't matter, really. Something medium size, unless you have an Irish Wolfhound. Apparently, my husband has always wanted one."

The woman's eyes go wide. "We actually got one in the other day. I just listed her on the website. She's about six months old."

"Can we see her?" I ask instantly.

"Yes, come this way."

We follow the woman through the door, down a hall, and into a large room with more cages. I hate the cages.

"Here she is."

In the back corner this predominantly gray fluff ball sleeps. I crouch down and let out a low whistle. "Hey, girl."

She picks her head up. "Come here." I look at the employee. "Can I go in?"

She nods and undoes the latch. Peyton and I walk in just as the pup stands.

"She's huge, Noah."

"She's perfect, Peyton. She's still a pup and we can train her. Their temperament is perfect for a family. They're non-aggressive, loyal, and very smart."

"I won't be able to walk her on my own when you're working."

I scratch under her chin. "I'll train her to stay at your side. If that doesn't work, we'll hire someone, but everything in me says she's going to be perfect."

"How do we get her?" Peyton asks the woman.

"We run a full background check on you before we agree to adoption."

"How long does that take?"

"A day or two. Sometimes three."

My heart sinks. I continue to focus on this girl and the way she's loving the attention she's receiving from me.

"How can we make one happen within the next thirty minutes?"

"Um . . ."

"A sizable donation?" Peyton suggests. "Your adoption fee is three hundred. I'll add a zero if you run the background checks on us now so my husband can take that little girl home."

"Did you just tell me you'd give me three-thousand dollars?"

"We'll double it," I say, without looking over my shoulder. "My wife has all my personal information to get this started."

"Okay. Well, in that case, follow me right this way."

Peyton and the woman leave. I stay in the cage with this sweet angel. She hasn't jumped on me once, nor has she bitten me. While sitting there, I look in her mouth at her teeth and gums, check her paws and belly, pushing on spots I've seen other vets do on television.

"Well, you look healthy, but we'll take you to the vet anyway."

She sighs and leans into me.

"You need a name," I tell her. "Not sure how we're going to come up with one since your new mom has asked me to come up with a list of names for our new baby."

At the word, baby, her ears perk.

"Did whoever have you before have a baby and then drop you off here?" I pet her head, scratch behind her ear, and then nuzzle her. "That won't happen with us," I tell her. "You're going to have a big family. You can swim every day, run in the sand, chase a ball, and have a best friend in Beau."

I know it's probably wrong for me to talk to her like she's already mine, but I'm unwilling to leave her. This is a sign. From whom or what, I don't know, but it has to be.

Peyton returns an hour later. "Let's go."

I don't move. "Is she coming with us?"

My wife keeps her expression stoic. "You're looking at our first child," she tells me.

A smile spreads across my face. I pump my arm in the air, startling the pup. "Look at that, you're coming home with us."

"First stop is the pet store. We need everything."

I scoop the pup in my arms and take her over to Peyton, who dotes on her. "Please don't steal my husband."

Moving the dog slightly out of the way, I lean down and kiss Peyton. "I love you. Thank you."

"You better be right about this, Westbury."

"Oh, I am."

We thank the woman as we leave. Peyton climbs in and takes the puppy from me, while I slip onto the driver's seat. On our way to the pet store, I say, "She needs a name."

"She does. I say we post her photo online and let your fans decide on what her name should be."

"Oh, this ought to be fun."

"Famous last words, Westbury."

At the stoplight, I look over at Peyton and our new puppy. Peyton's loving her, just like I knew she would. Now, all we need is for tomorrow to be just as good as today.

13

PEYTON

$\mathcal{N}$oah's on the floor with Stevie Nicks, playing with her tug toy. It's her name for now until something else sparks interest. I like it though. It's not Stevie, but Stevie Nicks and she seems to respond well to it.

Night one was interesting, and I think it is somehow preparing us for when we are parents. I know a puppy and a baby aren't even close in how they're going to react, but I imagine the crying at night and wanting to be held are somewhat similar.

We bought training books and a DVD, which we watched as soon as we arrived home with the multiple hundreds of dollars we spent at the store on dog-related items. Stevie Nicks is already expensive. Who knew dogs needed beds in every room of the house? I didn't and neither did the clerk at the store who asked why we have so many beds in our cart. I looked from the clerk to my husband and shook my head. With what we paid for everything we bought for her, she's pricey. But she's worth it. Noah's in love with her, and she seems smitten with him.

Noah's watching me, waiting. Using our puppy as a

distraction until the timer goes off. He looks at his phone and then me. I don't want to know how many minutes are left until I can look at the stick. The pit I feel in my stomach right now doesn't feel all that great. I've never been this nervous before. Not even when I propositioned Noah on prom night. That was easy compared to waiting.

"Time," he says as he stands. "Come on."

"You go look and tell me."

"As fun as that sounds, no." He tugs on my hand and pulls me up. "Come, Stevie Nicks," he says as we walk down the hall. She doesn't know what that means yet, but she follows us, nipping at Noah's heels as we walk. He calls them love bites.

We go into the bathroom. The culprit for our stress during the last four minutes rests on the countertop, with the news we've been waiting a week for.

"How are we both going to look?"

"We'll close our eyes. I'll hold it up and we'll count to three, then open them."

"Okay." I stand next to him with my eyes closed.

Noah stands behind me, wrapping his arms around me. I sag into his chest, needing to feel him this close. "No matter what, our journey isn't over," he says.

"Nope, we have a dog."

Noah laughs and kisses my cheek. "You know what I mean."

I nod against his scruff. "Ready?"

"One, two, three."

I open and stare until I hear, "You're going to be a mom," being whispered in my ear. I'm not sure what comes first, the tears or sudden rush of elation. Either way, my husband has me cocooned in his embrace, kissing the side of my face as I try to grapple with what he's said.

"Are you sure?"

"I am," he says and shows me the stick more clearly. The word on the little white stick blurs as the tears continue to fall down my face. "We're going to have a baby."

"We're going to have a baby."

I place my hand on my lower stomach, now my womb, as if I'm protecting our child. Then it all sinks in.

"Holy shit, Noah!"

"I know."

"No. I mean, holy shit. We're going to be responsible for another human. Like, it's going to depend on us for everything and then some, and then . . ."

Noah chokes out a half laugh, half cry. "Are you seriously coming to terms about parenthood now?"

"I don't know, I just—" I trail off and look into the mirror and down at Stevie Nicks who is the most chill puppy. "Am I going to be a good mom?"

She wags her tail. What does she know? She's only known me less than a day.

"Holy shit," I say again, this time to myself.

"Do I need to call someone?"

I turn sharply at his suggestion. Everyone knows we've done IVF and had the transfer. We can't keep this a secret from our family as much as I'd like to let this stay between us a bit longer.

"No, I'm fine, but we need to make some calls."

"Let's head over to your parents'. We'll call mine from there. We can tell them all at once."

I shake my head. "If we show up at my parents, they'll know. Then your parents will be upset they didn't know at the same time. Oh, this is hard." I wring my hands together.

Noah shakes his head and pulls out his phone.

"No," I put my hand over it. "My sister too."

Noah pulls my chin toward him so he can look into my eyes. "You're being frantic for nothing. Your mom hasn't called. Neither has mine. Let's take our girl over to meet her grandparents and Ollie, then we'll do one big group call. Okay?"

I nod but am certain this won't work.

We pile into the SUV, and by pile, I mean we pack enough essentials for an apocalypse. Noah seems to think that in the time it takes us to get to my parents and back, Stevie Nicks will run out of toys, training snacks, and beds. I say nothing because I made sure she had on her pretty doggie shirt. I might have gone a bit overboard with dog clothes that probably won't fit her next week.

The entire drive I have the urge to rest my hand on my stomach, as if doing so will make sure everything works the way it's supposed to. I'm not naïve in thinking this pregnancy will be perfect but now I can't let the what ifs and negativity cloud my mind. Until now, we didn't even know if I could get pregnant. We're at least moving in the right direction.

An hour later, we're pulling into my parent's. Quinn's bike is out front, along with my dad's. There are times when I appreciate that Noah doesn't own a motorcycle. He can drive one but has never had the urge to buy one. But then, there are moments when I think, damn he'd be really hot on a bike.

"Quinn's here so at least we don't have to find a way to bring him in on a call."

"Yep." He picks Stevie Nicks up and carries her over to the small patch of grass. After encouraging her to do her business he rewards her with a treat and a lot of love. I do as well because she's scruffy and honestly, I can't get enough of her.

Noah leads us down the path and into my parent's house. The TV's on, but no one is really talking. We head down the hall and before we turn the corner, Noah says, "We have a surprise." He holds our pup out, like the scene from The Lion King. Someone, I think it's my dad, starts singing.

"Oh, my you got a puppy!" My mom all but squeals as she comes to take her from Noah. Honestly, now that I think about it, getting a dog before taking the test was the best idea. No one is staring, waiting for me to give them the news.

Then our universe aligns. Beau comes bounding into the house, with Ben and Elle hot on his heels, followed by Nick, Mack, and Amelie. There are lots of hugs and when I'm about to ask what everyone is doing and why my sister didn't tell me she was back in town, Liam, Josie and Paige walk in. I glance at my husband, who wraps his arm around me.

"I thought this would be the best way to tell them," he says into my ear.

"And if it was negative?"

"Then my parents are in town, and we have a puppy to show off."

"I love you."

"I love you," he says, kissing me where his mouth was.

"Dog!" Oliver screeches. He pulls on her ears, and she cries out, causing Ollie to cry. My dad's there, teaching him right and wrong, and before I can grab her, Mack has her cradled like a baby.

"What's her name?"

"Stevie Nicks," Noah says proudly. "As one name though."

"Isn't she, like, old?" Paige asks, much to my dad and Liam's dismay.

"Child, we're going to have a music lesson when we get home," Liam says.

"Hey, where are the Davises?" I ask.

"Australia," Josie says. "Eden has an event."

"Oh." That totally sucks.

Elle comes over to me and puts her arm around my shoulder. "How are you feeling?"

"I'm good."

"Do you have something to tell us?"

I play it off. "No, why?"

"Um, seriously, P?"

"What?"

"You were supposed to take a test today."

"Oh shit. I've been so wrapped up with the puppy I totally forgot." I wave the thought away. "I'll do it when I get home."

"You've got to be kidding me." Elle throws her hands up in exasperation. It takes everything in me not to crack a smile, to stay as stoic as possible.

"Where's Quinn?"

"Right here."

I hear him yell from outside. I go out there and find him hosing off, still in his wetsuit. "Where's Nola?"

"Studying for an exam. She said she'd try to come over later."

"Oh. Come meet our dog."

"You gotta . . . oh my god, come see Uncle Quinny." My brother drops to his knees and crawls toward Stevie Nicks, who is eating up all the attention she's getting except from Oliver. He'll learn to be soft with her, just as he had to learn to be soft with Beau, who wants to play with the pup.

"Did you just call yourself Quinny to the dog?" Elle asks.

"I did. Do you have a problem with that?"

"Uh, as a matter of fact, I do," she says. "One, that's my nickname for you. Two, you don't act like this with Beau. You're hurting his feelings."

"Beau has Mack," Quinn says. "Stevie Nicks as her Uncle Quinny."

My sister isn't having a good day. Ben wraps his arm around her to console her.

Noah comes to me and leans in. "Are you ready to tell them?"

"Only Elle has said something. I think Stevie Nicks was a good distraction."

"I think they're not asking because they're waiting for us to say something."

"You know, as soon as we get their attention, Elle's going to know and I'm not going to be able to hide my smile."

"Do you mind if I do something?" he asks.

I shake my head.

"Okay, follow my lead."

Noah puts his arm around me and relaxes. "Hey, Dad. I think Harrison has bigger muscles than you. I think he can probably take you in a fight."

"Bullshit," Liam says. "Stand up, James. Take your shirt off."

"Oh my, you're a genius," I whisper to my husband.

Our dads stand and take their shirts off. Both start to flex, causing our moms to catcall their husbands.

"We need a measuring tape," Liam says.

"Just stand next to me. You'll see mine is bigger." He waggles his eyebrows and my mom's eyes widen.

"Harrison!"

"What?" Dad shrugs.

Noah shakes his head. "I've got you both." He stands and takes off shirt.

"Quinny, you next?" Elle asks.

"Nope, I'm good."

"Doesn't matter," Noah says. "I've got you all beat." He flexes and then moves his arms into a cradling position. "Because in nine months I'm going to have my child in my arms."

The room goes silent as everyone processes what he said.

"What did you say?" Josie asks.

"You're going to be a grandma," Noah tells her and for the briefest of moments, it's just him and his mom in the room.

The room is no longer silent. Everyone erupts in a chorus of congratulatory cheers, well wishes, and then my sister puts it all so eloquently. "Bitch, you could've told me."

"I could've but we wanted to tell everyone at the same time."

There are lots of hugs, along with tears. My dad is the last one to come up to me. He pulls me into his arms, and it takes me back to the time when he taught me how to take my anger out on his drums. He didn't care that I was five or that Quinn had punched someone for me. All he cared about was giving me an outlet to express the hurt I felt inside from losing my father.

He holds me for a long time, thanking me. When we part, I look at him. "You're going to have to decide what you want to be called."

"I know. It's going to have to be better than whatever Page comes up with."

"This isn't a competition among grandpas," I tell him.

"Sweetie, everything's a competition."

14

NOAH

The other day when we were at my in-laws, Stevie Nicks chased Beau around on the beach. He was so gentle with her, even though she's not exactly small and pretty close to his size. He let her catch him, then he'd run again. It was a repeating cycle of dog energy that made me tired just watching them.

And then he took her to the water.

At first, Stevie Nicks didn't care about her feet getting wet, and then a fairly large wave came ashore and scared the crap out of her. One of Peyton's requirements with having a dog was that they like the water. So, I did what I thought would be best. I picked her up and waded into the ocean, holding her against my chest like a moron. The scratches from her claws are deep and aching, but she likes the water now and even follows Beau when he chases the waves.

After a run on the beach where Stevie Nicks does most of the running—if we can call it running: She usually sways to one side, speeds away, falls, gets back up, nips at my heels, and then needs a nap—we're using the outside shower to clean our feet. Hopefully this is something she gets used to because I don't like the idea of her tracking sand into the house and with her shaggy hair, she's bound to be a magnet for everything.

"Peyton, we're back," I say when we get inside. I stay behind our pup while she navigates the stairs. Whoever had her before us must not have had stairs of any kind because she's very unsure of them. Our first day home, I showed her how to use them and placed training treats on each step as her reward.

"Come on, you can do it." I tap her hind end to give her a little nudge. She looks over her shoulder at me and huffs. I'm tempted to carry her, but in a few months she's going to be huge and I don't know if I want to carry a full-sized wolfhound around.

Who am I kidding?

"Do you want Daddy to carry you?"

My question stops me in my tracks. Up until now, I haven't referred to myself as daddy or Peyton as mommy but that's what we are: to Stevie Nicks and to our little one growing inside of Peyton now.

"Holy crap," I say to the dog. "I'm going to be a dad."

Stevie Nicks looks at me like, "Duh."

How is it just setting in?

I give in, scooping her up, carrying her to the main floor and setting her down. She's hot on my heels as I rush into mine and Peyton's bedroom. "Peyton." I say her name a little louder this time, but she still doesn't answer. I pull my phone from my pocket, tap the screen and then the icon to see where she's at. The whole "find my wife" (that's what I call the app) is great except it doesn't tell me her exact location, just that she's in the house.

"Peyton!" This time I yell her name as I walk through

the house. She's bound to hear me. "Fuck this," I say as I press her name and turn my speakerphone on.

"Hi," she says as soon as she picks up.

"Where are you?"

"In the bathroom."

"Which one?"

"Ours. Where are you?"

"Looking for you." I hang up and head back to our bedroom and then into the bathroom. I knock once before opening the door to find my wife on the floor with numerous pregnancy tests scattered around her.

"What's wrong?"

She shakes her head.

I'm on my knees instantly, pulling her chin toward me. "What's wrong?" My tone's demanding, something I rarely have to use and hate using with her.

"Nothing."

"Clearly, it's something." I look around at the tests on the floor. Leaning over, I pick one up. The digital readout says pregnant. Another one shows the right number of lines. "Did you take all of these this morning?"

"Yes."

"Why?"

Peyton sighs. "I dreamt last night that yesterday was a dream, that I actually wasn't pregnant and when I woke, I started to wonder."

"So, you spent the morning in the bathroom? Peeing on sticks?"

She nods.

I sit down next to her and wrangle Stevie Nicks in the gap I've created to keep her corralled. "This is normal," I tell her. "I read about it in one of the books or magazines.

Women take multiple tests, so you don't have a false positive. Were all of them positive?"

Peyton nods and a smile begins to form. "Yes."

I can't help but smile. "Want to know what I said moments ago to our pup?"

"What?"

"I asked her if she wanted Daddy to carry her upstairs. It hit me square in the chest—we are parents to her even though she's a dog—and in nine months, we're going to be parents to a baby boy or girl, and then someday within how many ever months it takes, they're going to call us mama and dada. Babe, we have new names."

"You're a goof," she says as she pushes on my leg with her hand. "But you're my goof and I love you."

"Speaking of names . . ."

"We have time," she says. "Grandpa and I talked when we were all at my parents. He said I shouldn't feel obligated if we have a boy to name him Mason. I pointed out that Mason might be a name you want for your son though."

I go quiet, remembering the last time I saw my uncle. I was ten but other than that, my memory's fuzzy. The night he died, it had been raining all day and I remember asking Mason about my game the next day.

The next day, Mason was gone.

And then I met Liam.

I clear my thoughts and try to disguise my inner musings by clearing my throat.

"You okay?" Peyton asks softly. I nod.

"I'll be honest, I hadn't really thought about him in a while."

"I know. It's been so long, and I don't really remember him."

"You saw him though."

Peyton nods and I say nothing. She believes she saw him while in a coma, and I believe her. It's not my place to discount what happened to her.

"When do you get your first ultrasound?"

"I'll call them on Monday to let them know the test was positive. They'll probably have me come in to have my blood drawn and then it'll be at the six-week mark, but we won't see much." She holds her fingers up about a quarter inch apart. "The baby will only be this big. I'll have another one somewhere between the sixteen and twenty-week mark. We can find out the sex then."

I let out a long sigh. "Twenty weeks?"

She nods.

"Are you worried about multiples?"

Peyton shrugs. "The chances are high. Honestly, I love my twin. Our bond is—"

"Like nothing I've ever seen. I'd be okay with having twins." This time I'm the one pushing my leg into hers.

Stevie Nicks whines, getting our attention. Or Peyton's. She pulls the pup into her lap and starts petting her. Within seconds, her little doggie eyelids flutter closed.

"Do you want to find out the sex of the baby?"

"What a tricky question."

"Why?"

"Because if I say yes, then you'll say yes and vice versa." Peyton nods toward the sleeping dog in her arms, who's snoring. "She's so cute."

"She is. Thank you."

"You don't have to thank me, Noah. I'm already in love with her."

"She's going to be best friends with the little bean in your belly."

"Bean?"

I shrug. "I want to call him or her something. It seems so callous just to refer to it as 'it' or 'the baby' and makes me think we don't already love them. I think someone should invent a pee test that tells you the sex of the baby now and not at twenty weeks."

"Are you saying you want to know?"

I look at her. Her eyes are hopeful. "Yeah, I want to know, and I want to have one of those gender reveal parties."

"You just want to have a party."

Her phone rings, waking the pup. "It's Elle," she says and then answers it. "Hey. Yeah, okay. I'll have to go in anyway. Yep. Bye." Peyton hangs up and looks at me. "Elle's going to start her shots on Monday."

"She doesn't have to wait for whatever cycle?"

Peyton shakes her head. "I guess not. She just asked me to go with her."

"If she gets pregnant soon, the babies will be very close in age."

Her lips turn up in a grin. "It's what we want."

Stevie Nicks leaves Peyton's lap and starts to walk around. "I should probably get her outside before she has an accident." I stand and then help my wife up. "I'll clean up in here if you want to go make breakfast."

"Deal." She rises up and kisses me. "Love you."

"Love you more."

After I take Stevie Nicks out to do her business, after which she was rewarded with a treat and lots of affirmations, I clean the bathroom as promised. For some reason, I check each test. I don't know if it's for my own curiosity or what. Each positive brings a smile to my face. In nine months, Peyton will give birth to our child, and while it was created in a Petrie dish, it's still one we created together. Thank God for science.

When Stevie Nicks barks, I rush out of the room and find her sitting at the end of the hallway, tail not wagging. I approach her slowly, peak around the corner and roll my eyes. My father is on all fours, acting like a dog.

"You're scaring her," I tell him and then look at my mom. "Really?"

"He's a child. Humor him," she says. She walks by, kisses my cheek and before she can ask where Peyton is, I point toward the kitchen.

"What are you doing here?"

My dad finally sits up and then beckons his granddog to him. Thankfully, she goes. "Uh, staying here."

"Oh. Did I know this?"

Dad shrugs. "Ask your wife."

We go into the kitchen where I find Peyton sitting at the island and my mom making breakfast. "Really?" This seems to be my word of the moment.

"She insisted," Peyton says.

I fight the urge to roll my eyes. I had a feeling my mom would baby Peyton.

"Where's Paige?"

"She and Mack went with Ajay, Jamie, and the kids to Disneyland today," Dad says.

"Damn, that would've been fun to do."

"I'm not going on any rides," Peyton says.

"Nope, but once you start showing, we can go and get you some ears and take a bunch of photos. Speaking of, come here." I take her hand and drag her back to the bedroom. "Take your shirt off."

"Excuse me?"

"Just do it. I want to take your picture. I saw a video this couple did. They took a picture every day so they could capture her bump growing. I want to do it."

Peyton takes her shirt off. Unfortunately for me, she's wearing a bra, and my parents are here. I snap a picture and then make sure it's saved. "Come here."

She does after she puts her shirt back on and wraps her arms around me. I hold the camera up and snap a photo of us. Right at that moment Stevie Nicks comes trotting into our room. Peyton picks her up and cozies up to me again for another picture. I show it to her and instantly save it as my wallpaper.

"Our first family photo," I tell her.

"I'm sure we'll end up taking a ton."

I nod. "I want to do it all. Everything from introducing Stevie Nicks on social media with a pregnancy announcement, the pregnancy photoshoot, and family photos with matching outfits. I want to be the cheesy family that does it all."

Peyton holds Stevie Nicks between us. They both kiss me at the same time. "There isn't anyone in the world I'd ever want to do this life with except for you, Noah Westbury."

I push strands of her hair away from her face. "I've known from day one you were mine."

PEYTON

en paces up and down the hall near the bathroom waiting for Elle to come out. My sister opted to spend the night at our place last night, wanting to take her pregnancy test here, rather than at her house. I didn't question her mostly for selfish reasons. Hell, yes, I want to be one of the first ones to know if she's pregnant, but I also have a sense from her that she feels like she's not and then I'll be here to console her.

"What's taking so long, Elle?" Ben asks at the door.

"I gave her twenty tests to pee on," I remind him. He lets out a long sigh.

"She just needs one."

"Yes, but then she'll end up taking another nineteen like I did. Give her a minute," I say this as if I'm some type of professional when it comes to taking a pregnancy test. I know I've taken my fair share of them, but what woman trying to have a baby hasn't?

The door opens and Ben almost falls in. "Everything okay?"

"Yes," Elle says as she comes out of the bathroom

showing him her phone. "Now we wait four minutes." She steps out of the doorway and heads into the living room where I'm waiting. Noah's taken the dogs down to the water to help them exert some energy. Beau may be older than Stevie Nicks, but he has as much energy as a toddler with a sugar high.

"Do we have to wait?"

"If you want them to be accurate," I tell him. "Come sit."

"I'll pace," he says.

"He's going to wear a hole into your floor," Elle says as she sits down. She reaches for a magazine and starts flipping the pages, closes it, and then opens it again. I sit next to her and place my hand on hers.

"Three minutes."

"That's a long time in the grand scheme of things."

"Yes, but now it's even less. I know it's easy for me to say."

Elle nods. "At least you already know."

"And you will soon." I've been able to do all my blood-work and confirm my pregnancy. The clinic did my first scan to make sure everything was in place, and then referred me to an obstetrician for my first appointment. While I've never been pregnant before, no one is taking any chances and considering my high risk due to the injuries I've had. It's hard not to wonder what the hell is going on in that region of my body, but I'm hopeful I can carry to term or at least long enough to give this baby a fighting chance.

"I don't know why I'm so nervous."

"It's to be expected," I tell her. "This is something you want."

Elle laughs. "Who would've thought?" She looks toward

the other room where Ben is. "He changed my mind about everything."

"Sometimes that happens."

"Not with you. Your life is as you planned it."

I give her a halfhearted shrug. "I don't know about that. While I'm eternally grateful to be pregnant, this isn't how I pictured things."

"I meant with Noah," Elle says.

"You know I'm probably only with him because of the accident. If that hadn't happened, he probably would've never admitted his feelings for me."

"Can you imagine being married to someone else?"

I shake my head.

"I can't imagine him being married to someone else either. I think that would be weird at family functions."

I brush Elle's hair off her shoulder. "Something tells me our family functions wouldn't be the way they are now. But who knows."

Elle jumps when the timer on her phone goes off. She stares at it for a moment, leaving the piercing sound to echo through the house. Ben rushes into the room and looks at her while I press the button to silence the alarm.

Ben extends his hand, holding it there for Elle to take. He helps her stand.

"I'm going to go down to the beach with Noah."

"No, I want you to stay," Elle says, unshed tears in her eyes.

I bring her into my arms. "You have Ben," I whisper into her ear. "Share the news, good or bad, with him first." I'm up and out of the room without looking back. I'm torn though. As much as I want to be there for my sister, this is something she needs to do with her husband.

Beau spots me before Noah or our pup, and I have a

feeling the only reason Stevie Nicks is running toward me is because she's chasing Beau. I crouch down and greet Beau, taking all of his love until my girl reaches me. I'm on my ass before I know what's going on, being attacked by dog kisses.

Noah hovers over me, blocking the sun. "Are you having fun?"

"The best time," I tell him as he helps me up. I brush the sand away and watch as he throws a ball, mostly for Beau. "Does Stevie Nicks chase the ball?"

"She does, but Beau's a bit faster so she runs behind him. It'll change though in a few months. She'll be so much bigger than him. Where's Elle and Ben?"

"Reading their tests."

"I can't believe you suggested she take so many."

I shrug. "She would've just done the same thing I did, so might as well get it over with."

"Yes, but at least start with one."

"Yeah, it is overboard, but it's Elle. She's the go big or go home type."

"True." Beau drops the ball at our feet and Noah picks it up with the fetch toy and tosses it again for the dogs. "Ben says she's not very confident the IVF has worked."

His words give me pause and I sigh. "I got that feeling from her as well. I'm certain it's why she spent last night here."

"She shouldn't have any problems, right?"

I shake my head. "I don't think so. Her egg count was higher than mine, as were their embryos. I suppose she could be in the same boat as me, who knows. I don't think she and Ben tried to have a baby before he got cancer."

"They weren't even together."

"Don't remind me."

"The only saving grace was we were in Portland during all of that and didn't have to play mediator."

I nod. "Believe me, I'm grateful. I wouldn't want to choose between them. It's funny, while we were waiting for the timer to go off, Elle said something about how my life is how I pictured it." Noah stops walking and looks at me. "There was a time when I didn't think I'd have this." I point between us.

"I know," he says. "But I also know I wouldn't have been able to hide my feelings for much longer. The only way I would've been able to do so was to stay away from you and as it was, that was hard."

"You almost married her."

Noah looks at the sand and sighs. "Which would've been a massive mistake on my part."

"I never liked her," I tell him. "I never liked any of the women you brought home. But Dessie was just plain evil. She saw me as a threat and when I had the accident she saw her future slipping away."

"Are you defending her?"

I shake my head. "No, what she did is inexcusable. But desperation makes people do the inexcusable."

"Change the subject," he says as he steps closer to me. Noah rests his hand on my stomach. "How's my bean today?"

"Fine, I think."

"When is morning sickness supposed to start?"

I lift my shoulder. "I think it should have by now? I'm four weeks in. Maybe it doesn't start until six weeks? That's normally the time women find out after missing their period."

"Maybe you'll be one of the lucky ones and won't have it."

"From your mouth to God's ears, Noah Westbury. I hate puking and while I know the end game, the idea of sticking my head in the toilet every day for who knows how long does not appeal to me."

Noah crouches in front of me. "Hey, little bean. If you could do me a solid and not make your mommy sick, I'd appreciate it." He stands and gives me a look. "What?"

"That's the first time you've spoken to the baby."

"No, it's not."

"Yes, it really is. You've said some things, but that is the first time you've spoken directly to him or her."

"Well, I'm going to have to rectify that. Do you think I should read Madden's autobiography or something else?"

I can't hold back my laughter or my eye roll. "While John Madden is a legend, maybe we should start with something more educational."

Noah covers his heart with his hand. "You wound me."

"You'll get over it."

We walk for a little bit more before turning around. I'm thankful Beau stays with us, which keeps Stevie Nicks with us as well. She's very attached to him and his ears. Poor guy.

When we get to our steps, Noah and I pause. "Do you think we should go in?"

I stare up at the house and nod. "It's either good news or back to the clinic for another round."

"Elle's a trooper," Noah says. "Nothing seems to faze her."

"That's not true," I tell him. "You see what she wants you to see. I see the real her. The parts of her she hides from everyone else. She even hid from Ben for a long time because she didn't want him to judge her. It took her a long time to really, truly open up to him. Honestly, it's no different with me and you. You see a completely different me, especially at home. You know my ins and outs, what works for me and what doesn't, and you know what I need. Elle wants a baby with Ben, especially after everything he's been through."

Noah pulls me to him and cups my cheek. "Your love for your sister is unwavering. All I meant was, the shots didn't faze her. On the off chance she has to go through the treatment again, she can do it. She's strong and determined. I didn't mean to insult her."

My hand grips his wrist and I turn my head slightly to kiss his palm. "I'm sorry. I forget that you've been there our entire lives. You know her too."

"Probably more than I should being her brother-in-law."

"True." We climb the steps and head to the outside shower. I brush Stevie Nicks while Noah works on Beau. We'll never get all the sand off them, and I resign myself to having sandy floors. "I'll sweep the floors later," I tell Noah when I give up.

He laughs, brushes off his feet then mine, and then we head into a very quiet house, which I take as a good sign.

"Hello," I call out.

"In the living room," Ben says.

Noah and I approach with caution and find Elle and Ben sitting on the couch. Neither of them looks at us or even each other. There's a single pregnancy test sitting on our coffee table, on top of a paper towel. My husband directs me toward the love seat before I can reach for the stick to see if I'm going to be an aunt or not.

"You're scaring me," I tell my sister. "Spit it out."

"Maybe I'm contemplating some grand reveal like you and Noah did."

"Noah planned it, not me."

Elle eyes Noah, who's grinning like a fool.

"Elle," I say her name softly. "At Thanksgiving I asked if you'd carry mine and Noah's child and you said you couldn't because you and Ben wanted to start a family. I said I wanted us to be pregnant at the same time if we could figure things out. Do you remember?"

She nods.

I swallow hard, looking for any sign, but she's stoic. Not flinching or even hinting at anything. Noah reaches for my hand. "You're killing me, Elle. Are we going to have our babies at the same time?" My voice cracks at the end. I cover my mouth instantly, already knowing what she's going to say.

"How does Auntie P sound to you?"

I'm not sure who I scare more with my scream, the dogs or Noah. Elle and I jump up at the same time, ignoring the men in the room. We hug each other tightly, crying into each other's shoulders.

"We're going to be moms," Elle says, and I nod. "I'm so fucking screwed."

16

NOAH

*A*lan calls, says he's in town and wants to stop by. Of course, I tell him yes because I'm a guy and I don't think about things, like how there are a hundred and one pregnancy magazines all over the living room or how the garbage is full, as is the sink because Peyton and I haven't moved from the movie room in a couple of days. She wanted to watch movies like *Three Men and a Baby*, and some others. I was happy to oblige her in every way possible.

Now, we're frantic. Peyton yells at me for moving slowly but honestly, I'm not sure what she wants me to clean. She thinks our house is dirty. It's not. Especially after I load the dishwasher and turn it on. I also gathered her magazines and put them in our bedroom. Sure, we haven't made the bed yet, but Alan is definitely not going in there.

"Babe," I say when she tries to brush past me. "Take a deep breath."

"It's perception, Noah. Alan's only ever been to our apartment. He's going to come in here and think we live like pigs."

"The apartment in Portland is clean because we're never home and have a maid. Here is where we live. This house looks lived in."

Peyton looks off to the side. "Should I hire a maid? I should. Shouldn't I? A professional would have this place clean in minutes compared to the hours it's going to take me. Yeah, that's what I'll do."

I have to wait for her to stop talking to and answering herself. "If we want to hire someone, we will. Tomorrow. Right now, Alan is coming over. Hopefully with good news."

"Right. I'm going to place an order for groceries because the refrigerator is empty. You know, because we don't go to the store."

"We're going to have to get better about some of this stuff, aren't we?" I run my hand through my hair and sigh.

Peyton frowns and places her hand over her stomach. "Yeah. We're going to have to be super adults."

"Shit," I mutter, and she starts laughing. "Not to mention we're going to have to watch our language."

"You"—Peyton jabs her finger into my chest and leaves it here—"have to watch your language. I'm perfect."

I grab her wrist and pull her roughly to me. "You like to say some pretty colorful things when we're—"

"Noah Westbury if you finish that sentence, so help me—"

"You'll what, babe? Spank me?"

Her eyes widen and she lifts her hand only to pause mid-swing when the doorbell chimes. As if on cue Stevie Nicks barks, and then she barks again having realized that she does in fact make that noise. It's been cute watching her develop her bark. The first time she did it, she looked around at us, unsure if that was her or us.

"We're going to have to train her not to bark."

"Yes and no. I want her to alert us when she's uncomfortable. Especially if someone's near the house or you and the baby. But I agree, she doesn't need to bark at every little thing."

"Go get the door before she thinks this is a game." Peyton kisses me and then goes to hold Stevie Nicks from running out the front door.

"Alan!" My agent stands there, looking around at the landscape, dressed in a three-piece suit and wearing aviators. I have a few choice things to say but bite my tongue. This guy is supposed to have my best interests at heart, but there are times when I wonder if he does or if he's only looking out for his commission.

We shake hands and I step aside to let him in. Long gone are the days of briefcases and satchels. Now everything is done on the phone or tablet, which he carries in his hand.

"Hey, Peyton," Alan says when she steps into the foyer, carrying our pup.

"Hi, Alan."

"Who's this?" he asks.

"Stevie Nicks," Peyton says.

"Hi, Stevie."

"Gotta add the Nicks part," I tell him. "We're doing the full name as one name."

Alan looks at me oddly, and I shrug. "We're keeping up with the trends, Alan."

He goes back to petting the dog for a bit.

"Is this, sit in the living room kind of business, or dining room table?" I ask Alan.

"Living room is fine," he says.

Peyton sets Stevie Nicks down and tells her not to jump. Alan asks some questions about her, which we answer on our way into the living room.

"Alan, can I get you anything?" Peyton offers.

"Water is fine. This won't take long."

His statement gives me pause. Why would he be in California if what he's about to say or show me won't take long? He could've called from his high rise in New York if that's the case. Still, we sit, and I say nothing until my wife is back in the room. Any decision I make, I make with her by my side. We are a team.

"Why are you here?" I ask as Peyton returns with three glasses of water. "Thanks, babe," I say when she hands me mine. When she sits down, she's next to me, with her hand on my thigh. It's comforting.

"I've been pounding the pavement, so to speak," he says. "There are four teams interested in you, who plan to make a run for you at the deadline. This means a mid-season switch, or you wait out your contract and see if the offers are still the same."

I cringe at words because it's unprecedented for a starting QB to leave mid-season. Every other position, yes, but not the leader on the field. And then it hits me.

"Have you spoken to the Pioneers?"

Alan shakes his head. "They're not returning my calls."

I glance at Peyton. She smiles softly, but it doesn't reach her eyes. I know she's worried. Hell, so am I.

"What are my options?"

Alan sits back and crosses his ankle over his knee. "Demand a trade, sit out until the deadline, or play your last year in Portland and hope for the best."

"The latter is a gamble." While we like to think we're

invincible, our bodies are not. We take hit after hit and recover "enough." Never fully. Something always hurts, creaks, or aches to the point where you can't move.

"Peyton," Alan says her name to get her attention. "Have they said anything to you?"

She shakes her head. "I wouldn't ask either and if I did, I wouldn't expect them to be honest with me."

"What if I retire?"

Alan's mouth drops open. "Seriously?"

I shrug. "Why not?"

"Well, for one, you're at the top of the game."

"If that was the case, the Pioneers would be all over my shit, either signing me to a new contract or trying to trade me for top dollar. They're not. So, clearly, I'm past my prime."

"Ridiculous," Alan says. "These teams want you." He shows me his tablet and the four teams who have expressed interest in me.

I shake my head. "Two of them drafted QBs in the last two years. They want me as a back-up." I glance at Peyton, and she tries to smile again. Baseball looks pretty good right now. Either that or coaching with Nick. "I think retirement is at the forefront of my mind," I tell Alan. "But I'll let you know before the season starts for sure."

"Are you sure that's what you want to do?"

I nod and stand.

Alan stands and shakes my hand. "All right. I'll keep working though so when you come to your senses, we'll have an avenue."

"Thanks." I walk him to the door, hold it open as he steps out.

He turns. "You're young, Noah. Teams want you."

"Just not as someone to lead their team. I need to let that sink in for a bit, Alan. I'll be in touch." I shut the door and rest my head against it. Seconds later, Peyton's arms wrap around me from behind and she rests her head in the middle of my back. We stay like this for a bit, just being one with our thoughts. I have a feeling I know what she's thinking, just as she probably has my thoughts all figure out.

"I'm sorry, Noah."

I sigh heavily and grip her wrist and tug her hand, so I can turn and face her. "You're the analyst. What did I do wrong?"

"You know I would've told you," she says. I believe her, but still feel like something is missing.

"Do you think you missed something?" I know she didn't, but I ask anyway.

"Let's go watch a game film," she says as she tugs me toward our media room. I sit in the chair, waiting for a game to come on screen. She finally sits next to me, with the remote in her hand, and gives me a stack of papers. "These are your game notes," she says as she presses play.

On the screen is a condensed version of one of our games. It's whistle to whistle, no commentary, commercials, or delays. Just the teams and the officials.

Peyton lets it play for a moment and then stops it. She stands and goes to the screen. "Here, you miss stepped and you released the ball too early, causing Julius to reroute slightly. If you had hit him in stride, he had an easy shot to the end zone. With this play, it took you five more downs to score."

I look down and read her notes. They're verbatim to what she just said.

"Here, Julius didn't run the route correctly. You noticed

and hit him in stride. However, Chase thought the throw was for him. He leapt and fumbled."

Again, her notes say the same exact thing.

"Okay, enough."

"Are you sure?"

"Come here."

She does and I pull her onto my lap. She straddles my thighs. "I'm sorry for doubting you."

Peyton runs her fingers through my hair. "Stop doubting yourself," she says. "Just because Logan doesn't want to sign you again, doesn't mean you're not one of the best quarterbacks out there. Logan's an idiot."

"He's your boss." I point out.

"He doesn't know the difference between a zone defense and man coverage. He thinks the defense just chases people around. I don't even know how he got hired."

"Maybe you should take his job."

She shakes her head. "It's not something I want. I'd be less involved and if I'm going to work, I want to be where the action is."

My hand slides under her shirt and up her back. I look into her eyes. "Is this okay?" I ask as my fingers play with the clasp of her bra. She nods and I slide the hooks loose, moving my hands quickly to pull her shirt over her head, along with her bra.

"Do they still hurt?" I press my lips to her breasts, mindful of the soreness she's talked about previously.

"Some, but that feels good." Peyton holds my head, keeping me near her chest. We haven't been intimate since . . . well shit I don't even know because I've made it a point to respect the changes her body is going through. I don't pretend to imagine or understand the emotions she's feeling right now. It's funny because I've never considered myself to be a patient man, but it seems I am.

Peyton grinds against my hard cock. I let out a strangled groan crossed with a hiss and bury my face between her tits. Her reaction is immediate and instinctive as she tilts her head back, a soft moan escaping from her parted lips. Her hands roam over me, tugging at my shirt until I give her enough space to take it off. Nails dig into my skin and then softly trace the contours of my back.

"I've missed us like this," I say into her flesh, reddened by my stubble. Her perfume fills my senses, a tantalizing mix of floral and all Peyton. Her fingers move from my back and into my hair, tugging harshly. She presses harder into me. The friction sends my mind reeling.

"Let's go to our room," I say against her flesh as I start to push us out of the chair.

"No, here. Now."

I am not one to tell my wife no and start maneuvering my joggers and boxers down until my cock springs free. Peyton grips my shaft, giving me a solid pump before sliding off my lap to take her shorts off.

For a moment, I stare at her. Taking her all in. I'm the only one, besides her, who can see the tiny bump starting to form. Every day, I've taken a photo of her, to mark the growth of our child. I reach for her, bringing her closer to me and place my lips on her belly. I don't know how I got so lucky, to be her husband and the father of her child. As cheesy as it sounds, she completes me.

"Babe," she whispers as her fingers brush through my hair. I pull away from kissing along her tan line and look at her. "I need you."

Peyton will never grasp the magnitude of what those words . . . hell, what any of the things she says to me mean. I sit back and bring her forward, again straddling me. She grabs a hold of my cock, strokes me a few times and then hovers over the tip. Painstakingly slowly, she takes me in. Inch by inch, until she lets out a contented sigh, and despite the disappointment I felt earlier with Alan, this feels right. Being home is where I'm meant to be.

17

PEYTON

$\mathcal{M}$y mom and Elle show up at my house early. I swear the sun has barely risen when my annoying sister bursts through my house, acting like we're planning her wedding or something. My head hurts and I'm afraid to take anything, and the homeopathic remedies only work part of the time. Lately, I haven't felt great. Some foods turn my stomach sour, but it's not like I'm puking or anything. The nausea comes and goes and is mostly non-existent. I guess I'm one of those women who can say their pregnancy has been easy. So far, minus the whole getting pregnant part, it has been.

I come out of my bedroom wearing a dress. We're going to see a venue today for Elle and Ben's vow renewal. She wants the whole ceremony, with our dad walking her down the aisle. I don't blame her one bit. It was a magical moment. Not only for me, but for our dad as well. Deep down, even though he's known Noah for most of his life, and with Liam being his best friend, I'm not sure my dad was ready to let me go.

As soon as I see my mom, she comes over and hugs me,

and then sets her hand on my non-existent bump. Noah says he can see a difference, but I don't and I'm not sure I believe him.

"I bet you can't wait to show off your bump," Mom says.

Do I want that? Part of me thinks I do, but then, I'm not so sure.

Elle scoffs as she walks into the room. "We match," she says as she points to her also non-existent bump. She's going to be the one showing her bump to everyone and not have a single care in the world about it.

Sometimes, I want to be more like her. Elle's confident in everything she does and doesn't show any fear and never holds back. That's not me. I'm not meek, but if something isn't going my way, I let it slide and just fade into the background. I don't like confrontation, and I definitely don't want any attention drawn to me. Noah and I have kept our growing family a secret. We want to control the narrative when it comes to what photos of me are out there. We have the ones we'd taken the morning we found out we were pregnant, but he's yet to post anything.

Our lives have always been so public, whether it be our dad's career or Noah and his team winning the Super Bowl, no matter what, we've always somewhat been in the public eye. While I accept that—I've grown up with it—the early days of pregnancy are so intimate and special, and I want to savor those moments with my family. I don't want to be the unwilling participant in Bump Watch in the showbiz columns just yet. Not when there's a doubt at the back of my mind that the really tough days of this pregnancy are yet to come.

"I wonder how long I can continue to look like this?" Elle looks in my hallway mirror. "If I start showing before the ceremony everyone is going to think I'm having a shotgun wedding," Elle says.

"You should wear a shirt that says, 'I'm already married to my baby daddy' to get attention," I tell her.

"No, she shouldn't," Mom says, completely unenthused with my attempt at humor. "Come on, we're going to be late."

Our mother keeps a tight schedule. It's something she learned when she moonlighted as 4225 West's manager or whatever the heck she was. She didn't last long—something about fraternizing with one of the band members—that's what we tease her about. The band doesn't actually have a policy like that in place.

Elle and Ben want to get married at a vineyard. It doesn't matter which one even though she has a list of requirements. The view being one of them. I can't fault her there. No one wants to get married with a road behind you or some cow pasture next to the venue. We've already toured a few, none of which sparked any real interest from my sister. The guys appreciated it though. Each time we toured one of the vineyards, Ben and Noah helped themselves to the free wine offered. In the words of my loving husband, "Ben and I have to double up since you and Elle can't drink." I sure do love him.

"Shotgun," Elle yells as soon as we get outside. As the oldest, I should be able to sit in the front. I look at our mom, who says nothing.

"Fine, but I get the front on the way back," I say to Elle.

"Only if you're fast enough to call it."

"Then I'm not going or I'm driving myself. I'm not sitting in the back both ways."

"Girls!"

We stare at our mother, both of us smirking. She sighs

heavily and pinches the bridge of her nose. I'm not sure what her issue is, it's not like we're fighting or asking her to come in between us.

Well, maybe I am.

"Elle you're in front for the first two stops, and then Peyton until we get home. If you don't like it, I'll stay home."

Mom looks at Elle when she says the last part.

"I'm good with that," I say as I make my way to Mom's car. "Come on, we're going to be late."

Elle likes to sit up front because she likes to control the radio or whatever streaming app she's using. We're halfway down the road when she plays a new song. I find myself bopping along to the beat and even pick up on the catchy chorus.

"Who is this?" I ask.

"Plum," she says. "You remember the all-girl band?"

"I do. I have them on my playlist. I like them a lot."

"This new single is going to drop next week," Elle says.

Mom looks in her rearview mirror. "Ask her who is on back-up."

I don't ask or look at Elle but she answers anyway.

"Quinn," she says. "He worked with them some last year but sings on this album. He also helped produce it. I think he has co-writing credits on three songs."

"Really? Dang, he's so talented."

"They're going on tour soon," Mom says.

I look at Elle for confirmation. She nods. "I'm not going with them. Or maybe I will show up at a couple stops. I don't know. I know dad raised us on a tour bus, but we were also older." Elle shrugs. "Besides, I worry about Ben. It's not like I want to leave a newborn with him and I'm not sure how he feels about tour bus life."

"What about a nanny?" I ask.

"Are you using one?"

I shake my head. "I'm thinking about quitting."

"What?" Mom screeches and I feel the car swerve.

"I know," I say with a sigh. "But we only had two embryos and I feel like I'm blessed to be pregnant now, I really don't want to spend ten hours a day away from this baby. And I don't want someone else to raise him or her."

"What if it's Mom?" Elle asks.

"Unless I quit that means Mom is moving to Portland with Oliver."

"As much as I love you both, I'm not becoming a nanny. Your dad and I are very much looking forward to being grandparents. Spoil them and send them home."

"Like you with Evelyn and Jamie?" Elle asks.

"Exactly," Mom says as she turns into the first vineyard. "We love Oliver, but he's a handful. I never realized how tired I was until he started walking."

"Any word on the adoption?" I ask as we get out of the car.

"Hopefully we'll hear next week. Your dad wants it done because I think the band is going to head back on tour. He doesn't want someone taking a photo of Ollie and having it plastered all over the web."

"The last thing you need is for his mother to come back," Elle says.

"That would break my heart in too many ways to count. At first, it's what I wanted, but now that he's been mine for a year and a half, I can't imagine my life without him."

Elle reaches for my hand. We walk side-by-side, with me in the middle and our mom on my other side. It's an odd formation but works for us.

"He's going to end up being a big brother to our babies," I say.

"If he's anything like Quinny, he'll be the best," Elle says.

"As long as we can teach him to be nice. He's in the pulling, biting, and hitting stage. I have no idea where he's learned any of this because it's not like your dad acts this way. It's definitely not a learned behavior."

"Maybe from the play dates he has?" Elle asks.

"Possibly, but I'm there with him. I don't see it. Although, sharing is an issue at those play groups. The other babies take his toys, and he cries, which I get. Technically, he's an only child and doesn't understand sharing. Your dad and I try to work on it, but I think it's different when it's toddler to toddler."

"Well soon you'll have a houseful," I tell her as we reach the door to the winery. "You'll be on full-time grandma duty while Elle and I are basking in the sun."

Mom lets out a soft chuckle. "I love you dearly, but no."

"Riiight," Elle says as we walk in.

As if on cue, Elle's contact walks out and greets us. She introduces us to Kerry, and we start the tour. She takes us through the vineyard, pointing out the different grapes, and tells us about the growing season. She details the history of the vineyard, what wines they produce, and introduces us to other employees as we walk the grounds. This is all fascinating, if not mundane. Every winery has the same story, it started with a dream, or it's been handed down through many generations. I'm not sure if Elle is even interested or just wants to see the spot where she would walk down the aisle and renew her vows with Ben.

When we finally reach what Kerry refers to as the grand wedding location, I'm not impressed. I have a better view of the ocean from my patio. It's hilly, uneven, and you can faintly hear the water. If Elle and Ben wanted to see the water, they'd have to walk to the edge and the ocean still wouldn't be in their backdrop.

Kerry takes us inside to show us where the reception would be. The room is small, not that Elle's guest list is overly large, but she'll have a live band or four and people will dance. Our father will have industry professionals there and I believe Elle and Ben are inviting some of Noah's teammates. There needs to be space and this room doesn't have it.

Elle glances at me and without her saying anything, she knows I'm not impressed. Sometimes it's hard to hide how you're feeling, but the website for this winery showed a very different picture of what they can offer.

As soon as the tour ends, Kerry urges Elle to sign a contract, saying dates are filling up. She's good at her job, but the winery isn't selling itself. At least, not to me.

"I'm still looking at other places," Elle tells her. Kerry nods. She gets it. Every bride has to do their due diligence. "I'll be in touch."

Once we're an earshot away, I say, "Not a fan. The pictures they have on their website do not match."

"No, they don't. I hate when businesses do this," Mom says. "It really chides my butt that they wasted our time."

"Whoa, Mom. Watch the naughty language," Elle says, and we both laugh. "Don't worry, I'll tell Ben and he'll mention how disgruntled his MIL was during the visit."

"MIL?" she asks.

"Mother-in-law," I tell her.

"Do you call Liam a DIL?"

Elle snorts. "No, but others call Dad and Liam, DILFs."

Mom looks at Elle strangely. I shake my head but know Elle's going to do it.

"Dads I'd like to fu—"

"Elle Miller so help me. . ." Mom walks off shaking her head.

"She's so easy to rile up," Elle says as she links her arm with mine.

At the car, Elle tells us Ben has started vlogging. It was something his therapist said would help as part of his recovery and acceptance. "You know since he lost his nuts."

"Elle!"

Elle cackles.

"That's pretty cool for Ben," I tell my sister.

Elle nods. "He's doing a pretty detailed account of everything. It's like journaling. At first, I thought it was a bit odd, but he likes it and I like reading and watching the videos he's made. He's taken a bunch of photos and videos on the sly and put them together."

"That's very sweet," I tell her. I don't bother to tell her that Noah's taking a picture of me daily so we can watch the bump grow in real time. It feels intimate and something that should stay between us. I know he plans to share it on his social media sometime after the baby arrives and I'm okay with that, but for right now, I like that it's private.

We pile into my mom's car, with Elle in the front. Instead of going to the next winery, Mom takes us out to lunch. In the back corner, the color pink has exploded, and the section is filled with women, presents and balloons shaped like baby bottles.

"We should probably talk about a baby shower or gender reveal parties," Mom says as we sit down. "We can schedule them after Elle's bridal shower."

"I love presents but don't need a bridal shower. A baby shower for sure," she says.

"I don't want a shower or a party."

"Wait, aren't you and Noah going to find out?" Elle asks.

I shrug. "We've talked about it. One day, we want to know and then the next we want it to be a surprise. Imagine the elation you'd feel when Ben says it's a boy or girl, and you're finding out for the first time."

"I get it," Elle says. "I still want to know though."

"For shopping," Mom adds.

"Definitely," Elle says. "I want everything bought and done so I can rest on maternity leave and not have to worry about anything. Just me, the baby and Ben, living in bliss."

"Part of me wants that too," I tell her and my mom. "But I don't know. There's something about the element of surprise."

Mom nods. "You have a very valid point. I don't care what you girls have, as long as they're healthy and my babies stay safe. It's all I can ask for."

"How does it feel knowing you're going to be a grandma?" Elle asks her.

"A lot better than it did when I found out I was having twins," she said. "Even though I wouldn't trade you girls for anything, having multiples scared the shit out of me."

"Ben wants twins," Elle says. "One of each and then we can be done."

"Noah wants a football team," I tell them. "He'll be over-the-moon happy with the one he's getting."

Mom and Elle laugh. We pick up our menus and have our orders ready by the time the server comes to the table. With our glasses raised, Mom says, "To my babies and their babies, I'm one lucky woman."

NOAH

Today, we are meeting Peyton's obstetrician. I'd met the one she used in Portland, but because she's pregnant now, she needs one in Cali. While I'm over the moon that we're having a child, I'm nervous about fatherhood. I know I'm going to be a good dad because I have some strong male role models in my life, however I fear that with my career I won't always be around when my child needs me. Which makes me feel like I should retire sooner rather than later, and just kick this football career to the wayside.

I'm scared for Peyton, though.

I'm scared about the changes her body will go through and how that'll affect her. Will she be in pain? Will her hips hurt which means she'll have difficulty walking? I remember her recovery like it was yesterday. I saw the pain on her face each time she went to physical therapy, each time she stood to walk. Seeing her like that about killed me because there wasn't anything I could do, other than blame myself for her being in the situation to begin with.

We walk in and while Peyton goes to check in with her

mountain of paperwork, I scan the room for two seats next to each other. There isn't one, and it's not like I'm going to ask an expectant mother to move.

As I look around, most of these mothers, with different sized bellies, are alone. This doesn't sit well with me. Yes, I know expectant fathers can't get the time off from work to go to the appointments, which just proves another issue with our healthcare system. I find a vacant seat near the window and in the corner and stand against the wall while I wait for my wife. When she walks over, her smile is wide.

"Sit here," I tell her.

"Or I could sit on your lap."

The offer is tempting. I shake my head. "Professionalism," I tell her, although there is no need. I know she's joking . . . at least I think she is. "Did everything go okay?"

She nods. "I have more paperwork to fill out."

My eyes roll hard. They sent her a packet of crap already, which took her an hour to fill out. Now, a clipboard rests on her lap.

"They want to know where you work and what you do?"

The question makes me laugh. It's as if my profession or any other spouse's profession make a difference in a woman's pregnancy. I suppose if I worked in the mines or something, it would.

"Professional gigolo," I tell her.

Peyton snorts. "You wish. I've seen you dance," she says quietly.

"It's not all about dancing. It's about how I move . . ." I trail off when she glares at me. The woman next to her stifles a giggle, which makes me smile.

I nudge Peyton with my knee. "You should put QB1."

"You're not in high school anymore, Noah."

"Good thing. Otherwise, you wouldn't be sitting in this waiting room." Many times over the years there have been instances where I wished I could say she was my high school or college sweetheart. There's something about the connection my parents have, or even Peyton's mom had with Mason. I remember watching Katelyn and Mason, always in sync with each other. It's funny to think about it now, though. I can't imagine Katelyn without Harrison. They're not high school or college anything, and yet you would never know it. Their relationship is so fluid, even in a room full of people, they gravitate toward each other.

Peyton kicks my foot with hers. A sign I should probably stop while I'm ahead or I'll end up paying for it later. The thought is tempting, but I'm not going to push my luck. Not today. She has enough on her plate.

She finishes the paperwork and takes it back to the reception desk. I stand there, making an error in judgment when I glance at the woman in the seat next to Peyton's. She smiles at me. It's not one of those nice kinds of smiles, the one where they're just being kind and whatnot. This smile shows interest, especially when her eyelashes flutter and she cocks her head.

Nope.

Besides the fact that I'm beyond happily married, and my wife is expecting our first child, something tells me this is not the place to pick up men. Maybe it's because I'm here and her partner isn't. For whatever the reason is, I don't like her flirting, and she's making me uncomfortable. Before I can pull my phone out of my pocket, Peyton returns. Her smile is the only one I want to see. It's the only one that does things to me.

"How long did they say?" I ask as she sits back down.

"Just a few minutes."

I nod and keep my eyes on my wife. Not that I mind looking at her. She's fucking beautiful and sexy, even sexier now that she's carrying my child. I reach for her hand, needing to touch her. It's weird. I have this fear she's going to slip away from me. I don't even know why, but it started when our journey to parenthood did. My thumb moves over the bracelet, the one the guru gave me. I have no idea if it's going to work, if it's going to protect her or not, but she wears it.

"Peyton Westbury."

As soon as her name's called, we make our way to the nurse. She's dressed in pink and blue scrubs with rubber duckies printed on them. They're cute. She holds the door for us and as soon as we pass by, she steps in front of us.

"I'm Stephanie, Dr. Ringman's nurse," she tells us as we follow her down the hall. "We're going to get you weighed." Stephanie motions for Peyton to step onto the scale and tells her this is her starting point, and they'll monitor her weight increase from this point forward. Being the good husband I am, I turn away. While I know how much my wife weighs, I don't need to look at the numbers and make her feel self-conscious about anything.

Stephanie directs Peyton to leave a urine sample in the bathroom, which leaves me standing in the hallway, like a weirdo. Maybe this is why the other partners don't come to the appointments. When Peyton comes out of the bathroom, the nurse brings us into a room, jotting down information on a piece of paper. Inside, she takes Peyton's blood pressure and checks her oxygen and her temperature, which I find odd.

"Do you have a fever?" I ask in a hushed tone.

Peyton shakes her head.

"The body produces more heat while pregnant,"

Stephanie tells me. "We like to track everything." She laughs.

"Everything?" I question.

"Everything," she reiterates. "Knowing how the body changes throughout the pregnancy helps."

"Interesting." I quiet down while Stephanie asks Peyton a series of questions, mostly the same ones Peyton answered on the pile of paperwork they sent to our house.

"Okay, I'm going to step out. Go ahead and strip down. Put this gown on, open in the front, and cover your lap with the sheets. Dr. Ringman will be in shortly."

"You have to get naked?" I ask as soon as the door closes.

Peyton shrugs. "This is my first time doing this."

"My bad. I wonder if one of our baby parenting books gives us some idea of what you should expect from each visit."

"Are you going to come to each visit with me?"

My eyes widen at her question. "Why wouldn't I?"

She shrugs and continues to undress. I watch her, reminding myself that this shouldn't be for my enjoyment. When she goes to sit on the table, I help her up.

"Why did you ask me if I'll come to your appointments?"

"Well, you didn't see any other spouses out there, and once we get into football season, you'll be busy."

"I don't care about other spouses or my job right now. I care about you and our child. Honestly, I don't want to miss any of this. If you decide we're one and done, I want to be able to say I was there every step of the way."

"One and done isn't just my decision."

I scoff. "It absolutely is, Peyton. I will not, in good conscience, ask you to put your body through anything you don't want. If you tell me this one is all we're having, so be it. I will not pressure you for another, let alone hint or ask for one."

She reaches for my hand. "How'd I get so lucky?"

Another scoff. "You have no idea how backwards you have things." I wink.

The door opens. A tall female wearing a skullcap walks in dressed in blue scrubs and a white coat. Stephanie comes in behind her and shuts the door.

"Hi, Peyton. I'm Dr. Ringman." She shakes Peyton's hand and then mine.

"Noah," I tell her.

"It's nice to meet you." She sits on the rollie chair and looks at the computer screen. "I went through the notes from the fertility clinic. It looks like things went smoothly. Congratulations."

"Thanks."

"It says they implanted two embryos?"

"Yes," Peyton says. "They were the only two viable."

The words hurt, but I fight to remain composure. We'd hoped for more. Well, Peyton had. I had a tough time coming to terms with having viable embryos we may not use.

"Hoping for multiples?"

"I'm a twin, so if we have twins, we'll be good," Peyton says.

Dr. Ringman nods. "Okay, let's get started. Do you want Dad to stay in the room?"

Dad . . . I'm not sure I'll ever get used to someone referring to me as Dad. Peyton looks at me. I smile softly. "Whatever you want, babe."

"I want him to stay." She doesn't take her eyes off mine. Right then, I wonder what Dr. Ringman thinks. Does she wonder if I'm forcing Peyton to answer this way? Does she think Peyton's in some abusive relationship? Now, I'm uneasy, thinking the worst. I swallow hard and step forward, clutching Peyton's hand.

Once Peyton's settled, she's back to staring at me and not paying attention to what the doctor's doing to the lower part of her body. When Peyton winces, I want to demand the doctor stop but know this is necessary.

"All done." Ringman moves away from Peyton and covers her lower half. "Are your breasts sensitive?"

"Yes. Some days are worse than others."

Ringman moves Peyton's arm, checks her breasts—which I think should be my job—and then covers her up before coming to my side. I step away but am back at her side as soon as Ringman's done. She moves back to the computer, sitting on the stool I desperately want to sit and zoom around the room on. I help Peyton sit up.

"Everything looks good, Peyton. Your due date is going to be around January tenth."

"Well, would you look at that?" I say so only she can hear. "I'm a cliché."

Peyton laughs. "Everyone on social media will blame me, saying I should've planned this better to have a spring or summer baby."

"Who cares what everyone thinks. We're having a baby. If he or she comes on game day, oh well."

"Peyton, I've copied your OB in Portland, per your request. Is your next appointment going to be here?" Dr. Ringman asks.

"Yes," Peyton says. "I'm here until August and can come back for the monthly appointments. It's the two-week ones that I'm concerned with."

Dr. Ringman nods. "Okay, the only concern I have right now is bed rest and premature delivery in the third trimester. As soon as you hit your second trimester, we're going to have you come in every two weeks to be on the safe side."

Peyton glances at me briefly, and then at the doctor. "Maybe I should just keep all my appointments here?"

"That might be an undue financial burden."

"My dad has a plane. It's okay." Peyton covers her face, shaking her head. "It's not a problem," she says.

I wait for Dr. Ringman to ask her to explain. She doesn't, which is probably a relief to Peyton. Truth is, we'll use the crap out of the private jet.

"Where do you plan to deliver?"

"Oh, um, I guess Portland."

Dr. Ringman nods and types. "We don't normally suggest the back and forth. I'm happy to see you until you return to Portland and then transfer your care over to your OB there."

Peyton nods.

"I'll see you back here in four weeks. Please don't hesitate to call if you have questions." She shakes our hands and leaves, along with Stephanie. As soon as the door closes, I help Peyton off the table and wait while she dresses.

"We had questions, and I forgot to ask."

"We can look at the books when we get home," she says. "I'm sure appointment expectations are in there somewhere."

Peyton stops at the check-out, gets her appointment for next month and then we're on our way. "What's on the agenda?"

"I want to go shopping."

I think the groan I let out can be heard all the way back to Beaumont.

"For baby stuff," Peyton says. "At least I want to look at

furniture. Get an idea of what's out there and what we might like."

"As long as I don't have to try anything on, and some dude doesn't ask me which way I hang. I hate that."

Peyton laughs as I help her into the SUV. "That's always a favorite question of mine."

"Of course it is." I shut the door and run around to the other side. As soon as I'm behind the driver's seat, I say, "Okay, mama, where are we going?"

"Beverly Hills."

Another groan, but I keep this one in check and let my ass pucker all the way to the store.

19

PEYTON

Someday, I'm going to look back on this adventure with Noah and ask myself, "Self, what the fuck were you thinking?" when it came to this damn road trip to Portland. It's not that I'm seven weeks pregnant and miserable. I know those days are coming and I have months to prepare for them. It's that we're driving with a puppy. A puppy who is still potty training and can't exactly ring the bell on the door when she wants to go out.

Noah's oblivious to her needs as he drives I-5. He's in the zone, thinking about Organized Team Activities. I tried to tell him he didn't need to be there, but under the circumstances, he wants to show the organization he's a leader. I question the latter because I swear if he could stick his head out the window like Stevie Nicks, he would. As is, we're stopping every two hours to take her potty, but then I worry she's not drinking enough water. And she's restless. Whining because she's cooped up in the car. I try to hold her, but that only lasts for a few minutes before she's moving to the back. When we got on the road, I had her strapped in. I found a cute dog seat and, being the responsible pet owner I am, bought it. Along with the suggested harness and a blanket. The latter wasn't needed, but it was sitting there on the app, so I figured why the hell not?

Stevie Nicks hates it.

Noah says it's because she wants to be with us, which I would agree with if she wasn't in the back trying to chew on things she shouldn't and acting all innocent when I scold her. And I'm the only one who can because Noah's driving, which makes me the bad guy.

"Why didn't we fly?"

"Because we thought it would hurt her ears," Noah says.

"Other dogs fly. Why did you talk me out of flying?"

He laughs. He didn't talk me out of anything. This was my grand idea.

"I'm crawling in the back with her."

Noah signals to shift lanes and then slows down.

"What are you doing?"

"Slowing down so . . ." he says, nothing else. He doesn't need to. It doesn't matter how many years have passed, the car accident is always at the front of his mind. I try not to think about it even though I live with the pain of what it has caused me.

I get into the back, much to Stevie Nicks' happiness. She crawls on my lap, kissing my face and hands, while I try to buckle my seatbelt. I hate being in the backseat and will probably end up closing my eyes. Maybe I can get her to lie on me and fall asleep.

"You good back there?"

"Yes." Probably not. I go through her puppy bag and find a bone for her to chew on. Everything with her is about redirection, rewarding her with a positive toy instead of scolding her.

"Bone," I say, echoing the command Noah's put on the buttons he's training her with. She gives me her paw and I reiterate my command. She finally takes it and melds into my side until she's slid down the seat. With one leg over mine, she uses my thigh as leverage to hold her bone in place. The jabbing or pinching hurts, but I ignore it. She's content and not chewing on the seatbelts, so I'll deal.

I'm tempted to ask my husband how much longer, but I know the answer. I've done trips like this before, going from city to city, state to state, in a decked-out tour bus. When the kids went on tour, each family had their own bus. Noah always stayed on the main bus with his parents, while Quinn, Elle, and I ended up in some rental. Ours still had bedrooms, a bathroom, kitchen and eating area, but it wasn't the cool kid's bus. Sometimes, I'd ride in Noah's bus during the day, but I never slept on it. Once the wives and kids went back to Beaumont, the band ditched the rental and went back to their custom tour bus.

I miss those days. They were carefree and fun. As kids, we had no worries as long as we followed the rules. Sometimes, we'd have a babysitter, but it was always someone from the record label, sent out at Liam or my dad's request, so they could take their ladies out.

One year, Noah didn't go on tour with us because he had football camp. That summer, he stayed with Nick, and everything changed. When we came home, Noah had grown. He was no longer a kid, but on his way to becoming a man, while I was still the pesky little kid who followed him around.

He never said that to me, but I suspected it's what he thought. When Noah started dating, I cried myself to sleep every night for . . . I don't know how long. Months on end. Elle was tired of hearing me sniffle and would complain to our mom. I never told her why, despite her begging for an answer. At eleven years old, I hated everyone, especially the girls Noah brought home. I would antagonize, torment, and act like a spoiled brat to and in front of them. It didn't matter how much trouble I got into. They were the enemy, and I didn't want him with any of them.

His high school reunion is going to be fun.

I lean forward, resting my head on the back of Noah's seat, and slide my hand between the seat and the door, to where I can touch him. He places his hand on mine and instantly everything seems right in the world.

He's the man I crave. Desire. Dream about. He's never close enough, and when we're connected, I swear it's not enough. I have this fear growing inside of me that I won't love this baby as much as I love Noah. It's irrational. This baby is the best of us combined, and I know my motherly instincts will kick in and he or she will be my entire world. Does that mean Noah won't be? I shudder at the thought.

I don't know how long I stay this way, hours possibly, with my head on the back of his seat and Stevie Nicks content with her bone pressed against my leg. Long enough to feel a kink in my neck and maybe even doze off. When Noah signals and slows down, I sit up and look out the window.

"Where are we?"

"Outside of San Joaquin."

"She's content. I don't think we need to stop."

"We're meeting the jet at an airfield."

"What?" I glance at Noah through the rearview mirror, and he nods.

"You're already tired and when we got Stevie Nicks,

one of the things we talked about was being able to fly. We need to start her on that now. Not later."

"But how did we end up here with the jet?"

"While you were sawing logs back there, I called your dad."

"I wasn't snoring."

Noah's eyebrow raises.

"Ugh. It's only because of the way my neck was."

"Whatever you tell yourself, sweetheart."

Noah drives a bit more and then pulls down a long road of nothingness. He parks in a parking lot with one other car and gets out. I hook the pup up to her leash and repack her doggie bag. After opening the door, I grab her, her things, and whatever else I can carry, and get out. There's a man with a luggage cart, helping Noah load our suitcases. He takes the things from my arms and smiles softly at me.

A couple hundred feet from where we are, the jet lands. I don't remember who it was, but one of the guys decided to wrap the outside in the 4225 West logo. Now, no matter where the jet is, someone always knows a family member is in town.

As we walk toward the airfield, the steps descend, and my brother appears. I look at Noah, who keeps his attention on the plane. Quinn meets us halfway and Noah hands him our keys.

"Thanks, man."

"What's going on?"

"I'm driving your car back, so it's there when you come home." Quinn leans down and hugs me. "I'll pick you up at the airport on Friday."

"You're the best!"

"I try," he says. "If you're all set, I'm off. It's a long drive back."

"Thanks, Quinn. I really appreciate you," Noah says as they bro hug.

We watch Quinn walk away before heading toward the plane. Secretly, I'm relieved. Noah's right, we wanted a dog that could fly, and this is the time to start her on doing so. When we get to the steps, she looks at them, almost as if they're going to bite her.

"You can do it," Noah says to her as he puts her paw on the first step. I step up, go to the third step, and wait for her.

"Come on, sweet girl." I give her leash the slightest tug to keep her attention focused while Noah taps her butt. She finally climbs the first, and then second, with Noah cheering wildly behind her.

"Give her a treat," he yells.

When she gets to the top, I have one in my hand and praise her. Who knew stairs were so challenging? While the plane is being loaded, I let Stevie Nicks sniff everything, including the pilot and the flight attendant. They love her and fall to their knees to dote on her. Noah sets out her water bowl and bed, even though we both know she'll be on my lap. He keeps asking me what I'm going to do when she's fully grown. The simple answer is nothing. I'm in love with her and want to snuggle with her all the time. What is likely to happen is she'll fall in love with the baby and won't want me anymore.

Noah and I buckle in and as soon as the engine roars to life, Stevie Nicks is on my lap. I hold her tightly, making sure she knows she's safe. Once we're airborne, the flight attendant comes over with a couple of drinks.

"She'll get used to flying. Another crew I work with, the owner of the jet, has six poodles. They all sit in their own seats. Nothing fazes them." She pets Stevie Nicks's head.

"That's good and exactly what we want."

"Beau travels well," she tells me.

Why hadn't I thought to ask Elle about Beau? "You're right. I forgot."

She leaves, only to return with some food. I hadn't realized I was starving until she put it down on the table in front of us.

"Thank you. I'm sorry, but I forgot your name."

"It's Sage," she tells me. "I've only been on a couple of your flights."

"Well, thank you, Sage."

When she walks away, I lean over and kiss Noah on the cheek.

"What's that for?"

"For being the best husband a girl could ask for."

He smiles. "I did it selfishly."

"Oh yeah?"

He nods. "I wanted you to sit next to me, but you moved to the back. I couldn't have that."

After we eat, I bring Stevie Nicks onto my lap. She lies across both of us while we watch a movie. Thankfully, the flight is short, but it gives me time to snuggle with my favorite human and our pup.

"Are you going into the office tomorrow?"

"I think Stevie Nicks and I might make an appearance. I think she wants to run on the field." Logan will lose his mind and he deserves it for the way he's treating Noah.

"What if Logan fires you?"

I shrug. "Then Stevie Nicks doesn't have to worry about a babysitter. Besides, I'd have a job before I even cleaned out my desk."

"Would you go to work for someone else?"

Another shrug. "I like the idea of freelancing. Getting

game film might be hard, but it's probably something I can manage with each team. We'll see. I'm not worried."

"I am," Noah says. "I'm worried how their lack of commitment in me might affect you."

I turn slightly and cup his face. "Babe, we are fine. I love how you worry about me but believe me when I say things will work out. If they fire me, so be it. I'm seven weeks into this pregnancy and I honestly don't know if I want to go back to work. If this is our only child, I want to spoil the crap out of them. I don't want a nanny raising our baby."

"It's odd. I can't imagine not playing next year."

"There are other things in the world we could be doing."

He kisses me. "Like moving back to Beaumont?"

"Have you thought about it?"

He nods. "A little. My mom is very excited. She's ready to be a grandma."

"I think my parents might move as well, once the adoption is final."

"That would be perfect. We'd just need Quinn."

My heart sinks a bit. "Elle and I would have to convince Nola it's an amazing place for her to be. I'm not so sure she'd agree, though. Sometimes I wonder how much she's given up to be with Quinn when he hasn't given up anything."

"Love makes us do some stupid things."

"Hey," I say as I slap his chest.

Noah laughs and pulls me to his chest. "Oh, Peyton. The things I did to you on your eighteenth birthday could've gotten me into a lot of hot water. I'd do them all over again, given the chance."

"You'd change nothing?" I ask, looking up at him.

"I wouldn't let you go," he tells me. "I would've taken

you home and told your parents I was in love with you and wanted to be with you. Damn the critics."

He could've lost everything. Part of me is happy we waited.

Just not the part that got damaged because we waited too long.

20

NOAH

We have to rethink apartment life in the city. In the week we were in Portland for OTAs, poor Stevie Nicks had too many accidents to count, which totally circumvented our potty-training efforts. I don't even want to think about what things will be like when Peyton's here alone, with a child, and trying to get our fur baby outside to go to the bathroom. I also don't know if I can stomach buying a house here.

As much as I love the city, Portland isn't my end game. My gut tells me I'm going to be somewhere else next year. Either with a new team or sitting on the couch, growing a beer belly, and having a pity party for myself because my career is over.

After a week in Portland, we're back in Cali for the long weekend. We're going to spend all of Saturday at Peyton's parents, with everyone in tow. It's weird because our house is big enough to host everyone, but we don't have direct access to the beach. Whereas Harrison and Katelyn's access is there the second you step out the door. Honestly, I'm jealous. Although, while their beach is supposed to be private, there are always lurkers. People who didn't see the sign or ignored it.

I come around the corner and rest against the wall when I see Peyton and Stevie Nicks having a moment. She's holding our pup in her arms, and I swear the way our pup's paws are, she's giving her mama a hug. They're swaying to the song playing from our sound system.

"You're going to be the best big sister, aren't you?"

Stevie Nicks kisses Peyton. She laughs and hugs her tighter. "You'll always be our first baby, though."

Yeah, she will.

Peyton turns and pauses when she sees me. I don't give her a chance to set our pup down. I go to my girls and pull them both into my arms. Stevie Nicks squirms. I give her the command to be still, something we've been working on to keep her calm. Mostly, it seems to work. Training her has been fairly easy. That was, until we got to our apartment, and she had more than one accident because she wasn't used to the environment she was in. I read in the training book we could put a pad out on our balcony, but I feel like this would confuse her when she's here.

Leaning forward, I press my lips to Peyton's and then nuzzle Stevie Nicks's coat. She's soft, thanks to the bath Peyton gave her earlier, and smells like the beach. "They make beach scents for dogs?"

Peyton laughs. "They make every scent possible."

"I like it."

Stevie Nicks squirms. Peyton sets her down and then wraps her arms around my waist. She looks at me, leaving me with no choice but to run my finger down the side of her face and lean in for another kiss. Touching her, kissing her, hell just being near her, is something I'll never get enough of.

"What's on your mind?"

I frown and shake my head slightly. "Work."

"Blah."

"I know, but I'm wondering if maybe you should stay here when I go back for OTA's."

She eyes me skeptically. I don't enjoy leaving her alone, mostly because I hate being away from her, but because she doesn't like to drive.

"Or head to Beaumont for a bit?"

"You know you don't have to be at OTA's, right?"

I nod.

She sighs and tightens her grip on my waist. "But you feel if you're not there . . ." Peyton doesn't finish her sentence and steps away. "I wish you didn't feel this way, Noah." She looks out the sliding doors at the view we have of the Pacific Ocean. Faintly, we can see people surfing. They look like giant ants from this far away. It's a clear day, with a gorgeous blue sky. The temperature is getting warmer and warmer every day and soon people will clog the beaches with their umbrellas, cabanas, and those sunshades that are impossible to put back together.

I step behind my wife and wrap her in my arms. "This past week sucked. Sitting in those sessions with the rookies, learning the ropes. But I was present, and I think Logan saw that. I answered a lot of questions."

"I get that, but they shouldn't make you feel like you have to be there. This is your down time. You should be recovering and taking care of your body. I know it's just meetings right now and when you move outside, you won't take contact, but still . . ."

"What are you afraid of?"

"The team breaking your heart," she says as she continues to look out the window. It wasn't the answer I expected from her. I thought she'd say something about me missing an appointment, which would never happen.

I pull her tightly to my chest and rest my chin on the top of her head. We stare out the window, with Stevie Nicks sitting at our feet. Poor girl can't see past the balcony wall, but that doesn't seem to faze her.

Do I tell my wife my heart's already breaking? That I feel like I've invested my life with this team, building connections, and working toward another championship, only for them to turn away from me? And for what? It's not like I've sat on the sidelines with injuries.

"Regardless, I think the apartment isn't the smartest for Stevie Nicks. You saw her when she had the accident. She cowered and hid in the corner. I don't want her to feel like that."

"I wanted to cry," Peyton says as she looks down at her, and then cocks her head to see me. "We'll figure it out."

I kiss the tip of her nose. "I suspect you want to stay here, but I worry about you feeling stranded."

"It's not like I can't drive."

Laughter rolls through me. Peyton jabs her elbow into my ribs, forcing me to step away from her. "You crack me up."

She rolls her eyes and reaches for the dog leash. "My faithful companion and I are going for a walk."

"She does pretty well off leash."

"I know, but there are people out there, plus it's windy, which means the waves are rougher. I don't want anything to happen."

Peyton slips Stevie Nicks into her harness and then

clips the leash on. I follow them out of the house and pause when we reach the steps leading to the beach.

"I assume you want me to come with you."

It's like time stands still. Peyton turns her head and her hair fans out. She greets me with a smile and my breathing hitches. She's all mine, and we're living this amazing life together. Peyton doesn't care what I do for work, as long as I'm happy.

"What?"

"Nothing," I say, shaking my head slightly. "Nothing at all." I place my hand on the small of her back and nudge her toward the stairs.

As soon as we reach the sand, Stevie Nicks spins in a circle and barks at us. "She wants to run."

"What if someone tries to take her?"

"No one will take her, babe. She won't go far. We've worked a lot on it." I crouch down and tell Stevie Nicks to sit. She does and eyes me expectantly with her big brown eyes. "You're free," I tell her as I unclip her. Still, she sits and waits for my hand command. Once I give it, she runs, turns, and runs back, with her tongue hanging from her mouth.

Peyton and I walk, and thankfully our pup stays in front of us. The few times she circles us, we watch her like a hawk. We head as far as the coastline allows until we run into a rocky outcrop and then turn around. Stevie Nicks remains by our side the whole time, being the goodest little girl.

After two hours of walking idly along the surf, we head toward our house. When we reach our patio, I veer off and start the outdoor fire.

"What do you want for dinner?" Peyton asks.

"Let's do pasta. It'll be quick and then we can sit out here and watch the sunset."

She nods and leaves the dog with me. I sit down, and before I can tell Stevie Nicks no, she hops onto my lap with her wet paws and sandy bottom.

"I probably should've taken you to the shower before I sat down." I run my fingers through her wiry hair, loving the feel. If Peyton stays behind while I return to Portland, she'll be able to take the pup to the groomers for a haircut.

When Peyton returns, Quinn and Nola are with her. Stevie Nicks jumps down to visit her friends, giving me a chance to brush the dirt off my lap.

"Hey, man!" Quinn and I bro hug. And then I give Nola a hug. "You guys staying for dinner?"

"Yeah, they are," Peyton says. "I ordered out. Makes things easier."

"We can go," Nola says as she sits down. "I told Quinn we're intruding."

"Are we?" Quinn asks us.

"Never. Our door is always open. Can I get you something to drink?"

Quinn asks for a beer. Nola wants water. I run into the bar area of our patio and grab what's needed and return. Nola eyes the beer in Quinn's hand.

"It's only one," he mutters, but doesn't twist the top off.

"So, what's up?" I ask as I sit down. With a beer in one hand, I reach for Peyton's hand with my free one. After Stevie Nicks has given her visitors the all clear, she comes over and hops onto Peyton's lap. Instantly, I wish I had stopped her.

"Ewe, gross."

"Wet dog, dirty dog, it all equals fun," I say, laughing.

"We should get a dog," Quinn says to Nola.

"I really don't want to take care of a dog," Nola says sharply.

I glance toward Peyton who meets my gaze. I think we're both trying to hide how awkward we feel right now. I don't know what's going on there, but something is definitely bothering Nola.

When I chance a look at Quinn, his eyes are down. If I had to guess, something's up between them. I suppose I could ask Quinn to come with me into the house, but I don't want to be too obvious and upset Nola.

"Nola, on Sunday, we're going to check out some more wineries if you're not busy and want to come with us?" Peyton asks.

"Thanks, but I have a final next week."

"Are you almost done with your masters?" Peyton asks.

Nola shakes her head. "No. I took time off to go on tour with Quinn, so I'm behind." She rubs her hands down the front of her shorts.

"Oh, no. Does that mean you'll have to take more time off for this next tour?"

Nola's head turns sharply toward Quinn, who's focusing on the fire. *Oh, shit.*

"What tour?"

Quinn twists the top off his beer and takes a chug.

"Quinn?"

"Sinful Distraction and Plum."

"Are you serious?" she asks in a hush tone. "Again?"

"It's part of the business. You know this."

"Well, I'm not going." Nola angles her body away from Quinn.

This is awkward and clearly something they should talk about at home, where no one is privy to their disagreement.

"Do you have to go potty?" I ask Stevie Nicks, looking

for a change of subject to ease the tension in the air. Her ears perk and then I believe she looks at me like I'm some kind of dumbass because we're outside and she doesn't need me asking. Still, I stand, as does Peyton.

"I left my phone upstairs," she says as she follows me down our cobblestone path.

When we're out of earshot, my eyes widen at her. "What in the hell?"

"I don't know," she says quietly. "Why didn't he tell her?"

I shake my head. "I don't know. It's not like Quinn not to tell her something like this." I think back to the conversation we had outside, and how Quinn and Nola seemed to be at odds with each other. Hopefully it's just a tiff and not anything more serious. "Did you really forget your phone?"

She nods. "Yes, it's in the kitchen."

"I think mine is as well. It's not in my pocket."

Peyton rises and kisses me. "I'll bring yours down when the food gets here."

"You're going to leave me with that?" I point toward the fire pit outside.

She nods and bolts up the stairs. Stevie Nicks leaves me as well, following Peyton. "You both suck," I mutter as I head toward Quinn and Nola.

"Peyton went to get her phone and check on the food."

"I'm actually going to go," Nola says as she stands. "I called an Uber."

"Oh, okay. Peyton should be in the kitchen."

"Thanks."

Quinn puts down his beer and then looks at the empty bottle.

"Need another?"

"Yep."

I head toward the bar and bring back a few in an ice bucket. "Wanna talk about it?"

Quinn groans. "I wish I could say something stupid like, 'What are you talking about' or 'Everything's fine' but I can't. Can I?"

My head shakes slowly.

"Fuck my life." He opens another bottle and drinks half of it down.

"Is it that bad?"

"I don't know what it is," he says. "I suggested we set a date for the wedding or start looking at venues, but she wants to finish this program. Which I get. I stupidly asked her what she's going to do when she's done, and she said work. Again, I get it. She wants her own money and wants to feel independent, and I'll support whatever she wants to do. But each time I try to talk to her about a wedding and tour, all I get from her is, 'I have school' and 'There are things I want out of life' but she won't tell me what those things are or give me a chance to give them to her."

"Oh."

"Pretty much all I can say, too."

"So, you didn't tell her about the upcoming tour?"

Quinn shakes his head and takes another drink, emptying the bottle. "I did not, which I know is a mistake, but I didn't want to deal with it."

"I thought she enjoyed being on the tours?"

Quinn shrugs. "I thought she liked a lot of things."

I turn at the sound of Peyton coming toward us with bags of food. I get up and take them from her."

"Why'd Nola leave?" Peyton asks.

"What'd she tell you?" Quinn asks.

"She has to study."

"Then that's it," he says to his sister without looking at

her. Peyton eyes me and I shake my head. This will have to be a conversation for later. One I am not looking forward to. The twins were cautious of Nola when Quinn first introduced her to them. The last thing he needs is for his sisters to put a wall up when it comes to his girlfriend. If I'm not careful with what I tell Peyton, that's exactly what will happen.

21

PEYTON

As much as I wanted Noah to stay with me, he returned to Portland and I decided to go home to Beaumont. I hate these feelings he has about his job. The organization is making him feel like he's done something wrong. I don't get it. And I hate being in the dark. I know I'm not privy to contracts and negotiations, but this is my husband they're messing with, and as a result me. I place my hand over my tummy. If Noah isn't in Portland playing, I'm not staying. I hope they understand this. They can't honestly expect me to stay on staff if my husband isn't there.

I miss the beach. The sound of the waves coming ashore. But I love being back in Beaumont at my grandfather's house, even if he's not home. When he said he was going on a cruise, I had no idea he meant a multi-month cruise. I'm happy he's out there living his life, but damn. His life is more exciting than mine.

Being in Beaumont means I have to drive. It's not so bad when the town is small, and traffic is all but nonexistent. I pull into the farthest parking spot and get Stevie Nicks out of the SUV. Of course, Noah makes me drive a tank. If I had to guess, he's had the sides reinforced or something.

When we get to the carts, I pull one out and tell Stevie Nicks to give me a hug. It's another command Noah's taught her, where she stands on her hind legs and if I'm crouching down, she'll put her paws on my shoulders, making it easy for me to pick her up. I'm sure the grocery store has a problem with her being in there, but I'm hoping they'll allow it since she's in the cart.

"Be good," I tell her as I give her a snack. She sits there, probably a bit uncomfortably. If there's a next time, I'm going to bring a blanket for her to sit on. We head in and instantly the employee gushes over her. I'm biased, but she's definitely a cutie.

"What's her name?"

This is exactly why I told Noah Stevie Nicks needs a pink collar and I'm glad I held my ground and added a bow. I didn't want to have to correct everyone each time they called her a boy.

"Stevie Nicks," I tell the young girl.

Stevie Nicks looks at the girl, almost as if saying *pet me now*.

She smiles. "That's the cutest name I've ever heard. Can I pet her?"

I nod and watch her lean into the young girl's touch.

"Am I allowed to have her in here?"

"Yeah, as long as she stays in the cart. The owners don't really care. Your sister brings her dog in here all the time."

"You know my sister?"

She nods. "Yeah, everyone does. She's at the school a lot, cheering for Mack Ashford."

Hearing this about my sister brings a smile to my face. I know Mack helps with Beau, but it really seems like Elle and Ben have brought Mack into their lives in ways no one expected.

"You go to school with Mack?"

The girl nods. I scan her shirt for her name tag but don't see one.

"And your sister-in-law, although we aren't friends."

"Oh." I'm not sure what to say to that.

"It's okay though." She shrugs. "If you need anything, let me know. I'll probably follow you around because she's the cutest thing ever," she says as she makes kissy faces at Stevie Nicks.

"Thank you. I'm sure she'll lap up the attention." I slip her another treat before being well-behaved and start pushing the cart through the vegetable section. I hate buying groceries when it's only me. Noah won't be back until the weekend and Elle and Ben are in Los Angeles at the moment. I know I can go to the Westburys', but I don't want to show up and expect them to feed me every day. Tomorrow, Josie and I are getting manicures and pedicures. She said I need to feel pretty at all times during the pregnancy because there will be times when I won't.

I also realize I don't like grocery shopping unless I have a list. I didn't make one, hoping something would speak to me as I zigzag these aisles. Yet, nothing jumps out at me. Turning the corner, I push my cart around a man in a suit.

"You people shouldn't be allowed to bring a dog into the store."

Ignore him.

I avoid making eye contact or letting him see any sign his words affect me. I get it. People don't like dogs in stores. Everyone's entitled to their opinions. Some dogs misbehave while others, like Stevie Nicks, sit in a cart and don't bother anyone. It's also not about dogs bothering people, but about cleanliness. Still, his comment is unwarranted. If he has a problem, he can go to management, and they can ask me to leave.

Only the man comes toward me. I turn slightly when he gets closer and freeze. It's weird, knowing someone you've never met, simply by the fact no one in your family likes him. It's disconcerting though. This man brings out a sense of fear in me, and I don't like it. I grip the cart as he stalks toward me.

He stops, only two steps in front of me. "You know who I am?"

I nod. At least I think I do.

"Where's Noah?"

"Um. . ."

"Um. . ." he mocks me. "Do you know, or are you the unintelligent one of the two?"

"Excuse me?"

"Ah, she talks. Where's Noah?"

I say nothing.

"He's my grandson, I want—"

"It doesn't matter what the fuck you want."

I lean to the side and see Liam stalking toward us. I've never felt so much relief in my life. He looks angry and ready to kick Sterling's ass. I'm here for it.

"You okay?" he asks when he's closer.

"Yes," my voice is weak, and I hate it.

Liam turns to Sterling. They're the same height, but you'd never be able to tell one is the son and the other is the father. They're the opposite of each other in every way. Liam's bicep bulges through his shirt sleeve as he raises his hand and points at Sterling, who's dressed in a suit.

"It behooves you to leave her alone. In fact, leave both of Mason's daughters alone."

Sterling scoffs. "What are you going to do? Hit me? I'd like to see you try."

"You'd be worth the battery charge, Sterling. All I need is two, one for me and one for my mother. Right in your fucking jaw. But that's after my son has had his chance with you. How dare you approach his wife the way you did, and then insult her? You've got a death wish, old man, and I'll happily watch them carry you out in a body bag."

Liam drops his hand and comes toward me.

"You believe her lies."

Liam makes eye contact with me and rolls his eyes.

"You ruined your life the day you knocked that girl up."

Liam turns and rushes Sterling. I react and grab him. "He's not worth it."

He raises his hand again. "You . . ." He pauses and collects himself. "Stay away from my family and don't you ever mention my wife again. Better yet, get the fuck out of my town. You left once, leave again."

Sterling sneers as I pull Liam away.

"Come, he's not worth it. Look," I say as I turn him around. "Isn't Stevie Nicks cute, sitting in the cart like a good girl?"

Liam scoops her up and holds her to his chest. I don't need to ask him what he's doing. I know. She's calming him down or he's using her as a shield. Something to hold him back from pummeling Sterling, who absolutely deserves to have his ass beat. I'm thankful Noah wasn't here. I'm not so sure how he'd react, especially if Sterling made a jab about his mom.

We get to the end of the aisle and pause. Liam stares straight ahead. "He's gone," I tell him. "Hopefully, he left the store."

"I don't know why he's still here," he says. "His son left

him. His wife left him. The last I knew, he moved. I don't know why he's back, but I don't like it."

I wish I had the answer for Liam. There isn't a doubt in my mind, he struggles when it comes to Sterling. Noah doesn't. He never had a relationship with him. My grandpa was more of a grandpa to Noah than Sterling's ever been.

Liam stays with me while I try to finish my shopping. I appreciate him doing so. But any appetite I had is long gone. I put a couple of things into my cart and then check out. The cashier eyes Liam. I like to think it's because of the way he's holding Stevie Nicks and not because he's famous. Everyone knows him around town, and no one bothers with him. Those days are long gone.

We walk to my car, and he puts Stevie Nicks into the back. "Come over for dinner," he says as he shuts the door.

"Okay. Let me take these bags back to my grandpa's and then I'll be over. Is it okay if I bring her?" I point to the backseat.

Liam laughs. "Of course." He pulls me into his arms. "Drive safely and do me a favor—text me when you get home and when you're on your way—I don't think I need to tell you why."

"Nope, you don't. I will. I'll be over soon."

He waits for me to get in and drive away. I do as he asks, and I text him as soon as I'm in the house and then text him when I'm on my way.

Betty Paige is waiting outside when I pull up. As soon as I'm parked, I get out and open the backdoor for Stevie Nicks. She still won't jump out, so I pick her and then set her on the ground.

"Come to Auntie," Paige says as she spreads her arms out wide. Stevie Nicks runs to her without a clue as to who she is. They've met once, but the dog doesn't care. She loves people and showers Paige with kisses as she tackles her.

"Just push her off when you're done."

"I'll never be done," Paige says. "I'm hoping Dad lets me get a dog."

He might after today.

"If there is anything I can do to help, let me know."

"Let me keep her overnight?"

I shake my head. "Absolutely not. You can come stay with me though," I tell her. "I'm all by myself in that house."

"Or you can stay here." I look toward the door where Josie's standing, leaning against the frame. If Noah was here, this is where I'd be, but I thought it might be awkward if I stayed here without him. "Come on," she says. "It's time for dinner. Paige, wash up."

Paige rolls her eyes. "She's bossy."

"She's being a mom." I help her stand and call for Stevie Nicks to follow us.

"Are you going to stay here?" Paige asks as we get to the stairs.

"I don't know. Should I?"

She nods. "I think Mom would like it. She misses Aunt Katelyn a lot, so having you here would sort of ease the ache."

I smile at my sister-in-law. She's right, I should stay here. "Okay, as long as your parents are good with having a puppy around."

"I'm going to be sick tomorrow so I can stay home and play with her."

"She's not going anywhere, ya know."

Paige looks at me and smiles. "I know, but I want her to love me, so when the baby comes and everyone's too busy with baby stuff, Stevie Nicks will know who loves her."

Her words give me pause. I look at my pup, who I love very much, and wonder if there's any validity in what Paige says. No, there isn't. Stevie Nicks is very much part of our lives and will be right by our side when the baby comes.

"When are you going to start showing, by the way?"

I look down at my stomach. "Not for a bit, I think. I'm not that far along."

"So, like you're not craving ice cream?"

I laugh. "I'm always craving ice cream. Come on, let's eat and then we'll make Liam take us to get ice cream."

"Oh, joy," she mutters as we go inside.

The fun teenage years have arrived. I remember mine clearly. All hormones and anger. I guess I have all that to look forward to.

2 2

NOAH

*I*t's been almost a month since I've seen my wife. Each day, I've had her send me a photo of her belly so I can keep up with my daily snapshots. When she first arrived in Beaumont, she stayed at her grandfather's until my mom invited her to stay at their house. I'm happy Peyton and Stevie Nicks went there, especially after my dad filled me in on the encounter with Sterling. He's never paid us any attention, not that we'd accept any, so I'm not exactly understanding why he did what he did. I'll never know either.

Peyton, Stevie Nicks, our little bean, and Mack are arriving in Portland today. Mack is attending a football camp put on by the Pioneers. This is one of the events I'm proud of and happy to be a part of. And I like the idea of Mack coming out. I miss the kid a lot.

As soon as the jet lands, I get out of the car. Not gonna lie, having something like this at my disposal is a perk that I'll never take for granted. The door opens and the steps descend. For some reason I hold my breath while I wait for my wife. Seeing her every day on video chat is nice but having her in my arms is a whole other ballgame.

Mack is the first one off the plane. He has Stevie Nicks with him and she's wagging her tail. I crouch down, praying she'll remember me. When they're close enough, I hear Mack say, "There's Daddy."

She's not so little anymore and if I had to guess probably as big as Beau. She rushes to me, and I let her jump on me because I need this type of affection just as much as she does. After a minute or so, I glance up and my wife is coming down the stairs. I stand and go to her. This is the longest we've been apart, and I hate it.

I meet her at the bottom of the stairs and Peyton leaps into my arms. I hold her tightly, pressing my lips to hers. "God, I fucking missed you," I say in between kisses.

"I missed you too."

I set her down and squat, raising her T-shirt as I do. "Hey, little bean," I say to her growing bump. "How's my baby doing? Yeah, I know you can't answer me, but Mommy tells me you're growing and doing everything you need to be doing in there. Daddy loves you." I rub my thumb back and forth over her skin, hoping I'm not bothering my wife.

After placing a kiss there, I rise and kiss Peyton again. "How are you feeling?"

"Fantastic."

"Your appointment is set for today, right?"

"Eleven weeks," she says. "And I feel wonderful."

"No morning sickness?"

She shakes her head. "Very little and only with certain foods."

"Perfect," I say and then correct myself. "You're perfect." I take her bag from her and head toward my rental.

The cargo team loads the few bags she and Mack brought into the back and tells us to have a good day.

Once we're inside and heading out, I look in the rearview mirror at Mack. He's had to grow up so much in the last couple of years, with his dad leaving for a bit and his parents' subsequent divorce.

"How are you doing?" I ask him.

"Good. I'm excited."

"Yeah, me too. You won't know anyone other than Julius's son, but he'll be in the lower age level, although he's going to be a fantastic wide receiver when he's older."

"That's cool. It'll be good. I'm here to learn from the best." Mack smiles at me. We hold eye contact for a bit longer and then I turn away. I don't feel like the best and have felt off this past month. Maybe it's because Peyton wasn't here.

The drive through the city is hectic, with bumper-to-bumper traffic. I'm annoyed. I want to get home, relax and be with my family. Maybe watch a little TV before Peyton has to go to the doctor's or play with Stevie Nicks at the dog park across from the building.

By the time I pull into the garage, we have an hour until we need to leave. I take Stevie Nicks into the courtyard and encourage her to do her business. All she wants to do is sniff and has no interest in going to the bathroom.

She finally goes, watching me the whole time. "Yes, you're the goodest girl." I give her lots of love but don't have a treat for her. "When we find your Mommy," I tell her. "She's got your cookies." At the mention of cookies, her ears perk. She nudges my pocket, looking for her snack. I hate that I'm already disappointing her.

The elevator ride to our apartment is quick and as soon as I step off, I yell for Peyton. "We need a snack."

"Do you want me to make you something?"

I point to Stevie Nicks. "She did her business, and I didn't have anything to reward her with."

Peyton laughs, goes to her purse, and pulls a bag of dog treats out of it. Stevie Nicks goes to her and sits. "Do you want to show Daddy your new trick?"

"Yes, she does," I say as I sit down.

"She's really smart," Mack says when he comes into the room. "I've been working with her after school, mostly when Beau isn't there or Elle doesn't need me to babysit him."

"Is that your job? Babysitting Beau?" I ask him.

Mack shrugs. "Nah, I walk him after school and will take him to the park if I don't have practice. If she's working late or if Ben has a meeting and she's stuck at the studio, I'll grab Beau on my way home. He's my friend," he tells me. "And now I have Stevie Nicks."

"She is pretty cute. Okay, my loves, let's see this trick."

"Stevie Nicks, whisper," Peyton says.

She lets out a very quiet bark.

"Are you shy?"

Her paw covers her eyes, and she dips her head. I can't help but smile.

After each trick, Peyton rewards her.

"Will you dance with me?" Peyton holds her arms out. Stevie Nicks stands on her hind legs, rests her paws on Peyton's arms and moves her back feet side to side.

"Oh my, this is amazing." I start clapping.

"Take a bow," she tells our girl. Stevie Nicks leans back, dips her head, and Peyton rewards her with another treat.

"This is what you've been doing for the past month?"

Peyton laughs. "She's so easy to train. Your mom and I were watching some pet show and saw a dog like her doing all these tricks. I made a list and started working with her. Each trick takes her a couple of days to master."

"Amazing." I crouch down to her level and give her a lot of love. "Good girl."

Peyton's timer on her phone goes off, signaling we need to go. I look at Mack. "Wanna stay or go?"

"I'll go and stay in the car with Stevie Nicks."

Mack gets off the elevator first to take the dog to the courtyard for another potty break. I tell him I'll pick him up out front. In the garage and because we're alone, as soon as we get to the rental, I turn Peyton and push her up against the side. Before she can react or ask me what the hell I'm doing, my mouth is on hers. She moans and opens for me, inviting me in. Our tongues meet, dancing together in longing, want, and need.

"I fucking missed you," I say as I break away and kiss along her jaw. "I wish—"

"Mack," she says as her hands slips under my shirt. I slow down and groan.

"Tonight, in the shower. You're mine." I kiss her again.

"In the shower?"

I nod and open the door for her. "Yes, the water will drown us out. Mack doesn't need to hear us having sex."

"You're right. Maybe we should wait until he goes home."

I glare at her, wondering how she became my wife with an attitude like that. I shake my head and shut the door. When I open the driver's side, she's laughing.

"You should see the look on your face."

"I'm sure I wouldn't find it very funny," I tell her as I start the car and pull out of the spot. "I've been cooped up with those juvenile men all day, every day, for a month. I need my wife."

"Yes, but Mack's with us and the apartment isn't that big."

"Locker room it is then."

"Absolutely not!"

"Your office?" I look at her. "We've done it there before."

"Yeah, when I was ovulating."

"What's the difference? Last time I was trying to get you pregnant. Now you are."

She doesn't have time to answer since I'm pulling up to the curb to get Mack and the pooch. Once they're in, I meander our way through the downtown traffic until we reach the hospital.

"Will we have time to go to the zoo?" Mack asks.

"If it's something you want to do," Peyton tells him.

"I want to take some pictures. I signed up for photography class for next year."

"Are you still using the camera my dad gave you?" I ask him.

"I am. It's been great. Liam taught me how to develop film. He let me do it in the basement and even though I'm not there every day, if he's home I can go into the dark room."

"That's awesome, Mack."

I park and leave him the keys in case he wants to get out and walk the ground. The hospital where Peyton's doctor is, is expansive with lots of open space. The elevator ride is quick. She checks in and barely sits before the nurse comes out and calls her name.

"Peyton, I was so happy to hear you're pregnant," Dr. Chan says when we enter the exam room. "I've been in touch with Dr. Ringman. She seems nice."

"She is."

"Hello, Noah. Congratulations."

"Thanks, Dr. Chan."

Peyton sits on the exam table, has her blood pressure and temperature taken, and then is told to pull her yoga pants down.

"Dad, you'll want to get your phone out for this and record."

I do as Dr. Chan says without question. Peyton reaches for my hand and shivers when some gel type stuff lands on her bare stomach.

"What's that?" Peyton asks.

"Gel. Nothing harmful," the nurse says.

Dr. Chan presses a wand to Peyton's stomach. "We may or may not be able to hear the baby's heartbeat. It's still early, but sometimes . . ." She pauses and nods to me. I hit the red record button. "Yes, there it is."

"What? That's the baby's heartbeat?" Peyton cries out and looks at me. I'm sure my smile is as wide as it can get right now. "Do you hear this?"

"I do." I crouch so I can be next to her. "This is the most amazing sound I've ever heard." It's up there with Peyton screaming my name while we're having sex, but I can't say that in here.

Whoosh, whoosh, whoosh, fills the room.

Tears fill our eyes as we listen to the sound of our child's heartbeat. I choke back a sob as I take it all in and wipe at Peyton's streaming tears. We did this (with the help of modern-day science) but we still created a life together.

I nuzzle Peyton's nose. "Thank you."

"Thank you," she says right back as she kisses me quickly. "That's our baby."

"Yeah, it is."

I've never been more thankful Dr. Chan told me to record this because now I'll have it forever.

Dr. Chan makes some notes on the computer and then takes the wand from Peyton's stomach, and then wipes the gel off. "Baby's heartbeat is strong, Peyton. Everything looks great. I'm going to send my notes to Dr. Ringman."

"Thank you."

"Anytime you need to see me, just call. I'll make room for you." She gives Peyton a hug and when she passes by me, I reach out and give her one. I don't even care if it's awkward.

As soon as the door shuts and it's only Peyton and me, I go to her and cup her face. "We heard our baby."

"I know," she said with tears in her eyes. "And he or she is strong."

"Of course, little bean is strong," I tell her. "With you as a mom, they're going to be the strongest ever. Bean is in there, learning from you. Thriving because of you. Honestly, I expect our son or daughter to be an over-achiever."

Peyton laughs. "I love you."

"Love you more, babe. Come on, we have phone calls to make!"

PEYTON

I love my sister and tell her as such when I put on my beautiful A-line dress for her wedding. She picked it out, to match her gown, hiding our growing bumps —well mostly mine—from any paparazzi lurking in the shadows. Elle doesn't care who knows she's pregnant, but I do. It's something Noah and I plan to tell the world when we're ready. We haven't even officially introduced Stevie Nicks yet, but he's posted her on his social media pages, sans name of course. Noah plans to make her famous, now that he's seen how much dog influencers can make. I have a feeling he's using her as his retirement plan.

Our dad comes around the corner, dressed in a tuxedo, and my heart stops. For a moment, I stare at the man who didn't hesitate to step up and raise Elle and I as his own. It's easy to see why my mom loves him so much. When Harrison James looks at you, he *looks*. He sees you, your soul, your heart, and he wraps it in his. He makes every pain, heartache, and sorrow disappear with the way he holds, comforts, and soothes you with his words. If it wasn't for him, I don't know if I'd be half the person I am today.

"Wow, Dad. You're looking hot," I tell him as I fan myself. "Mom is going to have a hard time keeping her hands off you."

"Who says she hasn't had them on me already?" Dad waggles his eyebrows at me and before I can reply, Mom comes around the corner, breathless and straightening her dress.

"Really? At Elle's wedding?" My eyes widen in horror at my parents. "What is wrong with you?"

Mom points to Dad. "Him. He's the problem."

To make this all worse, my dad smirks.

"I give up." Throwing my hands in the air I start to walk away, only for my parents to say my name. I turn and they're both coming toward me. It's as if they're walking like zombies, even though they're not, with their arms outstretched as they both go for my belly.

"Ew. Please tell me you washed your hands."

Dad laughs. "Of course."

"With soap and water?" I ask.

"It's like you don't have sex, Peyton," Mom says.

"Uh, gross and no. I'm not having this conversation with you. You're going to be a grandma. Doesn't that mean you stop?"

I'm not sure who laughs first. My dad's head falls back and my mother keels over. I can't with these people. Yet, I stand there because they have this obsession with my belly. At thirteen weeks, I have the cutest little pouch. If I wear anything tight, you can see I'm pregnant. At home, Noah insists I wear anything to show my bump off. He's in love with it and constantly touching or talking to the baby. I don't mind because it gives me ample opportunity to run my hand through his hair, which I absolutely love.

Dad cradles my bump and tells the baby how he can't wait to meet her.

"Her?" I ask.

"Yes, I want a girl," he says.

"And you?" I ask Mom.

"A boy."

"I don't know why," I say to them. "I thought the opposite."

"I already have you and your sister," Mom says.

"Yes, but you have two girls and two boys. I'm surprised you have a preference."

"Boys are easier." Mom shrugs.

"Well, I want a girl because I want Oliver to grow up the way Quinn did, protecting his sisters." Dad holds his hand up. "I know Ollie isn't going to be a big brother, but close enough."

I can't argue with his logic. Quinn was the best big brother either of us could ask for. Even before he was officially my brother, he punched some kid for saying horrible things about my father. He didn't have to do that, but he did, and I've always been so grateful for him.

"Do you want the opposite for Elle?"

My parents shake their heads.

"Interesting." Their thought process truly is. Dad wants granddaughters while mom wants grandsons. I just want a healthy baby.

"We should probably find Elle," I say and lead them toward her bridal suite. When I left, the hairstylist was fighting with her hair. I knock and then open the door.

"Is Ben with you?" Elle asks.

"Nope, just Mom and Dad. Noah has Ben tied up in the bar." We step in. I eye the stylist, who looks frustrated. I'm not sure if it's Elle's hair or Elle herself.

"Oh, great! He's going to be drunk."

"Unlikely," I tell her. "Ben doesn't drink, remember?"

"Well, he might on a day like today."

Dad kisses Elle on her cheek. "I'll go check and then I'll come back."

"Thanks, Daddy."

"Do you need help?" I ask the stylist. "We have the same type of hair, maybe I can get it to do what my sister wants." I step behind Elle and see that she's on the verge of tears. Leaning down to her ear, I whisper, "Don't worry, I got you."

"Thanks, P. I'm wicked hormonal and nothing is going right."

I pick up the curling iron and begin wrapping her hair around the barrel. When the light changes, I pin the curl and move to the next section of her hair. Our mom takes the stylist to the other side of the room, hopefully explaining Elle and her pregnancy hormones and how they're all over the place right now. She has morning sickness, sometimes all day, while I've escaped the curse, so to speak. I've gotten sick only a couple of times and it was because food didn't agree with me. Nothing more. But my sister . . . I fear this may be her one and only pregnancy, even though she has other viable embryos.

After a handful of minutes, I'm done curling. I give her pinned curls a light spritz of hairspray and give them a chance to rest.

"How's your makeup, do you like it?"

She shakes her head.

"Okay, I'll fix it."

I pull a stool in front of her and fix what I know she doesn't like. At one time, Elle loved the drastic look. It was an easy way to tell us apart. She used to opt for dark eyeliner and dark lipstick. This was during her grunge phase, when she couldn't figure out if she wanted to take the next step with Ben or not. Once they finally got together, she toned everything down and went back to the natural look.

Even though we're twins, I've always been jealous of her natural beauty, which is just like our mother's. Everything came effortless to Elle, whereas I feel like I had to work at everything. Except for understanding football. My knowledge there came from Noah, Nick, and Liam. I barely remember anything my father may have taught me and even now, all these years later, a picture of us only sparks a memory that I've learned from my mother.

Elle keeps her eyes closed and her breathing normal. Her hand rests on her bump and every so often she whispers, "I'm worthy of being your mother."

My sister is scared. She never saw herself as the motherly type or even a mother, and yet here she is, eleven weeks pregnant with her first child. A child, I might add, whose father is over-the-moon excited for. I thought I was a bit obsessive when I went to look at furniture for a nursery, but Ben has outfitted not only their house in Malibu but also at our grandfather's house until their newly built home in Beaumont is ready. Ben's bought two of everything so the baby isn't confused and doesn't prefer one over the other.

As if babies cared.

"There," I say when I finish the last of the touches. "Have a look and tell me what you think."

Elle turns slowly and waves her hands near her eyes. "You made me look beautiful."

"I didn't, really." I stand behind her. "You're so naturally beautiful all I did was highlight your best features."

"Thank you, P."

"You're welcome. Now what do you say we find you a groom and get you re-hitched."

"Yeah, I'd like that."

❦

ELLE'S WEDDING party consists of Noah and me. Quinn is the officiant again. He loved doing it the first time and said it was only right that he did it the second time as well. Elle wasn't going to argue with him. I always thought she'd be a bridezilla, but she's been so laid back and I think her attitude has a lot to do with the fact she and Ben are already married.

When Ben asked Noah to be his best man, there wasn't some grand gesture or heartfelt speech given, it was *hey man* and then they hugged. After Quinn, Noah is the closest person Ben has. He hasn't talked to his brother much, not since Ben's cancer diagnosis. The family dynamic saddens me only because we're so close. I can't imagine not speaking to Elle and Quinn every day, even when it's by text message.

I walk along the path, in between rows of grapevines, and turn toward the altar where Ben, Quinn, and my husband stand. Behind them is the Pacific Ocean, its blue water and frothy waves lapping over each other until they get to the shore. This is exactly what my sister wanted, to see the ocean, to feel the mist, and to hear the sounds of the waves while she married Ben.

Noah smiles when he sees me, and my insides turn to goo. He's so fucking hot in his tuxedo, with the waves in his hair blowing in the wind. Noah makes my knees weak and my stomach flip flop with anticipation. If I wasn't already pregnant, I would be by the way he's staring at me now.

God, he's gorgeous.

My steps are slow, mostly because I can't take my eyes off Noah. I want to take him home and do things to him, which seems silly since I can have him anytime I want. Above me, a bird squawks, breaking my eye contact with Noah. I smile at Ben, then my brother, and finish my walk.

Mom comes down the aisle next, escorted by Liam. I seek out my mother-in-law and wonder if my expression when looking at her son is the same as hers when she watches her husband. What is it with these Westbury men?

The music shifts and everyone stands. The melody Elle walks to is of Quinn playing the guitar. She told me she caught him playing it one day and recorded him, thankful she had because he hadn't written down any of the notes or chords. Quinn took the recording, played what he had created, and recorded it for Elle. The sound is soothing, almost like a lullaby.

My attention turns to Ben. I want to see his expression when my sister comes into view. I watch him as he waits for her. His gasp comes before his lips turn upward and then turn into a quiver. Ben needs this. He needs to have this moment with his bride. Honestly, Elle does as well. They didn't have this at their first wedding, given Ben was still in hospital. My hope for them, in this moment, is for time to stand still so they can take each other in. Married or not, this is different for them.

They deserve this.

Dad nudges Elle to move forward and she looks up at him and smiles. They reach Quinn, who clears his throat. Those of us who know him, laugh. He takes his role as officiant very seriously.

"We are gathered here today, among the grapes, the ocean, and the birds, to witness the vow renewal of Elle and

Ben. For those who don't know, I already married these two once before. However, anyone who knows my sister, knows she likes presents and being the center of attention, so here we are."

"Very funny, Quinny," Elle says while everyone around her laughs.

He clears his throat again. "All jokes aside. I'm happy to stand here and guide my sister and one of my best friends toward their happily ever after. I do so with honor and privilege, and I thank them for choosing me." Quinn looks out at everyone. "Who stands for Elle as she takes the next steps in renewing her vows to Ben?"

"Her mother and I do," Dad says as he gives Elle's hand to Ben.

"Thank you, Daddy." Elle kisses him on the cheek and then steps next to Quinn, facing Ben. He dabs at his eyes and Noah hands him a handkerchief.

Quinn continues with his elegantly written passages. His words about love and family aren't lost on me, but don't exactly have my attention. My focus is on my husband and the baby growing in my belly. Next month, we'll see our son or daughter for the first time, and we'll find out what we're having. I still haven't decided how we'll do a gender reveal but do know it's going to be something we tell people, in our own way, and when we're ready. For all I know, I'll blab the moment I find out.

Elle and Ben exchange vows, kiss, and, despite this being their vow renewal, they walk down the aisle for the first time as husband and wife. Noah and I follow, loving every minute of the celebration in front of us.

24

NOAH

aiting around to return to Portland for the season is like waiting to see if it's going to snow in California in the summer. You know the latter isn't going to happen, but that doesn't make the waiting any less painful.

Every day when I turn on ESPN, they're rubbing it in my face that the Pioneers have drafted another quarterback. Some joker of a sportscaster, who has probably never played a down outside of high school, seems to know more about my career than I do, and has no problem telling everyone who tunes into his show about it. He says I'm done in Portland. The shitty thing is, he's probably right. The even shittier thing is, I don't seem to care.

I don't know when it happened—when I lost the love of the game—but it's gone. I always told myself that when the game became a chore, I'd quit. Right now, it feels like a chore. However, I love my teammates, and I hate the idea that I might be letting them down. Sure, they'd survive. Some would even move on to another team, but to up and quit seems like I'm breaking up with them.

The thing is, if they retired or got traded, they wouldn't stop to consider my feelings. They'd expect me to move on to the next running back, wide receiver, or linebacker. It's rare for players to spend ten or fifteen years in the league and those that have, have escaped severe injuries. Knock on wood, I've been lucky. I've had a couple concussions, nothing major, but still enough to make me stop and ask myself if this is how I want to continue.

Is football everything?

This question is the easiest one I can answer right now. No, it's not. Peyton and the baby are everything. Honestly, I sort of like the idea of being home with them or always being around. Peyton shouldn't have to raise our baby by herself and while I know a lot of moms or dads do while the other works, we don't have to, thanks to our parents and my career. Over the years, I invested well. My dad helped me find someone to handle my money and in my rookie year, I lived off what I called an allowance. I didn't do anything extravagant. I made smart decisions and have continued to do so.

Peyton's done the same. And the more she leans toward not returning to work, the more I want to stay home with her. Or find something else to do because she may maim me if I'm in her space all day.

I flip the channel to something else and sink further into the couch. The anxiety creeps in as my mind replays the words the sports analyst said about me. *Washed up. Already past his prime. Could've been special.* The last one hurts the most. How was I not special? What was I supposed to do? I took my team to the playoffs every year and won the championship. Football is a team sport, not a me sport. I can't do it all.

The doorbell rings, saving me from flipping back to the

sports coverage. Before I can make it to the door, the bell chimes again and I groan. "Wh—" I say as I open it but stop. "Why'd you knock?" I ask Quinn as I step aside.

"I wasn't sure you were home."

"Ah, the car's in the garage. Peyton's been getting deliveries, and I didn't want to worry about someone coming down that incline and smacking into it. What's up?"

"Not much. I was in the area."

He's lying. We live out of the way from where he lives, works, and plays. But, if he says he was in the area, who am I to say otherwise.

"Want something to drink?"

He nods and follows me into the kitchen and heads right to the refrigerator. I don't care if Quinn helps himself. Sometimes he can be really introverted and it's like taking a bone from a dog to get him to open up.

"Where's Peyton?"

"She took Stevie Nicks to the park with your mom and Ollie."

Quinn grabs a bottle of soda and sits down at the island. I stand on the other side, waiting to see if he's going to open up or if we're just going to hang. I'm honestly good with either.

"I think I might miss the births of my nieces or nephews." He sounds distraught. I didn't think this would be something that mattered to him.

"Oh?"

He nods. "The tour. It's going to be for six months, I think. And it's going to start in September."

"What's Elle doing?"

"Uh . . ." Quinn runs his hand over his beanie. He's so much like Harrison, it's uncanny. "I think she said something about taking her last semester off."

"Trimester," I say, correcting him. "Pregnancies are tracked in trimesters." This is probably more information than he needs to know, but at least when Nola and he decide to have a baby, he'll be ready.

"Oh, right." He twists the cap off the bottle and takes a drink. "Can I ask you a question?"

"Shoot."

"You knew with my sister that she was the one, right?"

"I did. Are you thinking Nola isn't the one?"

Quinn shakes his head. "No, but I wonder if I'm her one. Something's off and it has been for a while, but she's my first real girlfriend and I don't know if I'm just looking too deeply into things or what."

"Maybe she's just under a lot of pressure from school."

He shrugs. "Maybe. I've told her she doesn't need her masters, but I also understand her need to be independent. Depending on someone isn't exactly . . . I don't know what word I'm looking for."

"I know what you mean. And I gather from the last time she was here, she's not excited about the tour?"

Quinn shakes his head again, but this time he's looking at me and his movements are much, much slower. "She's pissed, actually. I guess I didn't ask her and assumed she would go. She wants to spend time at home, which I get. I'm sure she's homesick. I've suggested her parents come out here, but I don't think they like me much."

"Why do you think that?"

"Because when I offered for us to go out there, she said it would be better if she went alone."

"Oh." Now that he's said this, I believe Peyton or Elle may have mentioned it. "Well, they're being ridiculous."

Quinn chuckles a bit. "I'm sure I'm not the picture they had in mind when their daughter brought someone home.

They're definitely prim and proper. Her brother wears a suit every day, and her sister is the lovely housewife, raising babies. According to Nola, she should've been married by now."

"So why not get married?"

Quinn scoffs. "I've tried. She wants to get married at her parents' property, which I get and I'm all for. However, the only time her parents have available are dates when I'm on tour. When I'm not on tour, her parents have their yard booked for other weddings."

"Oh." I am totally not good at this talking shit.

"See why I think they don't approve of me?"

"Yeah, it's becoming clearer. I stand by my earlier sentiment."

Quinn picks at the label on his bottle until he's pulled a corner clean and then takes the rest of it off. I reach for it and throw it away.

"You know, you're like a brother to me," he says, and I find myself wanting to give the guy a hug.

"Same," I tell him. Even though I'm close to a couple of my teammates, Quinn will always be my best friend. He's the brother I never had and always wanted. "Do you remember when we first met?"

He nods.

"I hated you," I tell him. "I was so jealous of your relationship with my dad, the only thing I could do was hate you."

"I know," he said. "And I was jealous because you had a mom. Well, two if you count Katelyn. Her and Josie were so good to me, accepting me right away, I couldn't understand why you didn't want to be my friend. I also didn't have any friends because I toured all the time and had a tutor on the bus. I thought we'd be band buddies or whatever until my dad told me you had just met Liam. It took me a bit to understand what he meant because I'd always known him and this world we lived in."

"Yep," I say. "That pretty much sums it all up."

"Look at us now." Quinn quips and makes a heart with his hand. "Should we get matching tats or something?"

"I think Peyton would kill me."

He laughs. "She probably would."

He spins the top of his bottle on the counter and sighs. "I don't know what to do."

"Have you asked her what's going on? Believe me, when I tell you communication is key, it's key. I avoid so many misunderstandings with your sister by communicating. Granted, she bottles shit up and sometimes I have to poke the bear to get it out of her, but nothing festers. We don't go to bed angry at each other. I don't think I'd be able to sleep if we did."

"We've talked but not in depth. I don't want her to feel like she has to go on tour. I'll miss her and will try to come home as much as possible, but we have shows every couple of days. There's no way I can fly back and forth all the time. I'd miss rehearsals. And once Elle leaves the tour, the last thing she needs is for me to fuck shit up."

"I'm sure Elle wouldn't feel that way."

Quinn looks at me and I feel like I should cower or something. "Okay you're right. Damn, you have the same look she does. Is that something Katelyn taught you?"

He laughs. "No, but I think I got it from Elle."

"Poor Ben," I mutter. "Have you heard from your boss while they're honeymooning?" After their ceremony they headed to Fiji for their honeymoon. The last I knew they hadn't decided when they would come back. Ben and Elle need this time away. They've been on the go since his cancer diagnosis and subsequent recovery. At this last scan, his body still showed no signs of cancer, which is a relief. I never want any of my friends or family to go through what he did. It was scary and really put a lot of things into perspective. Life's short—live it.

"I'm thinking of retiring," I say to Quinn out of the blue.

"Really?"

I nod and tell him how I've been feeling, how the draft went, and how the team has been incognito in offering me a new contract.

"Seriously? So, they're not going to renew you?"

"Doesn't look that way."

"So, you what, train this new guy and they're like sorry but not sorry, you gotta go?"

"Pretty much. They'll either part ways or someone will come in with a new contract and I'll go elsewhere."

"Okay, but if you don't play, then what?"

"I can retire. Maybe coach with Nick."

"In Beaumont?"

I nod. "We've talked about moving back."

Quinn groans and drops his head for a moment, then looks up. "If you move, my parents are moving, which means I'll end up moving. Which means . . ." He trails off, but it's clear what he's insinuating.

"Does Nola like it there?"

He shakes his head slowly. "Not so much," he says with a sigh. "I'm sure it's because we stay at your parents' house. It's not like I own something there or my folks do."

"I imagine it can be awkward."

Quinn leans back and groans again. "Why is life so complicated?"

"There is no answer, my friend."

"Ugh. Maybe Nola and I will just move to South

Carolina or something. This way, she can see her family whenever she wants. I'll just stay home like a hermit."

"That's not fair to you. The staying home part."

"I know, but I love her and if being there will make her happy, I'll do it."

25

PEYTON

The summer is fading quickly and before I know it, Noah will have to pack and return to Portland. I'll go with him, but not as a member of the Portland Pioneers. Giving them my resignation was easy and probably one of the best decisions, aside from marrying Noah, I've ever made. Our baby is due at the end of the year or early into next year and I'd miss the end of the season and potentially playoffs, where I would be needed the most. I did offer to freelance for them, since I'd be at most of the games, or they could send game film to me for the ones I don't make. As soon as word spread, offers from other teams came pouring in. I'm weighing all of them, just as I'm weighing myself now.

The number on the scale continues to go higher, which is good. I'm gaining healthy weight to support my expanding belly. One night, I went to bed with a somewhat flat stomach and woke the next day looking like I had put a small balloon under my shirt. Only, I hadn't. Our baby had grown or shifted or whatever it's called. As soon as Noah saw my bump, he had the camera out, taking pictures from every angle.

It's weird, up until now I haven't felt pregnant. The baby didn't move around enough for me to feel the flutters other mom's talk about experiencing and my little pouch was just that, little. I looked bloated most days, but now . . . now I get to stand in the mirror and cradle my belly.

We still haven't really told people outside our family and a handful of friends that we're expecting. Mostly because I want to get to the twenty-week mark or my first ultrasound. Technically, I still have another four weeks, but I managed to convince Dr. Ringman I need the ultrasound before we return to Portland for the football season.

Noah finds me standing in front of the mirror, rubbing my hand over my bump and then holding it. It's the most magnificent thing I have ever seen in my life. Knowing a life we created is in there, thriving, makes me feel like I can do anything in this world. I have no worries. Not about Noah and whatever decision he makes about his career. Not about whether or not I decide to be a consultant with the Pioneers.

He stands behind me, fitting perfectly against me. His hands hold my stomach as he looks at me through the mirror. "Are you ready for today?"

I nod. Today, we'll see our baby for the first time and learn if we're having a boy or girl. I'm both anxious and excited to finally reach this point in my pregnancy. I think because of the IVF and knowing right away, it feels like getting to this point has taken forever.

"Well, you should get dressed," he says. "I know how much you like looking at yourself in the mirror with no shirt on, but something tells me you don't want anyone else looking at you this way." Noah kisses the top of my head.

"It's so hot out but I want to try and hide my bump for a bit longer."

Noah heads into the closet and comes back with a dress. "What about this one?" He holds a long flowy dress in floral print by the hanger. "It doesn't look form fitting."

"No, we leave those to Elle." Everyone knows she's pregnant even though she won't confirm it. Each time she posts a picture on her social media, you can see her bump. She's not hiding it. This is one of those times I wish I were a bit more like her. Elle still finds a way to control the narrative, whereas I would cave and gush about the details.

"Are we posting today?" Noah asks as he takes the dress of the hanger and hands it to me.

"We can, but not the sex of the baby. I want the news to be a surprise to our family."

Noah nods. "They're all taking bets anyway. Paige says we're having a girl. Mack says girl. Dad says boy. Mom says she doesn't care, she just wants to hold the baby."

"My dad wants a girl and my mom a boy."

"What do you want?" he asks as he walks toward me.

I caress his cheek. "A healthy baby. I don't care if it's a boy or a girl. When this is over, I just want to hold our baby in my arms and tell him or her how much they are loved."

"Me, too." He kisses me quickly. "Come on, we gotta go."

Noah drives us to the doctor's office. I have the window down, the music playing, and I'm enjoying the nice weather. Noah presses a button on the console and the song changes. Our dads' voices come through the speakers. I roll my eyes.

"Seriously?"

"What?" he asks as if he doesn't know what he's done. "It's their greatest hits. It hasn't even been released yet."

"And you're what, giving them free promo as we drive down the Boulevard?"

Noah laughs and taps the steering wheel to the song playing. I can't help but move along to the beat and recite the words. They're not even my favorite band, and I still know all the words to their songs. He turns it up, likely to drown out my nasally sound, but I don't care. I sing louder.

By the time we reach the office, the twelve-track compilation has finished and we're both happily laughing at how silly we act sometimes.

While we're walking in, Noah says, "I'm going to call my parents and tell them to get to town so we can tell them all at once."

"Tell them to plan on tomorrow," I say as I text my mom and tell her. "This way we have one night with the news before we have to share it."

"And I can come up with the ultimate way to tell them. The whole we're pregnant reveal was pretty kick ass if I do say so myself."

"Yes, Noah. You totally slayed the reveal." I roll my eyes and step out of reach as he tries to grab me and rush toward the elevator.

"Don't run," he yells down the hall. "You'll give the baby a concussion."

My mouth drops open as he approaches. "You know that's not possible, right?"

He nods. "But it got you to stop running."

I roll my eyes. "You're ridiculous."

The elevator door opens, and we wait for the people to step out. One does a double take when they pass by Noah, but I pull him in, press the button and then jam my finger against the close button. Normally, I don't care except today.

Today, I want us to be expectant parents. I want my husband to be normal and to be treated as such.

In the office, I check in and then sit down. My bladder is full of the excess water I had to drink and I feel the need to squirm in my seat. My husband, though, stands and goes to the water fountain for a drink. And then another. Sometimes I want to berate him for acting like a child, but he doesn't do it on purpose.

Noah brings me a cup of water. I shake my head.

"I'm not thirsty," I tell him.

"Doctor said you should stay hydrated."

"Believe me, I am. I drank a bunch for this appointment. A full bladder is required for this ultrasound."

Noah nods as if he understands. He drinks the cup he brought me and takes it to the trash before coming back to sit next to me.

"I'm nervous."

"Me, too," I tell him. "But everything is good."

I lean back and tap my fingers against my growing stomach almost as if I'm playing the drums, just like my dad taught me to do when he first met my mom. I still remember how he sat me on his lap and let me beat the drums with his drumsticks. He didn't care if I did any damage. This was my outlet for the rage I felt after my father died. I can't wait for my dad to teach his grandchildren how to play the drums and write songs. It's my hope this child has either musical or athletic talent. I wouldn't mind having a basketball player in the house or a piano player. Noah and I agreed we won't pressure our child to do anything. Whatever they want to do, they can and when they want to quit, as long as they have a reason, we'll let them. Knowing how Liam was raised is something Noah and I don't want for our child.

When I see the nurse come out, I sit up, anticipating my turn only for her to call for another patient.

"We'll be next," Noah says.

"I know. The nerves have turned into anticipation. I'm excited."

He reaches for my hand. "I'm probably going to want to buy one of these machines."

I laugh, but I know he's serious. "I'd never get any work done nor would we ever leave the house."

"Nope. You'd be hooked up all day and night so we could see our little bean, growing and thriving."

"Peyton Westbury." The nurse calls out and I want to rejoice at the sound of my name.

Noah helps me stand and keeps his hand on the small of my back as we follow the nurse. We stop at the scale and then head into the room. "The tech will be in shortly. Please take everything off from the waist down and sit on the table. We'll be right back."

It's always a sprint when you have to undress and put a gown on or a lap covering. In my case, I should've worn a shirt. After taking my dress off, I slip into the gown and tie the top strings to keep the girls somewhat hidden.

Not that he needs to, but Noah helps me onto the table and covers my legs with the medical blanket. He barely sits when the door opens.

"Hi, Mom and Dad, I'm Baxter." He sits down on the stool and wheels toward me. "Before we start, are we finding out the sex of the baby?"

"Yes," Noah and I say together.

"Okay so no big gender reveal party? You want to know?" Baxter asks.

"Yes, we're not keeping it a secret," I tell him.

"Excellent. All right. How's the bladder?"

"Full."

"That's what I like to hear. You're already my favorite patient of the hour."

Out of the corner of my eye, I see Noah look at his watch. He smirks. If I had to guess, the hour changed and we're Baxter's first patients since. Baxter's a funny guy.

He angles the computer so only he can see the screen and tells Noah to stand next to me. Baxter drops a blob of gel onto my stomach and then sets the wand on there. Instantly, the room fills with the sound of the baby's heartbeat.

"Best fucking sound in the world," Noah says to me as he presses the button on his phone. I have to agree.

"Do you want to record it, Dad?" Baxter asks.

"Already recording," Noah told him.

"I'm going to take some measurements and then we'll have a look," Baxter says.

I turn toward Noah and hold his hand while we listen to the whooshing sound play around us. I swear I could listen to it all day and night.

"All right, Mom and Dad, let's see what we're having."

Baxter turns the screen, giving Noah and I a chance to look as well. He sets the wand on my stomach again and the black screen turns a fuzzy white.

"Well, would you look at that?"

I'm looking and it takes me a minute to recognize anything.

"Is that?"

"Yes, it is," Baxter says as he presses a series of buttons. "I'm printing pictures now." Baxter presses the wand a bit harder into my skin.

"Uh, I'm going to pee if you do that."

Baxter laughs. "I'm trying to get your son or daughter to

cooperate so we can see . . . ah yes, thank you baby." He presses another button and the screen freezes. I sit up on my elbow so I can get a better view. He brings the screen closer, showing us the details.

"If you can't see for yourself, let me know and I'll tell you."

"Holy shit," Noah says as he squeezes my hand. "Peyton, do you see this?"

I nod slowly as tears form. "I'm going to be a mom."

NOAH

The past twenty-four hours have been the hardest of our lives. Knowing what we're having and having to wait to scream it from the rooftop. Of course, it's our fault for the situation we're in. We want to tell everyone at the same time and the only way to do it is to have everyone gather at the Jameses. In hindsight, I should've told my family to be there yesterday because waiting is killing me.

I don't even want to imagine what it's doing to Peyton.

Once I have everything in the back of the SUV, I help Peyton get in. Now that I've seen our precious cargo, I want to wrap her in bubble wrap and keep her locked in the house. She glares at me as I hand her the seatbelt. I can't help it. I want to make sure she's safe.

"You love me," I tell her.

"I don't know, Westbury. You're driving me nuts."

"I know," I say and wink. "But you still love me."

She rolls her eyes.

When I get in, I glance at her and smile. Up until

yesterday I didn't think I could be any happier, but the sheer elation I feel is indescribable. I can't wait to be a dad.

"We need to make a list of names," I tell her as I head toward her parents.

"Should we each make a list, pick the top three from each list and then draw one out of a hat?"

"We can, but who is going to draw?"

Peyton turns and looks at Stevie Nicks who is sitting in the back. "She doesn't have opposable thumbs so she's out. Unless we can teach her to reach into a bucket and pull something out."

"I could do that. That would make a cute video."

Without looking, I know my wife is rolling her eyes. She doesn't give two shits about social media. I sort of like it, until I do something stupid on the field and people leave me ridiculous comments about how I should be better at my job. You know, because they're freaking Heisman winners themselves.

"If you can train her, I think that would be fun."

"I'm on it, babe."

At the stoplight, I reach over and rub my hand on her belly. Dr. Ringman said Peyton will be able to feel some kicking soon, which I'm looking forward to. The fact I'll be able to feel the life we've created growing inside of her blows my mind, and I know once it starts happening, it'll take everything I have to stop myself from permanently keeping my hand there.

The drive to Harrison and Katelyn's takes us no time, thanks to the minimal traffic. Thankfully, someone thought to leave a parking spot for us in the driveway. By the looks of it, everyone is here, which is perfect. The more the merrier. After helping Peyton out of the car and getting Stevie

Nicks, I grab the necessities I need to pull off the ultimate gender reveal.

"We're here," Peyton yells as we walk inside. The pup takes off, knowing she has friends to play with. We walk toward the back of the condo, where most of the hanging out takes place, and find everyone outside.

As soon as we step out, Katelyn rushes to us. She pulls Peyton into her arms. "You can tell me now," she says. "It's my right as a grandma."

"You get to wait, with everyone else."

"I don't even know," Elle says as she gives Peyton a hug.

We make our rounds, hugging and shaking hands with our family. No one is missing from this event, even our world trotting grandparents are here. They're back from their cruise and already planning their next one.

"I'll be right back," I tell Peyton as I head back inside to prepare my plan. Once I have everything ready, I summon all the men. When they're all in the kitchen, I hand them white T-shirts.

"Here's the deal," I tell them and proceed to fill them in on what their job is. None of them seem thrilled other than the grandpas.

"Remind me not to have you plan any reveals for Elle and me," Ben says as he does what I've asked. I tap him on the back and laugh.

As soon as everyone is ready, I lead them outside and yell for everyone to gather. I thought about dragging this out for hours, but I'm far too eager to hold the news in any longer.

"What on earth?" my mom asks.

I clap my hands to get everyone's attention. "As you can see, the men in your family look pregnant. Each of them has a balloon under their shirt, filled with either blue or pink water."

"Ooh, a wet T-shirt contest. Sign me up," Elle says.

"I'm with you," Yvie adds.

"My first adult time fun," Paige says.

"Leave, now," our dad points to the house, while everyone laughs.

"You too, Little One. You're still a baby in my eyes," JD says.

I happen to glance at Rush, who blushes.

"I've seen him without a shirt on, Daddy," Eden says.

"I didn't need to hear that!" JD sighs.

"Anyway, Peyton and I know the gender. Here's what's going to happen; I'm going to count to three and the men in our family will pop their balloons. Their shirts will either turn blue, pink, or remain white."

"Wait, what?" Mack asks.

"What did you think was going to happen?" Nick asks him.

"Ah, man." He shakes his head as he looks to the ground, avoiding eye contact with Paige. Everyone laughs at him.

I make sure my phone has the best angle to get everyone's reactions and turn on the video to record.

"Guys, are you ready?" They hold up their safety pins. "Assume the position."

Their hand moves next to their fake bellies, ready to jab.

"Go."

The collective sound of each balloon popping and water sloshing, mixed with gasps is a pretty cool sound. I look at my dad and Harrison, waiting for them to realize what we're having. And then everyone starts talking.

"You're having a . . ."

"Boy."

"Girl."

"Wait."

"Oh my God."

Peyton and I let them try to figure it out. She comes to me, wrapping her arm around my waist.

"Peyton, what's going on?" Katelyn asks.

She puts her hand on her stomach and looks at me.

"You tell them," I say to her.

"Yesterday, we found out we're having triplets," she says excitedly. "Two boys and one girl. The boys are identical."

Our parents rush over to us, crushing us in hugs, with tears and congratulatory sentiments.

Katelyn cups Peyton's face. "I'm so happy for you."

"Thank you."

"Twin boys, really?"

Peyton nods. What she doesn't tell them is we only had two embryos.

"And a girl?"

Another nod.

"You're going to need so much help."

"I know," Peyton says through tears. "You'll be there, right?"

"Every second of every day," Katelyn tells her before pulling her into her arms.

While my mom talks to Peyton, my dad shakes my hand. I can't recall any other time he's done this, except for maybe the first time I met him.

"I'm proud of you," he says. "Damn proud of the man you've become."

"Thanks, Dad."

We stand there, like we did on our wedding day, talking

to everyone. Nick, Mack, and Amelie, who is excited to babysit as long as her dad is around to help. Eden and Rush, who probably aren't interested because they're teens and hopefully nowhere near this stage in their relationship. JD and Jenna, who promises us she will keep JD far away from the babies. Xander and Yvie, who says our babies have free dance lessons for life.

Quinn hugs Peyton tightly and then comes to me, so Nola can talk to Peyton. Nola's excited and asks to touch Peyton's stomach.

"Are they kicking yet?" she asks.

"Not yet," Peyton says. "I'm ready though."

"My sister says it's the oddest feeling at first, then you love it, and then you want it to stop." Nola laughs. "I'm so happy for you and Noah."

"Thank you, Nola." They hug.

"Things good?" I ask Quinn.

He nods and smiles, and he looks so much better than he did the last time I saw him.

My sister makes her way over to us. There are more hugs, tears, and promises that she'll babysit whenever. We know it'll never happen. No one her age wants to watch three babies at the same time, but then, it could be a great deterrent from having sex.

The future great grandparents don't promise to babysit, but all say they can't wait for our family to expand.

Elle and Ben bring up the rear. There are lots of tears between the sisters. It's fitting we're having twins. Now maybe I can figure out the twin language while my sons develop their own.

We're about to head over to the food table Katelyn and my mom put together when Harrison comes toward us. He's still wearing his wet shirt. The only pink one. He hugs me and then goes to his daughter and holds her for a long time. He holds his arm out toward me and I step toward him.

"I know you know this, but I feel like I need to say it, ask for help. We will be there. You don't have to do this alone."

"Thank you, Daddy." Peyton hugs him again.

We finally make it to the food table, where Peyton is told to cut the blue and pink cake. She brings me a piece and then sits next to me.

"That was a cute reveal."

"Thanks." I kiss the tip of her nose. "I wanted it all to happen at the same time. Create mass confusion."

"Oh, there was some for sure. It was great."

Mack returns, with both dogs on his heels. He's like the dog whisperer or something. Of course, now that he has a plate of food, they want whatever he has, even though I know he doesn't feed them.

"You know, this time next year, the babies will be crawling."

Just as Peyton says this, Oliver runs by screaming as Harrison chases him.

"We'll have three of those," I say, pointing to Ollie.

"It's never going to be quiet in our house again."

"Bring it on," I tell her. I don't care what my life is going to be like, I'm ready for our babies to get here. "We need to go shopping."

Peyton laughs. "I think we need our own place in Beaumont."

I take a drink of my water. "Yep, on it. We'll figure it out before the babies get here. I promise."

"Thank you."

I look at her, pushing a strand of her hair behind her ear. "There isn't anything I wouldn't do for you and our babies."

"I know and we love you for it."

We end up staying at Peyton's parents for a few more hours. My parents and sister, along with Nick and the kids, all come back to our house, which is bigger than Harrison & Katelyn's. By the time we crawl into bed, I'm exhausted, which means Peyton must be running on fumes.

We're lying on our sides and, I'll admit, I'm jealous of the pregnancy pillow she has right now. I'd rather her wrap her body around me but I know she can't.

"I've been so excited about the triplets I haven't asked if you're happy."

"I don't think happy is the right word, Noah. We've gone through these stages in our life together, from dating to being engaged, to getting married. Kids were always on our list and then we struggled. I wasn't sure we'd make it to this stage. I prayed, hoped, mediated. All I wanted was to have a child with you, to create a life that is the best parts of us."

Peyton puts my hand on her bare stomach.

"We created three. Two boys and a girl. Our family is beyond complete. Having three at once doesn't scare me. I'm so eager to have all three in my arms, in this bed between us while we watch them sleep. I am counting the days until I see you holding our daughter, protecting her. Teaching our boys how to be men."

"The man in me wants the boys to be born first," I tell her. "I want them to be big brothers to our little girl."

"I think, no matter what, they'll be the best big brothers. They have you and Quinn as role models."

"And JD."

Peyton rolls her eyes. "He'll teach the kids some weird Britishisms and we won't have any idea what they're saying."

"This pregnancy is going to be harder than we thought."

Peyton nods. "I'll be on bed rest."

"I don't like that I won't be with you all the time."

"I know, which is another reason I want to go to Beaumont. I know my parents are here, but unless my mom moves in, it'll take an hour for her to get here. Plus, she has Oliver. I know she'll come when I call, but I think that puts a lot of pressure on her."

"We'll find a place. I'll start tomorrow."

"I'll stay in Portland for a bit. I'm not ready to give up on watching you play football just yet."

I can't help but smile.

"Are you okay with me posting our pic?"

Peyton nods. I lean over to the nightstand and grab my phone. I have a series of photos in my drafts. We go through them and pick one together. It's of us kissing, her bump is showing, and Stevie Nicks is sitting in front of us. We took it one morning last week after the pup and I went for a run on the beach and Peyton did yoga. It's very us in our normal lives.

Introducing Stevie Nicks. Our newish addition to the family.

"What do you think?"

"I approve of the 'newish' term."

"How many times do you think people will ask if you're pregnant?"

"Many, even though as soon as you post it, Elle will comment with the pregnancy emoji."

"God, I love her."

I publish the picture and wait about thirty seconds for the likes and comments to come in. Sure enough, Elle is first, and she comes through with the emoji. Followed by Paige saying she can't wait to be an auntie.

Peyton clicks on Paige's profile. "How does she have so many followers?"

"She's popular on the apps," I tell her.

We watch the comments roll in and respond to the ones from my teammates. I turn my phone off and give all my attention to my wife.

"Now, let's talk names."

27

PEYTON

The rideshare drops me off at the side entrance of the stadium, the one employee's use. Although, I'm no longer employed. For all I know security won't let me through and they'll send me around to the gated entrances with the hordes of people. I suppose if I hadn't quit, the owners would be happy to have me at the game. We're not exactly seeing eye-to-eye at the moment. They were happy to send game film my way and agreed to pay my fee. However, when they found out I had been contacted by other teams and players, they tried to pull some non-existent contract bullshit on me. It's funny, I never remember signing one, and they couldn't produce one when I asked to see it.

I make it through the first door and walk around the corner, grinning like a fool when I see one of the guards I know. "Kevin!"

"Oh my, would you look at your bump."

He holds his hands out like he wants to touch me. I nod, letting him. Normally, I'd say no, but I want him buttered up, so he lets me in. I really don't want to walk to the other side where family members can enter.

"When are you due?"

"Technically, January. But I'll have them early."

"Them?" he asks.

"Triplets," I tell him as I point to my side. "Twin boys." And then I point to my right. "A girl."

He's in shock as his hands rest on my stomach. "Noah must be excited."

"We are over the moon, Kevin. So happy!"

"I heard you're not working here anymore."

I shake my head. "I'm going to be on bed rest soon and the babies will be here during the season. I honestly don't see myself going back to work."

"I don't blame you. Stay home with your family. I hear your sister is pregnant, too."

Nodding, a smile spreads across my lips. "And I know what she's having, but she's sworn me to secrecy."

"Is she going to do one of those big reveals?"

"No, she's waiting until she gives birth. She wants everyone to be surprised."

Kevin shakes his head slightly. "She definitely keeps your family guessing."

"Ha! You have no idea."

He motions behind him. "Go on," he says. "Just remember I want to meet those babies when you have them."

"You got it, and thank you, Kevin. For everything."

"You'll always be my favorite, Peyton."

I make my way toward the field, which I'm allowed to be on thanks to the pass my husband secured for me. Noah had asked me earlier to come out here. I think he secretly wants to show off the bump. Honestly, I don't mind. He's very proud of his swimmers for getting the job done effectively. This will be my only go at being pregnant. Having three is more than we could've hoped for. Having two boys and girl will make our family complete.

As soon as I step onto the field, Noah throws the ball toward me. He's lucky I know how to catch and not so lucky I know how to throw a spiral. I hurl it back to him and a couple of the new guys, who I haven't met or worked with, want to know when I'm signing my contract.

"I don't know why you do that," I say to him when he gets close.

"Because it reminds me of the time we spent all summer working on my drop step, back home."

"Oh yes, when you wooed me?"

Noah kisses me. "Did I really have to woo you?"

"Sort of," I say, shrugging.

He laughs and kisses me again. "When was the last time you watched a game from the stands?"

I shake my head. "I don't even know. Did you find out who's coming?"

"Dad, Grandma, and Mack."

"Is Mack still spending a lot of time with your dad?"

Noah nods. "They're besties."

"Does that bother you?"

He shakes his head. "Absolutely not. I love that kid." Noah leans down and kisses me a third time. "I gotta run. I love you." He drops to his knees and cups my growing belly. "Okay, boys. Don't cheer too hard. I don't want you to hurt your mommy. And my sweet girl, when your grandpa says hi, kick him."

I swat Noah. "That's mean."

He laughs and runs back to the field. I watch him for a moment before making my way toward my seat. I don't get very far when the players I've known for years stop and congratulate me. The only one I let touch my belly though is Julius. He gives the boys fist bumps and then taps his fingers twice where our girl is.

"That's a love tap," he tells me as he heads back to the field.

Watching him, it makes me sad that we're leaving Portland. Noah and I are confident the Pioneers aren't going to resign him, even though they say they're ready to negotiate a new contract. Oddly, Noah's okay with it. He talks a lot about retiring, especially now that he knows we're having triplets. He wants to be there for the babies. All the time, not part-time or when the season's over. I know it doesn't help that I want to move back to Beaumont. While I know my mom and dad aren't there, Noah's family is and so are my grandparents, who aren't getting any younger. I really want my babies to know my grandfather before it's too late. He's the last part of my father, which is odd to say since Elle and I are still around, but we barely remember Mason. It's sad to think sometimes.

"Peyton!"

Looking up at the sound of my name, I find Mack waving his arm like a mad man. I head up the stairs and through the gate the security guard holds open for me, and toward Noah's family. Bianca gushes when I come into full view, eyes wide with unshed tears.

"Honey, you look ravishing. Pregnancy agrees with you," she says as we hug. "Tell me, do they have names yet?"

"Unfortunately, no. Right now, we have baby A, baby B on the left. We are calling them the boys right now. Baby girl on the right."

"I can't wait to meet them."

"Me, too."

"Okay, my turn," Liam says. He gives me a hug and then says hi to the babies before I sit down next to him and Mack.

"Do you want to say hi to the babies?" I ask him.

Mack shakes his head. "No, thanks," he says as he looks at me from the corner of his eyes. "Don't be mad."

I laugh. "I'm not mad. But I hope when they arrive, you're not afraid of them."

He looks at me sheepishly. "I remember when Amelie was born. She made a lot of noise. Cried a ton."

"Yeah, babies cry."

"Will they cry at the same time?"

Great question. I want to know as well. "I don't really know. I'll have to ask my mom. Make her think back to when she had Elle and me."

"Betty Paige is really excited to be an aunt. She says she's going to babysit all the time."

"Is she now?" I love the idea of her wanting to babysit. I'm not sure she will actually be able to do it though. I'm not sure how I'll be able to handle three babies, and if I don't know how, neither will a teenager.

"Yeah, she says it's a rite of passage or something."

While I babysat back in the day, I never considered it a rite of passage. Some of my classmates went as far as taking a Red Cross course on how to care for a baby. Everyone seemed to call Elle and I to watch their kids though, and I have no idea why.

"How come Paige didn't come with you guys?"

Mack shrugs. "She's been helping out at the café and spending time with my sister."

I lean in and ask, "Are you jealous?"

Mack tries not to smile. "No, not really."

"How's Talisa?"

He does smile this time. "I like her a lot. She does every-thing for us, but we help her. She has somehow turned chores into something fun and she teaches us how to make all kinds of food. It's funny though, when she hears a word she doesn't know the meaning to, and once we teach her, she uses it all the time. She makes me laugh."

"I'm excited to get to know her," I tell him. "How's school going?"

"Lame. I don't know why we have to go every day."

"They're preparing you for adulthood when you have to do the same thing, over and over again."

"You and Noah don't."

"No, but that has to do with the jobs we have. Noah still has to train, stay in shape, and do a bunch of community events. Like the camp you went to over the summer. A lot of contracts require players to do something in the community."

"Noah would do the camp regardless."

"You're right. He would." I smile at Mack.

"I wish Noah could come to my games."

You and me both, kiddo.

"I'll be there this week," I tell him as I bump his shoulder with mine. "Noah will be there when he can."

We stand for the national anthem and cheer when the guys take the field. At halftime, the Pioneers are up by one touchdown. I find it hard not to critique my husband or even the rest of the team. It's no longer my job but shutting my mind off from those thoughts is easier said than done. I hope Noah asks later, but if he doesn't, I won't say anything.

I think.

Autumn and Kelsey make their way over to where we're sitting. They gush over my belly, ask about names, and tell me how much they miss having me around.

"I do miss coming to work, but I like the freedom and flexibility of doing whatever. At least until I'm put on bedrest."

"Dang, really?" Autumn asked.

"Yeah, my OB says it's pretty much a given now since there are three and with the damage that was done in the accident. It's more for me than them. She's not sure my body will be able to hold the weight of them up."

"So, what are you going to do?" Kelsey asks.

"We're moving back to Beaumont," I tell them, only to realize my mistake. Immediately, I start shaking my head. "It's not what you think. Noah will stay in Portland and once I have the babies and we can travel, we'll come here during the season."

"Oh, phew," Autumn says. "I thought you were telling us Noah got traded."

"What? No. That's not even an option."

Autumn looks down at the ground quickly and out toward the field. "Autumn?"

She looks at me.

"Did you hear something?"

She gives me a slight grimace. "Just rumors, according to Julius. You know how the guys gossip."

"And what are these rumors?"

Autumn squirms. I can tell she doesn't want to say anything but the cat's out of the bag now so she might as well spill.

"Just that the owners are pissed you left, and the guys think Noah's going to bail on them."

"I left because I'm about to have triplets and being with them is far more important than coming into work every day and watching game film when I could do that from home. This is why we need more women in sports management and ownership. Family oriented women at that. My decision has nothing to do with Noah and his position on the team."

I turn toward the field and cross my arms, resting them on my growing belly. The anger I feel is at the club, not at Autumn, even though it may seem it's all directed at her. I turn back and apologize for my outburst. She's been pregnant before. She understands how easily the hormones can take over.

"For what it's worth, Julius doesn't want to lose Noah as his QB."

"He's not going anywhere." This may be a lie, but I'm not going to send my husband down the creek without a paddle. When the guys return from halftime, we hug, and they head back to their seats. I sit down next to Liam and sigh.

"It'll be all right," he says as he pats my leg. "If the Pioneers don't want him, others will. It's the name of the game."

I appreciate his confidence because I'm not so sure I have it. Noah waves and we return the gesture. He's down there, playing the game he loves and winning, for a team who doesn't seem to love him back.

28

NOAH

When I was younger, I loved Halloween, it's because I got all the candy I wanted. In high school, there would always be some costume party and I hated trying to figure out what to wear and often went as myself. One time, I went as my dad. It was freaky because my female classmates acted like groupies, and it was unnerving. In college, we didn't dress up, but partied. In Portland, we only get the kids who live in the building knocking for candy, but now that I'm going to be a dad, I'm so damn excited for this holiday. I can't wait to take the babies out next year. They'll be alert and looking around, and I'm looking forward to picking out their costumes with Peyton.

Speaking of, she's waddling (her words, not mine) around my parent's house in a pumpkin costume. It's probably the cutest thing I've ever seen. The novelty of her being a pumpkin, with her ever expanding belly humors me.

She pauses mid-step as she comes toward me and grimaces. I'm out of my seat instantly and rushing toward her. "The boys?" I ask as she holds her side and nods.

According to her doctor, because she has three babies growing inside of her, space is very limited, and she'll feel them moving and kicking more versus there only being one.

"They're brutal on my ribs," she says in between deep breaths.

"I'd take the brunt of it, if I could."

She offers me a weak smile. "I'm fine. Everything is perfect."

"Perfect" is how she describes everything as of late. I agree with her. Our life is perfect, even though we have a lot going on. The Pioneers have one loss, we're getting close to the playoffs, and even though I don't have a contract the owners assure me one is in the works. None of that even touches the fact Peyton and I are about to be parents. How can life not be perfect?

"You know, you're the cutest pumpkin in the patch," I tell her as I keep my hand on the small of her back and guide her to the recliner my dad bought for her. It's one of those remote-controlled ones, where it will literally help her stand. When he brought it home, she cried until she used it and then thanked him profusely.

"Your mom said the same thing when she brought the costume home for me."

"Are we handing candy out?"

She nods as she sits down. "Your mom and I are going to sit on the porch. This way the kids don't have to knock, and Stevie Nicks won't bark."

"I think Mack is taking her out tonight."

Peyton frowns. "I'd rather her stay home, Noah. Mack's a great kid and I trust him, but others . . ." she pauses and shakes her head. "It'll be dark, and I'll worry about her."

"Okay. She'll stay home. Mack will understand." I sit down on the couch, as close to her as I can get. Peyton presses the button to recline and I'm instantly jealous because the chair looks comfortable. "Maybe we'll get one of those for the new house." We were able to find a house perfectly situated between my parents and Nick, which I really like in case the babies need him in the middle of the night. We won't move in until renovations are done.

My grandma Bianca, offered to sell us her house—the one she shared with Sterling—and while it's big and perfect for our growing family, it's not perfect for my parents. My dad experienced so much childhood trauma there, not to mention how uninvited my mom felt. I wouldn't want to see my parents' agony when they came over. If they came over. It's much easier for my grandma to sell the house.

Peyton has her eyes closed. "So, you can rest your eyes while you're watching whatever sporting event is on TV?"

I chuckle. "Yep, while I'm shirtless and the triplets are snoozing on me."

She opens one eye. "I'm already pregnant. You don't need to keep trying to knock me up."

"If only," I say, laughing.

I turn the volume down, so she can take a nap. I know she's tired and exhausted most days. The triplets take a lot of her energy, and her hips are starting to hurt. She doesn't tell me she's in pain, but I can see it sometimes, especially when she's been on her feet for too long or when the boys start kicking her. So far, our little girl is an angel and only gives her mama love taps, as Peyton describes them. I do think she's kicking the crap out of her brothers though and showing them who's boss. She's not even here yet and she knows she'll be the princess of the family. While the kicking eventually starts to hurt Peyton, I love to feel the babies kick. It's such a unique feeling and very trippy to watch. Sometimes I feel like I'm not doing my part as their dad and

Peyton's partner. Right now, all the burdens are on her, while I sit back and wait. When she's really uncomfortable, I'll talk to the babies or read to them in hopes they calm down. It's all I can really do right now, besides massage Peyton's back.

When the front door opens and screaming ensues as well as barking from Stevie Nicks, I realize I had fallen asleep as well. Peyton looks at me, wide eyed, as I stand to go see what the commotion is in the kitchen.

"You can't tell me what to do," Paige screams at the top of her lungs just as I enter the room. "That's all you ever do, tell me what I can and can't do and I'm tired of it."

"Go to your room, Paige." My mom points in the general direction of where the stairs are.

Paige crosses her arms and leans her hip against the counter. "No."

Oh shit.

Mom looks at me and then back at my sister. "I'm going to make things really simple here, Paige. My house. My rules. You will go to school. You will get good grades. You will respect your teachers. If these rules in regard to school are something you can't live by, then by all means see your-self out."

"You'd kick me out because I told my teacher to fuck off?"

"Paige!"

She looks at me. "What? Like you've never said fuck?"

"It's not that," I tell her. "You don't disrespect your teachers."

"Right! But he can disrespect me? Got it!"

"No, I'm not saying that. It's all in how you handle things. If he says something you find inappropriate, you tell Mom or Dad, and let them deal with it. You don't get yourself in trouble over something you can't control. Believe me, I've had my fair share of asshole teachers. They're out there and you'll always have one. But saying stupid shit back to them only makes things worse. You have Mom and Dad for a reason. Use them."

Paige's expression changes and she wipes at her cheeks. I hadn't noticed she was crying. "You don't get it."

"What don't I get?"

"You're you and you were this amazing quarterback and pitcher. Everyone loved you. These teachers look at me and ask me what I'm going to do because of Dad and you. Like, why am I not enough? Why do I have to be famous or some standout sports player? Why can't I just be me?"

"You can," I say as I step closer and wrap my arm around her shoulder. "You can be whatever you want to be. No one says you have to follow in mine or Dad's footsteps. I didn't."

"But you did, Noah. He played football and broke all these records. I can't even walk down the hall without seeing your names everywhere and then these teachers look at me and they don't see me, they see Liam Page's daughter or Noah Westbury's sister. The shadow is suffocating."

"I'm sorry," I tell her. "This isn't something Dad and I can control."

"I know."

"So, why take it out on Mom?"

Paige looks at our mom, who has tears streaming down her cheeks. She pushes off the counter and collapses into the outstretched arms of our mom. They hug and cry while I stand there, wondering what in the hell just happened and who this teacher is.

Do I pay a visit to the school? Is that the right thing to do?

Probably not, but then what adult asks a teenager how they're going to live up to what her brother and father did?

The front door slams, I jump, and Stevie Nicks starts in again, making sure everyone in the house knows someone is here. My heart races, knowing exactly what's going to happen. "We're in the kitchen," I say before my dad can holler anything. I meet him in the dining room and instantly step back when I see the rage in his eyes.

Shit. Is this what I have to look forward to when I'm a parent?

"Who was it?" Dad demands as Paige steps out of Mom's hold.

"Mr. Pendelgraf."

"Wait, what?" I ask.

"He thought it would be funny if he asked your sister if music was in her future or if she planned to take the path of a groupie."

My mouth drops open.

"Why didn't you tell me this in the car?" Mom asks.

Paige shrugs. "Because it's ... his wife read that stupid book that lady wrote about Dad and . . . all I could think was to tell him to fuck off."

"So, you'd rather fight with me than tell me what's going on?" Mom covers her face with her hands. "Jesus, Paige. I'm not the enemy here. I'm your mom. I'm going to protect you from everything I can, especially fuckers that say shit like that."

"How did you find out?" Paige asks Dad.

"Mack called me," he tells her. "You should've called me."

"I was angry and then sad, and then just pissed off because sometimes I really hate your job. And yours," she says as she looks at me. "I'm this ordinary person and my teacher thinks I'm going to be some groupie. Like, is that how he sees me?"

"As long as it's not how you see yourself, you shouldn't care how others see you. Especially some middle-aged teacher who should know better than to imply . . ." Dad pauses. "Things."

The door opens again causing Stevie Nicks to bark. I head into the other room, hoping Peyton doesn't get up and almost collide with our dog as she races me to the front door. By the time I round the corner she's sitting in front of Mack, waiting for him to attach her leash so he can take her on a walk. We make eye contact briefly and I get the sense he knows what's going on right now.

"I'll be back in an hour," he says. "You have my location on your phone?"

I nod. "Yeah. Be careful," I tell him. There seems to be a group of teenagers who think it's okay to speed down the residential streets and not pay attention to the crosswalks. The town is working on hiring more police, but the process takes time, and the teens don't seem keen on listening to others.

As soon as the door closes and before I can head into the living room to check on Peyton, my dad stalks toward me.

"I'll be back later," Dad says.

"Liam, where are you going?" Mom asks, as he shuts the door. "Go with him," she says as she looks at me.

"Peyton."

"I've got her. Make sure he doesn't do anything stupid."

Heavy charge, especially since I'd like to do something stupid. "All right."

Outside, I jog to him as he swings his leg over his motorcycle. "Mom says I have to go with you. So, I'm either riding on the back or we're taking my car. And I don't want to piss

Mom off any further," I say as I rock back on my heels. When he doesn't answer right away, I place my hand on his shoulder and get ready to claim the seat behind him.

"Fine." Dad gets off his bike and stomps toward my SUV. He gets in, slams the door before I have a chance to get in, and glares out the front window.

"To the school?"

"Yep."

I nod, start my car, and put it into drive. None of this is smart, but I'm also not a parent yet. On behalf of my sister, I'm pissed, but there are other ways to handle shit. Showing up at the school may or may not be the right way. I suppose it all depends on how my dad plans to handle things.

It doesn't take long before he's directing me to pull up in front of the school. I do and shut my car off. "What's the plan?"

The normally calm and collective Liam Page stares out the front window. "As her father, I need to protect her from men like that."

"And as her brother, I agree. However, storming into the school and confronting this piece of shit isn't the answer. Neither is waiting for him in the parking lot."

Dad's chest rises as he huffs out a breath. "He needs to know he's in the wrong."

"So, let's calmly walk into the office and see if Mr. Pendelgraf has a class right now. If he doesn't, they can ask him to come to the office, where witnesses will be present to hear what we have to say."

Dad must like this idea because he gets out of the car and once again slams my door, causing me to cringe. I'm afraid he's going to bust out the window with his aggression.

I get out and have to run to catch up with him at the door to the school. It's locked, which is honestly a good thing. Anything to slow my dad down. I press the button on the wall and wait for someone to come onto the intercom. When no one answers right away, I press it again.

"May I help you."

"Hi, yes. Mr. Westbury to see Mr. Pendelgraf," I say, not knowing who the current principal is or I would've used their name.

"And if he's not available, we need to see Mrs. Gayle," my dad adds.

The door buzzes and we walk in. Long gone is the freedom we used to have at school when you could walk in and wander the halls aimlessly. Now, there are stanchions attempting to prevent you from entering the atrium and directing you to the front office. Dad must know this because he doesn't even hesitate to head toward the office.

As we walk in, I'm assuming Mrs. Gayle is heading toward us, with her hand up. "I know why you're here. I've taken care of the situation, Mr. Westbury."

"How?"

"I sent Mr. Pendelgraf home and told him he can't come back until there's been a hearing with the school board, which Paige will be asked to attend."

It's like all the gusto has escaped from my dad. He lets out a long breath and nods. "Thanks. I came in here ready to fight for my daughter."

"Believe me, I'm fighting for her and all the others. What happened isn't okay and I won't tolerate it."

After they talk for a few more minutes, we head back to my car. Inside, Dad sighs. "The best thing you can do for your children is be their advocate. Whether you agree with the situation or not, you stand up for your kids, no matter what. The worst thing you can do as a parent is not support your child."

"Do you not believe Paige?"

"I do and even if I didn't, I'd still be here ready to beat the shit out of the teacher. I don't care who you are, you don't disparage people. More so, you don't do it if you're someone in a position of authority, which a teacher is."

We sit there for a moment. I absorb his words. I never really think about the years I spent without him, at least not as much as I did when I was younger. Mason was there for me, filling in the hole left by Liam, even though he had no idea. And then there was Nick, who is still active in my life. I glance at my dad and realize he has no one. His dad isn't in his life and my grandpa Preston doesn't really do much with him.

"I'm going to need your help with the triplets," I say.

He looks at me.

"Peyton and I don't know what we're doing and with three of them . . ."

"Your mom and I will be wherever you need us to be. As will Katelyn and Harrison. We're not going to let you and Peyton fail or struggle. I believe the grandmas have already started a calendar so they can be there to help, especially in the middle of the night. Same with Harrison and me. We have some time off and we're going to be there."

"Thanks, Dad."

He grips my shoulder. "I won't let you down or fail you like my father failed me."

Tears threaten to spill over. "I know you won't."

29

PEYTON

In a matter of days, I'm going to be a mom. The countdown is on and very real, and tonight is one of the last times it'll ever be Elle and me, doing nothing but watching movies. It's not going to matter what the movie is, we'll both cry because everything makes us cry these days. We can't help it. We're emotional but after tonight, we're going to be different. Our lives will have forever changed. But tonight, we're two very pregnant sisters who are going to veg out on the oversized reading chair my husband bought me, and just be.

Elle waddles into the room and collapses dramatically onto my new chair. She thinks she's big, but she's nothing compared to me. "I'm tired of being pregnant," she says with a sigh. "I mean, I'm not, but I am."

"You're preaching to the choir," I tell her. "But I don't want it to be over. It feels like it's too soon."

"It is," she says. She kicks her shoes off and then maneuvers next to me. Within seconds, our mom comes into the room with a bowl of popcorn and two bottles of water. Both moms are here, on standby, to help us go to the bathroom when needed. Which is honestly too many times to count during the day. I don't know what I would do or would've done without Josie being at my beck and call twenty-four-seven. My mom was here when she could be, but with the adoption of Oliver not yet final, she hated being away, and the rambunctious toddler is a lot to handle right now.

Elle's next to me, with a bowl of popcorn between us. She takes a few pieces, sticks them in her mouth, and then throws a handful at me. Normally, I wouldn't care, but we're sleeping here and it's not like I can easily roll over to get rid of popcorn kernels. Stevie Nicks appreciates her aunt's gestures though.

My sister turns her head and looks at me. "Are you scared?"

I do the same, facing her. "No," I say and then add. "Sort of."

"They're going to cut you open, P." She reaches for my hand and holds it.

"I know but this scar will be different. I want this one."

"I wish things were different."

"If they were, I wouldn't have the triplets. I don't think I'd change anything right now because I'm getting them. As painful and scary the accident was, it brought me Noah and now the babies. I really can't imagine my life any differently."

"You almost died on me."

"It's going to take a lot more than an accident to get rid of me, Elle. I'm forever going to be a thorn in your side as your big sister."

Elle sets her hand on my stomach and feels one of the boys kick. "He's going to be a hell of a drummer," she says.

"And this guy," she moves her hand a bit higher. "I have a feeling he's going to be a poet or writer, someone who's laid back and just chill all the time." Elle slides her hand over to our girl. "And my niece, she's going to be fierce and determined to outshine her brothers and I'm going to help her every bit of the way."

I place my hand over hers. "The only girl among the boys."

"The instant princess. This little girl isn't going to have to ever lift a finger. There isn't a man in this family who won't dote on her."

"She's going to be spoiled."

Elle nods. "By me as well. I can't wait for her to be old enough to go shopping."

"Noah's ready for them to be three already so we can take them to Disney."

Elle puts her hand under her pillow. "Do you remember when Dad took us?"

I nod even though my memories are fuzzy. "The first time I remember parts of it. I think when we went around ten or eleven, I remember those trips better and definitely when we've tagged along with Ajay and Jamie to take the kids. I'm ready for us to do something like that with our babies."

Elle smiles. "They'll kick us out with our entourage because you know Mom and Dad will have to come with us. Josie and Liam will be there, too. Knowing our parents, they'll hire a videographer to capture every moment."

"Dad's ready to be a grandpa."

"Do you think Mom is?" Elle asks.

"Yes, I am," we hear her yell from the other room. We both roll our eyes.

"Are you going to name one of the boys Mason?" Elle asks.

I shrug. "We haven't decided on names yet."

"Peyton! You're having them in two days. They need names."

"I know." I groan and cover my face. "Nothing sounds right, and I only get one shot at this because I'm not doing this again, so they have to be perfect. We'll know what they're names are when we hold them."

"Noah Jr.?"

I shake my head. "No. He doesn't want a junior."

"Well, I think little miss would make a fine Elle Jr."

I laugh hard and have to hold my stomach to keep it in place. "Of course you would."

My sister shrugs.

"You could go all out with Elle Paige."

"I could or I could take a page out of *Breaking Dawn* and do something like Joskate."

Elle laughs. "No, LynJo."

"Okay, then one of the boys could be Pagison."

Neither of us can hold our laughter and it only gets worse when I yell, "I gotta pee!" Our mom and Josie come running. I don't need both of them to help me, but Josie is used to doing it and I know my mom wants to be the one.

When I come back, Elle's eyes are closed. Mom helps me into my spot and adjusts my pillows. She kisses my forehead and then tells the babies she loves them.

"Soon you can say it to them."

"I know I can't wait," she says as she moves my hair away from face. "Sleep now because you're going to need it. I love you."

"Love you, too."

WHEN I RETURNED to Beaumont to live, doing so put me in a conundrum with my obstetrician. With Dr. Ringman being in California I would have to find a new one in Beaumont or somehow make it back there to deliver the triplets. With Nick's help, I found a new one and I love her to pieces.

While the sun still sleeps, Dr. Harmon greets us at the entrance of the hospital. I'm in a wheelchair and hate it, but the weight of the babies hurts my hips and it's painful to walk. Noah offers to carry me however I don't need him straining a muscle and missing more time than he is now.

The saving grace when it comes to having triplets is I'm being induced. This means we were able to choose a date that coincides with Noah's schedule. Luckily for us, he's off for a few days due to the holiday and when he returns to Portland, he'll be a dad.

Sounds like a damn good few days off to me.

"Good morning, Peyton. Noah." Dr. Harmon leans to the side slightly. "And the rest of their family."

Yes, I'm the one who comes to the hospital with my family in tow. I don't know why I thought Noah and I would do this by ourselves. What a silly notion, especially with the family we have.

We follow Dr. Harmon down the corridor and into the elevator. Not everyone can fit so they take another elevator. Noah's behind me, with my parents on each of my sides, while Elle rests against the wall with her ever growing belly taking up space. I'm thankful Ben said he'd come later. I worry about him getting enough rest with the lifestyle Elle keeps. I told Elle she didn't have to come. Noah would call her after I had the babies and could have visitors, but she insisted. It's the same with my grandpa and Bianca. They're here so they don't have to wait for news on their first great grandchildren.

Somehow, the rest of our family beats us to the floor. I think about making a fat joke, but Elle's cranky in the morning and I don't want to hear it from her.

Dr. Harmon leads us to my room. It's private and something Noah stressed we needed. I'm not certain but I think either Liam, my dad, or the band donated money to this wing because they didn't make a fuss when my husband made the request.

We get to the end of the hall and Dr. Harmon stops. "The private waiting room is here," she says as she points into a room. And the guard will stand here."

"Guard?" I question.

"Just so we have privacy, Peyton," Liam says.

I understand, but then I don't. We're in Beaumont. No one should bother us here.

"I'm going to take Peyton, get her changed, and go over the procedure with her and Noah, and then you may come in," she says as she looks at me. "If Peyton wants you in there."

"See that, I'm in charge."

Elle cackles.

"After surgery, she'll be in recovery and then she'll be able to take a visitor or two at a time. However, I need you all to remember, there are women on this floor in active labor, and some who have given birth. Unless the babies are in the NICU, they are in the rooms with their mother's. Please keep your voices low."

"I feel like we've been scolded." I hear my father say to Liam. Leave it to these two to make jokes right now.

Dr. Harmon doesn't wait for them to agree before she

motions for Noah to continue pushing me into the room. There are blue and pink roses on the nightstand and a banner that reads: Welcome Westbury Babies, hanging from one corner of the window to the other.

"Isn't this a bit premature?"

"I think our moms wanted you to feel the love before you had them," Noah says into my ear.

"Okay, Peyton. We're going to get you changed and hooked up to these monitors."

Noah helps and takes advantage of seeing my bump for one last time. "I'm going to miss this," he says as he kisses my stretched skin. "But knowing I get to hold them today is pretty freaking awesome."

"Yeah, it is."

Noah leads me to the bed and helps me get settled. A nurse comes in and tells me she's going to start an IV. I've been poked and prodded so many times, needles don't bother me as much as they used to. Still, Noah has me focus all my attention on him.

"Can you believe these three still don't have names?"

"I know. Does that . . ." I take a deep inhale when the needle pinches my skin. "Are we going to be bad parents?"

"Nope," he says as he shakes his head. "As long as we call them something one, two, and three, we'll be okay."

"It's Thing One," I tell him.

"Nah, I'm sure that's trademarked or something. We need to come up with our own moniker for them."

"Elle says boy A is going to be a drummer."

"He can be whatever he wants as long as he's healthy."

"They're healthy," I tell him. He wasn't in town when I had to get the steroid shots to help their lungs develop before today. "Dr. Harmon is convinced they're done cooking."

"She would know, right?"

"She would."

I'm so busy focusing on Noah, I don't realize until I hear the sound of rushing horses echoing in the room.

"Those are some strong heartbeats," Dr. Harmon says. "What do you say we go meet these three?"

Noah and I nod as my bed is pulled away from the wall and heading toward the door. I expect to see our immediate family, including Nick and the kids. But when I see Quinn, I start to cry. Elle told me not to expect him because of the tour.

"Quinn," I cry out as I reach for him.

"Hey, kiddo. You didn't think I'd miss your big moment, did you?"

"Elle said—"

"Sometimes I like to keep you in suspense." Elle interrupts. "Now go have those babies because someone has to get back for his show tomorrow."

Quinn rolls his eyes. "I'll be here when you're out. I'm not leaving until I've met my niece and nephews."

"We'll be back soon," Noah says.

We continue down the hall. I'm taken into one room, while Noah follows a nurse into another. I look around in a panic and pause when I see three cradles in the corner, each with three nurses. They're waiting for my babies. I close my eyes, afraid I'm about to hyperventilate if I watch what everyone is doing around me.

I smell Noah before I hear him. "Open your eyes," he says.

He's sitting next to me, dressed in a blue gown, but with a pink hat. "They had both colors. I couldn't pick."

"Are you ready for this?"

He nods.

"I've never been more ready for anything since I said I do."

"Peyton, we're going to start now," Dr. Harmon says. I give her a nod and keep my eyes on my husband as he takes my hand and squeezes it.

3 0

NOAH

here's a board or a wall of some type blocking Peyton's view, which is a good thing. She doesn't need to see what they're doing to her body, and frankly, neither do I. When it's time for me to cut the cord, I will, but I won't be the father who will tell his children later in life that he watched their birth. I saw what a c-section looks like during some parenting class we took—that was more than enough for me.

I want to touch my wife, but I can't. I spent five minutes with the nurse, scrubbing up so I could be in this room, I'm not about to jeopardize anything, especially with them cutting Peyton open.

"I love you."

"I love you too," she says right back.

C-sections are safe. I know this. I did the research, but there are instances where things can go wrong. To say I'm worried about Peyton would be an understatement. Her body has been through a lot, and I'm honestly surprised she was able to carry the triplets for as long as she has. She was diligent though and worked her ass off to protect them, to

299

keep them growing inside of her as long as possible. Her moving to Beaumont was the smartest thing she could've done and I'm forever grateful to my parents for being there for her.

"Okay, Peyton," Dr. Harmon says.

The next sound we hear is music to our ears. Crying fills the room and everyone seems happy to hear it.

"Baby boy A is out. Dad, do you want to do the honors?"

"I'll be right back," I tell my wife, longing to kiss her or squeeze her hand.

I move behind the screen, where Peyton can no longer see. The baby is tiny and won't even take up the length of my arm. I do my best to keep my worries buried. We knew they'd be small, but knowing something and seeing it first-hand are entirely different. I want to hold him but the staff is busy making sure he's perfect. I think he is because he's my son. I look him over as if I'm the inspector general or something. Ten fingers and toes. Knobby knees, puffy cheeks, and kissable lips. He stretches, his tiny fists closed as the team wipe him down.

My throat seizes as tears stream down my face. I have a son. *We* have a son. We created a life and while I know there are two more coming, this guy is my first and will always hold a special place in my heart.

"Noah?" Peyton's voice pulls me to the present.

"I'm coming, babe," I tell her. "Just checking out our boy." As soon as I sit down next to her again, her eyes fill with tears. "He's perfect. Look." I move out of her line of vision so she can see where they've taken him. "They're going to get him cleaned up and then they'll bring him over to you."

"Okay."

We hear more cries and somehow, I know it's my other son. "Be right back," I say to Peyton. "Duty calls."

Baby boy B is small as well and I guess it makes sense. They were crammed in there tightly and Peyton isn't very big to begin with. Again, I inspect every detail of our middle child. I don't know what it's like to be a middle child but I read it can be tough. Not for this guy. I won't allow it. I'll have his back, no matter what. Even when his princess of a sister is picking on him.

"He's perfect, Peyton." Again, I'm out of the way so she can watch the staff with our son. "One more to go and then they'll bring them over here."

Another wail and for whatever reason, a smile spreads across my face. I move to the other side of the screen and glimpse my daughter, *our* daughter, for the first time. She's bigger than her brothers, which is comical in the sense Peyton wanted them to protect their little sister. I think it's going to be a good chunk of years until that happens.

"Peyton, she's gorgeous."

"And perfect?"

"Yes, perfect."

The staff take her from me, and I go back to my wife. "Ah, babe. They're perfect. With all ten fingers and toes. The boys don't have any hair, but our daughter does. She looks just like you."

While they finish putting my wife back together, three nurses come over pushing incubators. Each takes one of the babies out. You can tell they're pros at this and know exactly how to put all three babies with their mother. Tears stream down my face and while I know she'll hate me for this now, I take a selfie of my wife with our children.

I sit behind, thankful for the stool on wheels, and rest

my chin on her bed. "My god, Peyton, look at what we made."

"They're so tiny."

"Baby A and B are three and a half pounds, which is really good when there are three. Baby girl is four and a half pounds. You did really well, Peyton," the nurse says.

"Thank you."

"We're going to take these kiddos to the NICU. Dad will be able to come up and see them in about thirty minutes. Mom, we're going to take you to recovery. Dad, you can join her after you've notified your family."

I show Peyton the photo and then kiss her. "Thank you. So much."

"You helped," she says, smiling. "I should be the one thanking you."

"I'm going to go see everyone and then I'll come to you."

She shakes her head. "Go to the babies. They need you a bit more than I do right now."

"Peyton."

"Please, Noah. I'll heal faster knowing you're with them."

I nod and kiss her again as they start to wheel her out. I don't bother taking off the paper gown, the hat, or the booties. I've seen men do this on TV so many times, I figure why the hell not. Before I go out there and share the amazing news with our families, I pause and lean against the wall, bending at the waist to try and keep my emotions in check. To no avail though because tears stream down my face. I'm over-the-moon happy but I also feel an over-whelming sense of sadness. I'm going to miss Peyton's bump. I'm going to miss talking to my children and reading them stories. Sure, I'll be able to talk to them while I hold or feed them, but something hits different knowing I could do that while they were growing inside of her. Like, maybe I had a part in their development, too. I know I have the daily photos, and videos of them babies moving, but pressing my hand to Peyton's stomach and feeling them kick me is something I miss greatly.

"Are you okay?" I glance at the feet next to me and then stand tall. It's one of the nurses from Peyton's delivery room.

"A little overwhelmed."

"It's expected. Your wife is in recovery. You can see her."

"She wants me with the babies."

The nurse smiles. "Most of them do. I'll take you to NICU."

I glance at the door. "I need to tell our family first. They're waiting."

The nurse nods and points down the hall. "When you're ready, I'll be at the desk there. If I'm not, another nurse will take you. Congratulations."

"Thanks."

After another minute or so, I push my way through the double doors, praying my eyes are not red rimmed. The last thing I want to do is strike fear in Katelyn and Harrison, wondering if their daughter is okay.

My mom is the first to stand, followed by Katelyn and Elle. Slowly, everyone starts to gather.

I clear my throat. "The boys are tiny. They weigh just over three pounds. The girl is a bit bigger at four and a half. They're in NICU, which as you know is standard."

"And my daughter?" Katelyn asks, her voice breaking. "How's my baby?"

"Peyton's in recovery. She's seen and held her babies." I pull my phone out, bring up the photo, and hand it to Katelyn, sensing she needs confirmation of Peyton's well-being more than anything. She covers her mouth to hold back a sob as she studies the photo.

"She looks like my girls."

"She does." I confirm. "I know you can't see her hair, but it's dark. The boys are a bit bald, but hopefully that will change soon." I scratch the top of my head and laugh, enjoying how my hair has grown out since I shaved it in solidarity with Ben when he went through chemo.

Katelyn turns the phone to my mom. "Look at what our babies did," she says in a hushed tone. Both grandmas start to cry and hug each other. I imagine for them this moment is pretty indescribable for them. From being best friends to now grandmas. My dad takes the phone and Harrison huddles around him. They're heads are down but I hear sniffles. I step closer, only to have both of them look at me. I've only ever been afraid of Harrison a handful of times—this is one of those times.

"You're going to be a damn good father, Noah," Harrison says. I take this as a statement of fact. If I'm not, he's going to hurt me. The threat is there and understood.

"Welcome to the Hot Dad's Club," my dad says as he gives me a hug. Leave it to him to make light of the situation. It seems everyone hears him and laughs.

Harrison and I hug, and he congratulates me. When we part, Elle's standing there with worry on her face.

"Is my sister okay?"

I nod. "She's perfect. She's in recovery and wants me to go be with the babies while they tend to her."

Elle hugs me, bump and all. "I'll see if they'll let me in recovery. I don't want her to be alone."

"I appreciate that," I tell her.

Quinn hands me my phone, which I had honestly

forgotten about. "I think boy B looks like me," he says, smiling.

"Definitely." We hug hard and he pats my back with his fist.

"Damn, I didn't think I'd be this emotional over my sister having a kid."

"Three," I point out.

"Yeah," he says, shaking his head. "I can't wait to hold one of them. Hell, all three."

"Me, neither."

It's like everyone needed to digest the magnitude of the moment and once they did, my family was well before they started in with a round of congratulatory remarks, pats on the shoulder for a job well done, and then cigars. My dad opens a box and hands them to everyone waiting.

"Names, yet?" My mom asks.

"No, not yet. Once we get a chance to spend time with the babies, we'll name them. We have a list of finalists."

"All I know is my niece has my name as her middle name," Elle says proudly.

"She does," I tell her. "At least she has a middle name."

Everyone laughs.

We have a round of hugs and I promise to take a lot of photos and send them so the grandparents can gush about their grandchildren.

I head to the nurse's station and as promised the nurse takes me to the NICU where the babies are. I pass by the large window and peer into the room of cradles. At quick glance, there are four babies in there right now, three of which are mine. Briefly, I wonder why the other is there and quickly pray he or she is okay.

Before we enter the nursery, the nurse shows me where to wash up, and tells me to put gloves and a mask on. After doing so, she takes me to my three children, boy A Westbury, boy B Westbury, and girl Westbury, all in the same incubator.

As I look around, I see how open this place is and how anyone can stand at the window to look in on the babies. Peyton has a ton of privacy, but the babies don't.

"I'm sorry, I don't mean to be a pain, but is there something that can be done about their privacy?"

She nods and closes the curtain surrounding them. "Whenever you or Mrs. Westbury aren't in there, we'll have a staff member with them at all times."

"I appreciate it."

The nurse goes over the rules and then tells me Dr. Ashford will be in to speak with me shortly before leaving. It warms me to no end, knowing Nick will be the one caring for my children. I'm torn on what to do. I have three children who need my undivided attention and there's no way I can give it to them at the same time.

"Shit."

On the other side of the curtain, I hear giggling and find myself smiling.

"Don't worry, Mr. Westbury. You're not the only father we've encountered with multiples. One at a time is your best and only bet," the voice behind the curtain says.

"Right, okay then." I pull the chair toward the incubator and reach my hand in. The space is warm and honestly feels inviting. I touch each of their cheeks as tears spill over. I think about what I want to say to them, but the words don't come easily. Do I say, "hey guys?" or is that insulting to my daughter? I know she doesn't know the difference now, but eventually she will.

With a deep breath, I lean toward the opening and say the cheesiest thing I can. "Hi, I'm your dad." I feel awkward and rather silly, but I know it needs to be done. Peyton and I learned about early bonding through the books we read and the classes we took on parenting.

I clear my throat, take another deep breath, and let the tears slide down my face. Silly or not, I need to do this. They need to know who I am and what my voice sounds like.

"Like I said, I'm your dad and I'm so happy you're finally here. Your mommy is resting but she can't wait to hold you. So, until she can be here with you, you're stuck with me, and probably your grandparents. That's the thing you'll never fully grasp, but you have this massive family. They're all waiting in the lobby to meet you. Your Aunties Elle and Paige are going to love you to pieces and spoil the crap out of you, and then there's your Uncle Quinn—he wants to teach you all about music and art. You'll get your sports knowledge from me and Uncle Mack. We love our sports, but you know what—your mommy is the smartest when it comes to sports. I wouldn't have the career I do without her.

"I know you don't understand a single thing I'm saying. I wish you did though because then you'd know how much you are loved. How your mommy can't wait to hold you. You see, I know she loves me, but once she gets her hands on you three, I'm moving down the line in the pecking order. I'm supposed to be the one protecting you and being a macho dad, but I'm going to need at least one of you to have my back. Especially when it comes to your mom.

"I don't know much about being a dad, but I know what it's like to be a big brother, and boys let me tell you this, it's your job to protect your sister. She's going to look up to you. Your mom and I will protect the three of you, but you need to have each other's backs, always." I continue to caress their cheeks, hoping my time is spread equally among them. "Thank you for making our family complete."

"Mr. Westbury?"

"Yes?" I clear my throat.

The curtain parts and another nurse steps in. "Your family is at the window. Would you like to show them the babies?"

I look back at my three. "What do you think?" I know they're not going to answer me, but at least I gave them the option. After nodding, the nurse opens the curtain and then pulls the incubator toward the window. Despite the thick glass, I can hear each and every one of them oohing and ahhing. They wave, tap the glass, and say, "Hi baby," as if the triplets can hear them.

The nurse removes the top of the incubator and encourages me to tilt each baby up. I do, giving our family ample viewing.

"When can I hold them?" I ask her, while I have my daughter on display.

"As soon as Dr. Ashford gives you the okay. But from what I've seen, you'll be able to hold your daughter soon. She's very strong."

Like her mother.

PEYTON

When I wake, it's dark out. The curtains to my room are open and my husband is cast in a glow thanks to the moonlight streaming through my window. I try not to move much, my stomach hurts where they stapled my stomach back together. Lightly, my hand touches my now empty womb and I find myself fighting back the tears. I know the triplets are here, but that doesn't assuage the pain I feel from not having them inside me anymore. And it definitely doesn't help that I haven't been able to hold them. I saw them briefly when I came out of recovery, thanks to my family. They insisted I be able to at least see them through the window. At least Noah was there with our babies, talking to them. Loving them.

I blink and refocus my eyes on my husband. He's sleeping in a chair and shirtless. For a moment, the sight of him confuses me. That is until I see he's holding something. No, not something, but one of our babies.

"Noah." My voice is hoarse. My throat is dry from the meds. I clear away the roughness and say his name again. I'm about to say it for a third time when I stop myself. He's sleeping and whomever he's holding, is sleeping as well. The book says never to wake a sleeping baby unless you're trying to get them onto a different schedule.

I press the arrow on the control and raise the head portion of my bed. The noise doesn't wake him and while I am thankful, I'm sort of not. I want to hold the baby and bond with my child. My options are limited. I can't get out of bed without help and I don't want to yell. So, I stare at my husband and wait for him to wake.

And I wait.

And wait.

And wait some more.

Finally, he stirs and that's when I see it—the pink hat. My heart zings and races while my throat tightens with emotions. I yearn for her, to see and touch her. To have her with me. I want to nurse and develop a connection with her. The boys as well, but it'll be days before I can hold them. It should've been days before Noah could hold her.

"Noah," I say again, but this time louder. He opens his eyes and a slow, sexy grin spreads across his face.

"Hey, babe." He stands and his gray sweatpants sag a bit. I'm thankful it's just us in the room. He comes toward me, his large hand holding our daughter to his chest. She's so tiny compared to him. He'll have no problem holding all three babies at the same time, where I know I'm going to struggle. Tears spill over, wetting my cheeks. Noah by my side instantly.

"Hey, what's wrong?" Noah sits in the chair next to my bed. I want him next to me, on this same mattress but I can't move, not without assistance at least.

"I don't know," I tell him. "So many emotions." I wave my hands in front of my face, trying to quell the tears.

"Do you want to hold her?"

I nod furiously and hold my hands out for her. Noah sets our daughter in my arms, and he works to cover her up. "Hi," I say quietly as my mind works through a barrage of emotions. She's . . . everything. I choke back a sob as I take in her dark hair, button nose, and puffy cheeks. Her fingers are itty bitty and she's light as a feather. My finger trails down the side of her face and I swear her cheek lifts in a smile. It's probably my imagination, but I'm going to let it run and believe my daughter smiled at me.

"We were doing the skin-on-skin bonding," Noah says as he stands next to me. "You should do it."

I nod and he unsnaps my nightgown, exposing me. His hands guide her to my chest. At first, I shiver and then it's like a flood of heat and energy washes through me and into her. Another wave of emotion washes over me when I feel her heart thump against my chest. It's hard to describe and I can only liken it to fulfillment. I'm meant to be a mother. I feel that deep in my bones.

"She's so tiny."

"She's strong and mighty," Noah says. "Very strong. Already breathing on her own."

"The boys?"

"They're thriving. They're with our dads right now. Our parents are taking shifts."

"Are they going to be okay?"

"They're already perfect, Peyton. Nothing out of the ordinary. The steroid shot worked. Their lungs are fully developed. You did your job as their mama. Now the staff here will do theirs."

"I want to hold them."

"You can, in the morning," he tells me. "We'll go down to the unit and spend the morning with our babies, as a family."

"We need to name them," I say as I nuzzle my daughter's head.

"I know. I brought our list."

I look at Noah. He leans down and kisses me. "We're parents."

"I know," he says with a smile. "Of three. We definitely don't do things the easy way."

"Easy is boring."

There's a light knock on the door and a nurse comes in. "Hi," she says quietly. "I've come to take baby girl Westbury back to her brothers."

"Oh?" I don't move a muscle to let my daughter go.

"Only for monitoring and bonding. We like to keep multiples together. They flourish better," she says.

I look at Noah, with unshed tears. "Just until the morning," he says as he takes her from me. He sets our daughter into the cradle and the nurse closes the top. I sob quietly as she takes her out of the room.

"It's for her well-being," Noah says as he sits next to me. "They'll feed and change her and put her back in the incubator with her brothers. And in the morning, we'll have breakfast and then spend the morning with them."

Noah takes my hand and kisses it. "We need to rest because once we go home with these kiddos, we won't rest until we move them into their dorm rooms in eighteen years."

"I just woke up."

"Yeah, I know. But just think, if you close your eyes and sleep, when you wake, you'll get to meet your boys."

"Do they look like you?"

Noah smiles. "I think they look like us. Our daughter, though, she looks like you. I said it from the second I saw her."

"How do you feel about that?"

"Like the luckiest man alive."

THE MORNING GOES EXACTLY to plan with a little extra. I take a much-needed shower, welcoming the pounding water on my back to work out a kink from the uncomfortable mattress and go for a walk around the maternity ward, where I spent more time crying than walking. It's hard walking by rooms, hearing babies cry, and not being with mine right now. Knowing they're in the hospital with me isn't as comforting as one might think.

Noah wheels me to the NICU. He thinks it's funny and tries to do wheelies and pulls the "no hands" trick when we go down a ramp. When I balk, he says something ridiculous about boys and pranks and all I can think is I'm in for it. My hope is our daughter will side with me. I definitely need a sidekick in this family now.

We go into the NICU, wash up and put on the appropriate attire. It's quiet in the nursery minus the sound of machines beeping or humming. Noah pushes me toward a curtained area and when he pulls it back, I gasp at the sight before me. It's not our children that has my attention, but our fathers and my brother. They're all asleep and shirtless, sitting upright in a semi-circle near the incubator the babies stay in. Each of them holding one of the babies. I tap Noah's hand and he leans down.

"Take a picture."

He does as I request, hopefully snapping a few.

The boys are with our dads, while Quinn holds our daughter. When I look closer, her tiny fingers are wrapped around his index finger. Tears well instantly. Those two are going to be close and I love that for Quinn.

"Did you get a good one?" Noah hands me his phone. I heart every single photo, loving each one for different reasons.

I don't know if it's our presence or the fact that Liam senses us staring at him, but he startles and our son whimpers. Cue another wave of tears and emotions. I thought I was emotional during my pregnancy, but this crying shit is for the birds. Hopefully, once my body adjusts the waterworks will slow down.

"Morning," Noah says to his dad. "Which one do you have?"

"Boy A," Liam says and then adds, "Who needs a name or I'm going to start calling him Rocketship."

"You will not," I say to my uncle. "He'll have a name today." I reach back and pat Noah's hand. We have a list and after I spend some time with my babies, they'll have names.

Our voices wake Quinn and my dad. Quinn smiles sheepishly when I give him a fun pointed look. He smiles and shrugs.

"She's my first niece," he says. "She'll need me to keep the boys away."

"Won't her brothers do that?" I ask him.

"Sure, when they're older." Quinn makes no attempt to move our daughter from his chest. "She looks like you and Elle; it's in my nature to protect her."

"I appreciate you."

Now he stands and takes a few steps toward me. I expect him to hand me my daughter, but he holds her tightly to his chest. Quinn leans down. "I'm so damn proud of you," he says and then kisses me on my forehead.

Liam kicks my dad's foot. He startles, looks around, smiles, and closes his eyes again. Looking extremely content to stay there with his grandson on his chest.

The nurse comes over and doesn't say anything about the scene in front of her. She giggles though, which makes me laugh as well.

"Okay, gentlemen, I think mama wants some time with her boys."

My dad and Liam grumble something unintelligible and stand, and if I had to guess, reluctantly hand the boys over to the nurse. She sets them in their incubator, and then two bare chested, tattooed men block my line of vision. They both lean down and press their lips to my cheeks, each thanking me for making them grandpas.

"Have you decided on what you want to be called?" I ask them.

They look at each other and smile. "I'm going to be grandpa," my dad says.

"And I'm going with gramps. I like the shortened, much cooler version. And we both know I'm way cooler," my father-in-law adds.

"Shut the f—" My dad stops himself before dropping the f-bomb in the nursery. "Let's go round up our wives while we discuss the level of coolness you think you have." My dad puts his hand on Liam's shoulder and gives him a slight push. "Quinn."

"But—" Quinn protests and then sighs. "Here's your daughter," he mumbles as he hands her to me. "This isn't fair." He reaches for his shirt and then mutters, "Someone has to go back on tour," in a high-pitched voice meant to sound like Elle.

"I'll miss you," I tell him as he kisses my cheek.

"I'll be here until tomorrow."

"Okay, we'll be out in a bit, to tell everyone their names."

"One better be Quinn," he says, laughing.

When everyone is gone, the nurse helps me get situated in the chair. "Do you want to do skin-on-skin?" she asks.

"I do, but I want to hold them first," I tell her.

"This is boy A," she says as she places my son on my right side. Noah's there, with our daughter in his arms, looking at us.

"And this is boy B. I'll give you some time." She pulls the curtain shut behind her.

Noah pulls a stool up next to me and sits down with our daughter. I take each one of our babies in and let the tears roll down my cheeks. It's hard to tell who the boys look like, they're definitely a cross between the both of us, and I know the older they get, the more defined their features will be.

"They're perfect."

"They really are," Noah says as he touches the boys with his finger. "Mighty and tiny is what I've said to people. You did good, Mama."

I kiss the boys. It's easy to bring them to my lips with how light they feel. Boy B grunts or mumbles, it could've been either and something he's already picked up on from his uncle.

"Has Elle seen them?"

"Only through the window."

"Oh, that's so sad for my sister. She'll get lots of auntie time before she delivers."

"I don't think she's worried," he says. "She's more concerned with you."

"Really?" I look at my husband.

"Before I brought her in—" Noah looks at our daughter. "Elle was asleep in the chair next to your bed, and she tried to go be with you in recovery, but they wouldn't let her. I know it's a twin thing—your thing with her. She needed to be with you. I imagine she's a bit torn up inside."

"Wow."

"I really hope the babies have the same bond you and your sister have. While a mystery to most of us, seeing you two together is something of a marvel. The way you're always in sync with each other, know what the other is feeling or know when you need your twin. The bond is unbreakable. I want that for our babies."

"They'll have it," I tell him. I don't know how, but it's a twin thing and I'm praying our daughter is included in it.

Noah suggests I do some skin-on-skin with the boys. He helps maneuver them and then reclines my chair. I'm holding them and basking in our body-to-body contact when he places our daughter in the middle.

"Now mommy has her babies," he says as he wipes at my tears. "This is my picture-perfect moment, Peyton. Seeing you with our children."

"Really? It's not because my boobs are out?"

Noah laughs and then deadpans. "I say something nice, and you have to ruin it with a joke?"

I nod. "I'm so emotional right now I need some humor."

My husband sighs. He kisses me, and then kisses each of the babies. "Nothing but perfection," he says.

We stay like this, with the babies on my chest and Noah next to me, until it's time to feed them with the little droppers of the colostrum the nurse helped me pump earlier in the morning. After their feeding and the light pats on their back to get them to burp, Noah and I give them a sponge bath, which none of them care for. Their cries sound like they're saying la, to which the nurse assures me will change to screaming in months, if not weeks.

After the babies are settled, Noah looks at me. "It's time."

I sigh. "Pull out the list."

He takes a folded sheet of paper from his pocket and sits down next to me.

The nurse hands us a pen. "We've been waiting too," she says, laughing.

"All right, let's name our children," I say to Noah. "And pray they like their names when they're adults and we don't scar them for life."

Noah chuckles and then reads the list of names we've compiled over the months.

3 2

NOAH

*N*ormally, I don't consider myself a smooth talker. I'm not the guy who is going to flirt to get his way or even bat my eyelashes when I need something. I've seen Quinn do it with his sisters and those two turn into a puddle of whatever Quinny wants, he gets. Yes, I will do some puppy dog eyes at Peyton if I'm not getting my way, but she's my wife and it's expected of me.

With that said, I know when to turn on the charm.

Peyton has written out the three names we chose. We've said them out loud and given them to the nurse, who promptly wrote up new cards and handed them to us for keepsakes. The original name cards will remain the same for privacy reasons.

With a big sigh, I look at Peyton. "We should tell our family."

She nods and reaches out for me to help her move from the chair to the wheelchair. While she complains about using it, I think she secretly loves it because I'm at her beckon call. She likes being ushered around by me. Truth be told, I don't mind.

"I just wish they could meet the triplets at the same time," I say loud enough for the nurse to hear me. "Your sister really wants to meet her niece and nephews."

Peyton glances over her shoulder at me with a confused expression on her face. I give her the eyes, like I need her to play along with me. When she finally understands, her lips morph into an "O" and she nods.

"And she's leaving this evening with Quinn. Is there any way we can bring her in?"

Granted, this isn't the best argument since Quinn was in here, but it's what my mind came up with, so we have to run with it.

The nurse chuckles. "All you have to do is ask," she says, clearly onto our game. "I'll go with you. The triplets can't leave the incubator, but everyone will be able to see them, and the babies will hear everyone."

"Thank you," I say to her. We wait while she unhooks the incubator and then we leave the NICU and head back to the maternity ward where everyone has decided to hang out instead of going home. It has to be incredibly boring for them waiting around. Although, I think our parents stay because they want to be here if we need them or monopolize any free time with the babies.

My dad is the first to stand when he sees us coming. Katelyn stands next, and then everyone else does. Elle steps forward and I stop Peyton in front of her sister.

"Are you good?" Elle reaches for Peyton's hand. "Tell me you're good because I'm freaking out."

Peyton nods. "I'm sore, but good. Can't wait to get back into the gym. Thank God for Xander, huh?"

"I knew my brother-in-law was good for something," Harrison says while everyone laughs.

Elle and Peyton hug, and then Katelyn shoos her daughter out of the way to get to her other one.

"Where's JD and Jenna?" I ask, hoping they would've arrived by now.

"Delayed," my dad says. "Eden had a test this morning she couldn't miss. They'll be here later."

It saddens me they're not here. We try to include them in everything our family does, but Eden keeps them busy. She's a hell of a surfer and now that surfing is an Olympic sport, she's busting her ass to make the team. I know she can do it and her being there will give us an excuse to travel. I'm not sure any of us would miss seeing her compete for a gold medal.

It's my mom who notices the babies first. Her eyes widen and she covers her mouth in surprise. Maybe shock? I look over my shoulder and can't help but smile at the three of them.

"You bought the babies," Elle states.

"I hear you haven't been in to see them," Peyton says to her sister. "How come?"

Elle takes Peyton's hand. "Because I wanted them to see you first."

"I love you for that," Peyton says to Elle. I sniffle and blink my misty eyes. "Go meet your niece and nephews."

The nurse pushes the cradle into the family waiting room, allowing everyone to gather around. They coo, wave, say their names for the babies to hear, all while Peyton and I stay off to the side. As much as we want to be in the middle of it all, we'll have our time. Our moments with the babies will come as the days go on.

After what seems like an hour but in reality, is only a few minutes, I clear my throat and push my wife toward the cradle.

"We have names," Peyton says as she beams at me. "No comments from the gallery if you don't like them. We do and they're fitting."

"Baby A, our oldest is Maverick Liam Westbury."

We let Maverick's name settle onto his gramps. My dad wipes at his eyes and nods. Knowing him the way I do, he's too emotional to say anything about it right now and will likely write a song about his grandchildren.

"Baby B," Peyton continues as she looks at her dad. "Is Jace Harrison Westbury."

"Oh, thank heavens," Katelyn blurts out. "I thought you were going to call him Harry Westbury and I just couldn't wrap my head around it. The poor boy would've been teased relentlessly."

Peyton looks at me and blanches. Neither of us thought about anything like that. *Shit.*

"And my niece?" Quinn asks.

"You know her middle name's Elle unless Peyton did me a solid and named her first born daughter after her lovely sister," Elle says as she bumps his shoulder with hers.

Quinn scoffs. "Maybe Quinnella," he says.

"Please no," Katelyn says and then covers her mouth. There's a look of horror on her face. I shake my head, hoping to ease the dread she might feel.

"Our little girl is Juniper Elle Westbury."

"Yes," Elle says as she fists pumps. "I told you!" She jabs her finger at Quinn. "Wait, Juniper? Not Elle? I mean I knew Elle was in there, but I really thought—"

"Juniper," Peyton says. "We'll call her Junie or Junie Elle. I didn't want to call her Ellie, and she needs her own identity."

"I love it," Elle says.

My eyes meet Paige's. She's staring at the cradle but not

saying anything. I go to her, wrap my arm around her shoulder and pull her away from everyone.

"I'm guessing the tears are because Juniper has Elle for a middle name?"

She shrugs. "I don't know. It's silly. Elle's her sister so it makes sense, and I think I sort of knew it but hearing it out loud. I don't know. Like I said, it's silly."

"The one thing you and I will never understand or have, is the twin bond. It's freaky and indestructible. No one will ever come between them, and this is Peyton's way of honoring her sister."

"I get it. I think I was just caught off guard."

"I'm sorry, Paige. But do you want to know something?"

"What?" she asks.

"You'll spend a lot more time with the triplets than Elle will. We're going to raise the babies here, which means until you go away to college, you have full access to them. Elle has her own life and will be a mom soon. You," I say as I point to her. "You get to be auntie every day, anytime you want. They're going to be attached to you."

"I guess that's something even though this isn't a competition."

"I think dad and Harrison have made it one."

Paige rolls her eyes. "They're ridiculous. I think Mom and Aunt Katelyn have told them to knock it off a million times. Then, when Nick came to see how everyone was doing, they tried to get him involved."

This time I roll my eyes. "Come on, let's go see what the rowdies are up to."

We head back around the corner. I smile when I see Peyton and head toward her. "I'll tell you later," I say to her.

"Beautiful names," my mom says as she comes up to us.

"You guys did good." She comes over and hugs us. "Thank you for making me a grandma."

"Is that what you're going to be called?"

She shakes her head. "Grammie will suffice. Katelyn wants to be grandma."

"Gramps and Grammie it is," I say to her.

Before the nurse takes the babies back to the NICU, my dad, in his infinite wisdom says to my father-in-law, "You know Maverick being the first born and having a name like that means he's superior."

Harrison rolls his eyes. "Whatever you say, Gramps."

"Grandpa!"

"It's like they're fighting but in the old man sort of way," I whisper in Peyton's ear. "Do they even know what they're arguing about?"

She shakes her head slowly. "Nope, but it's entertaining."

Harrison rubs his hand up and down his torso. "Grandpa or not, I still got it."

"Hey!" Katelyn shouts.

"Too far, Harrison," I say quietly to Peyton.

"She'll kick his ass later."

Harrison puts his arm around Katelyn's shoulders and pulls him to her. "You're one hot grandma."

"Time to go, Noah," Peyton says, laughing.

I heed her demand and take her back to her room. Once she's settled, there's an army of people who come in and out all day. It's mostly our family bringing flowers and presents. Peyton had opted not to have a baby shower, mostly because we could afford everything and with the grandparents buying anything not nailed down in the store, there wasn't any need. Not to mention, Christmas is less than a month away.

Still, that doesn't stop the gifts from coming in. Everything from matching outfits for the boys, to frilly dresses for Juniper. While people visit, I begin to return texts and messages, and with Peyton's permission post a photo of three pairs of baby feet. Within seconds, my notifications go crazy. Also, with my wife's consent, I send the family photo I took of the five of us earlier in the NICU to our friends, knowing they won't share it with anyone.

While I'm checking my emails, I receive one from People, asking for an exclusive. "Peyton, the magazine wants an exclusive. It says here, they want to come to the house, interview us and take pictures. They'd like to be the ones to introduce the babies first."

"How much?" Elle asks without looking up from her phone.

"Say two mil."

"Nah, send it to me. I'll negotiate something better. Two is peanuts. They'll move the needle or we'll go with some other mag."

"Uh, Peyton?" She hasn't said whether she wants to even do this.

She shrugs. "Something to consider. We can donate the money though like we talked about, you know helping others with fertility."

"See, that's at least a five million dollar offer," Elle says. "I'll get you at least that."

I wait for Peyton to tell me what to do. She nods and I forward the email to Elle and let her do her thing.

Peyton asks for my phone. I give it to her, and she brings up Instagram. "All these comments. I'm glad they're all positive."

"Of course they are, you just had triplets. If anyone has anything nasty to say Paige will delete them." My sister is very good at managing my social media. Of course, she gets paid to do it and takes her job very seriously.

"Paige is dynamite on the socials," Elle adds. "We hired her to run the agency's account, as well as the FMG Records. Smart cookie."

I make a mental note to tell Paige about what Elle said, hoping to ease what she feels on the name sleight.

There's a knock on the door, which is surprising. It opens before we can say for whoever to come in. I see the cradle first and then Nick, in his white doctor's coat.

"I thought we'd stop by and say hi to mom and dad for a bit." Nick gives me a hug and then kisses Peyton's cheek. "We just took some vitals and did some testing. Things are looking great."

"When can they go home?"

"Juniper probably by the end of the week. The boys, I'd like to keep them for two weeks, but if they keep improving the way they are, end of next week at the earliest."

To be honest, I'm pretty damn happy Nick is their doctor. There isn't anyone else I'd trust with my children.

"Are they healthy?" Peyton asks. "Any longterm issues?"

Nick shakes his head. "None that I can see or even predict. It'll be a bit before the boys catch up with Juniper, but they're eating well and gaining slowly. You did everything right, Peyton." He gives her a soft smile.

There's another knock and this time Mack and Amelie, followed by Talisa come in.

"Can I hold them?" Amelie asks and then frowns when Nick shakes his head.

"Not until they go home, then it's up to Peyton."

"Uh, congratulations," Mack says awkwardly. "I think?"

Everyone in the room laughs.

"How's Stevie Nicks?" I ask him.

"She's good. She really loves playing with Beau."

"Because he's the best," Elle says, still not looking up from her phone, which she has resting on her rather large belly.

"I would love to come to your home while the children are at school and help you, Miss Peyton," Talisa says. Peyton looks at me, then to Nick, who nods.

"Consider it a gift," he says. "I know you didn't want anything, although Amelie has spent a fortune at the store on gifts. Talisa is home during the day and wants to help."

"Are you sure?" I ask Nick.

"Of course, we're family. It's what we do."

"I'd love the help," Peyton says. "Thank you."

Talisa claps her hands together. "Ooh, I can't wait to hold them."

I spy Mack, looking at the cradle. I go over to him and point to my oldest who is wearing a navy-blue hat. "That's Maverick," I tell him. "And this one is Jace."

"Perfect footballer names," Mack says.

"Or baseball," I add.

"Or doctor!" Nick throws his hands up. "How come none of my kids want to be doctors?"

"Too much school, Dad," Amelie says. "No one likes to read except for you."

We all laugh until Elle blurts out, "Will you freaking stop kicking me!" and then jabs her hand into her side.

"Yep, that's the one thing I'm not going to miss."

PEYTON

Talisa bustles around the living room, straightening and organizing candles and magazines she has already straightened and organized. I think she's more nervous than Noah and I are for the People interview. Granted, I am on edge about the entire thing. Having someone come into our new home, which we've only been in for a couple of days, take photos, and ask us questions is a bit unnerving. What if people on the other end don't care for how we decorated or like the theme we chose for the nursery? Or how the boys are in one room and Juniper is in her own?

Noah tells me I have nothing to worry about, especially where outsiders are concerned. If they don't like how we did something—that's on them—not us. Easy to say. Harder to accept.

Juniper came home first, one week after she and her brothers were born. Each morning, the two of us bonded over decaf coffee, breastmilk, and a screamfest while I gave her a bath. I'm thankful for my in-laws. Liam and Josie have been my saving grace, especially since I couldn't carry

Juniper around. Every day after school, Paige took over, giving me a moment to myself, but honestly, I could never go far. It's like my heart ached for her.

And my boys. I missed having Noah, Maverick and Jace in the house with Juniper. Granted, the house would've felt crowded and probably would've driven Liam out the door, but I needed them. Video chatting with Noah, while he's still in Portland is not a substitute for having him in Beaumont. Beside the fact that I miss him, he's missing moments with his children, and I hate that for him. I know I could've stayed in Portland, but not without a ton of help—the help I have in our hometown. Having family surrounding us twenty-four seven is the perfect way to heal.

Maverick and Jace came home right on schedule—my strong little warriors. Nick says they're going to be just fine and growing the way they should. Each morning, I give the boys my undivided attention, trying to make up for the week Juniper had all by herself.

It's funny to watch their little personalities come through each day. Juniper is an eye roller and Elle says she gets that from her. I don't disagree. Each time one of the boys begins to fuss, Junie rolls those baby blues, but then seconds later starts her own fussing.

Right now, when I'm sitting down, I can hold all three. It's the best feeling in the world having them snuggled on my chest. Noah loves it as well and when he's home for the one to two days a week he can get in, it's all he wants to do. This husband of mine sits on the couch, with his feet up and has a chest full of baby with his pup by his side.

Stevie Nicks is amazing with the triplets, as we suspected she would be. While we were at my in-laws the babies shared a room. Now that we're in our new home, the twins share, and Juniper has her own. The rooms are next to each other, joined by a jack and jill bathroom. This bathroom is where our dog sleeps, right smack in the middle so she has easy access to both bedrooms. We tried to bring her back to our room, but she won't have it. Stevie Nicks is wherever the babies are, standing guard and protecting them. I know they'll end up being her best friend, especially when they're highchair age and dropping food onto the floor for her.

Noah and I went with oval cribs and a color scheme of soft navy-blue and cream for the boys, and lavender for Juniper's room. It's a color Paige picked out and I fell in love with it.

In the few days we have lived in our new home, Talisa has come every day once Amelie and Mack leave for school. I love having her here. She's someone to talk to and seems to know more about babies than anyone I know. I marvel at how she can carry both boys and still do things around the house.

Noah comes out of the bathroom, freshly showered and smelling like sin. He didn't dry his hair fully in the back and water droplets sit on the ends of his hair, dropping eventually to the collar of his shirt. He's dressed in a red and white plaid button down with a green sweater over the top. I stand there, staring at my gorgeous and sexy husband, who looks like a Christmas ornament.

"I love your sweater, and your shirt, but not together," I tell him. "Not with the house being decorated for Christmas. You should wear something neutral."

Noah throws his hands in the air and groans. "Do you want to dress me?"

I can't help but laugh. "Wear your sweater. I like it and it'll match the boys. Put a white shirt under it."

"You got it," he says and then kisses me. "What do I need to do to get the babies ready?"

"Nothing," I say, shaking my head. "Talisa has the boys now and my mom is with Juniper getting her dressed. I just need to change."

Noah waggles his eyebrows at me, looking all mischievous and not at all sexy. Any other time, I'd fall for the tactic, but not today, and not yet. I'm still firmly in the no zone.

"Horn dog."

"You know it."

He takes my hand and leads me into our walk-in closet which I'm embarrassed to say is as big as a bedroom. My husband has a lot of clothes and for someone who is only here a few days a month, he takes up most of the space. I change into an ivory-colored dress and add a green scarf to give our family portrait a bit of cohesiveness. This will be our first professional photo and I want our family to look somewhat put together.

The doorbell rings and my stomach drops. I'm nervous I'm going to say something I shouldn't, and I honestly don't want people to judge me. Noah must sense my jitters and pulls me into his arms.

"Everything is going to be okay," he says as he kisses the top of my head. "Easy peasy. They're here to show the world our lives and let people meet our babies. They're not trying to embarrass us."

I nod and then smile when I hear Elle's voice. She's super pregnant and due in four weeks. Elle's scared to be a mom, but Ben's ready to be a dad. He's come to see the triplets every day because he wants them to know who their Uncle Ben is.

"P!" Elle screams at the top of her lungs. I close my

eyes, count to three, and wait for one of the babies to scream.

Silence.

"Were you holding your breath?" Noah asks.

"Yes. You?"

He nods. "I'm going to get her back for that stunt."

"Yeah, we are."

We head downstairs and find the interviewer already setting up and the photographer taking photos of our tree, stockings, and other decorations. We signed a waiver, giving them access to almost every space of our home, except the front. We don't want people to find out where we live, although if they came to Beaumont, it would probably be fairly easy.

Talisa comes downstairs with the boys and my mom with Juniper. She hands her to me once I'm seated and then Noah takes the boys from Talisa, who stands off to the side, ready to help when one of them gets fussy. Honestly, I never thought I'd need someone like her, but I do. I'm so thankful Nick asked her to move back with him.

The interviewer introduces herself as Liana and doesn't waste any time jumping into questions about Noah's career, mine, and what it's like being parents to three newborns.

"Peyton's my super woman," Noah says. "We decided to move back home to where my family is because we knew she'd need support while I finished the season."

"Do you have a full-time nanny?" Liana asks.

"Not full-time, no," I say. "Talisa comes during the day to help. She's been a lifesaver. Noah's parents as well, and mine are here when they can be. It's definitely been a village."

"Your home is lovely," Liana says. "What made you decide to remodel instead of build something new?"

Noah looks at me and smiles. "This house is close to our family. My stepdad Nick, who is also the babies pediatrician, is a few short blocks from here which we really like. And when we want to take the babies for a walk, we're not far from downtown, which my parents are actively revitalizing and helping small businesses owners open their own places."

"There's a rumor your dad, Liam Page, is going to run for mayor."

Noah laughs. "Who knows with him. Right now, I think he's happy being a grandpa, making music, and helping artists achieve their recording goals. He and my sister-in-law, Elle, have a great program set up at the studio. And Elle's working hard to bring more concerts to the area. We're really trying to put Beaumont on the map."

"Peyton, do you see yourself going back to work?"

Noah squeezes my hand.

"Right now, I'm going to freelance. I love helping players and if they want my help, I'll give it. At the moment, I don't see myself working outside of the home."

"And you, Noah. What does your future hold?"

This time, I squeeze his hand. "One game at a time, Liana."

There are a few more questions and then a series of photos are taken. We give Liana and her crew a tour, pose the babies, pose as a family, and take some sweet candid shots. When all is said and done, the entire thing took weeks of stress and less than an hour.

"Well send over the photos for you to see and mark the ones we plan to use. None of them will have anything distinguishable as far as where you live, so you have nothing to worry about there."

"Thank you, Liana." Noah and I shake her hand, and

then she goes to talk to Elle, while we head upstairs with the babies to change and put them down for a nap.

"I think that went well," Noah says as we enter Maverick and Jace's room. Noah sets each one down in their cribs, staying with Jace. I set Juniper next to her brother and somehow, they instantly gravitate toward each other.

"Let's put them in their sleepers and then in their pack 'n play. Give them some time together before it's time to eat," I say to Noah. "Yes, you want that don't you. Do you want to play with your brothers?"

"Is she answering you?"

"Not yet," I say with a sigh.

"Peyton!" My mom screams my name. It's not a normal scream, but one that strikes fear.

"Can you take care of them?"

"Yep, go," Noah says.

I'm halfway down the stairs when I see my mom, Elle, and Talisa slowly making their way to the door.

"What's wrong?"

"Miss Elle's water broke," Talisa says. "We need to get her to the hospital."

"Oh," I say as the news settles in. "OH! I'll call everyone and meet you there. I'll be right behind you."

I rush back upstairs, pausing when I reach the stop landing and grimace at whatever mess there might be on my kitchen floor. I'm going to have to clean it before I leave. Down the hall, I hear Noah talking to the babies. He's telling them about his game last weekend and how he wished it wasn't so cold out because then they could go.

"Babe," I say as I come into the room. "Real quick, Elle's water broke and she's on the way to the hospital. Can you call Ben while I go down and clean the floor? And then maybe your parents can come over and help with the babies?"

"Are you good driving yourself to the hospital or do you want me to take you?"

"I'm good. It's only a couple of blocks."

Noah nods. "Go, go be with your sister. I'll clean up and then I'll meet you there."

I rush to him and press my lips to his. "I love you."

"Love you more, Auntie P. Now go."

I wish I could say I broke all the speed limits getting to the hospital, but I didn't. Thanks to handsfree, I'm able to call our dad and tell him what's happening and luckily for us, he's at Liam's. My in-laws offer to keep Oliver with them while they come over to our house. I love my little brother but fear his grabby hands might be too much for the triplets. Deep down, I know I have to trust Josie and Liam. They're not going to let anything happen to their grandchildren.

The hospital parking lot is packed, and I end up circling until I find a spot. When I finally make it to the maternity ward, my parents are in the waiting room, pacing.

"Hey," Dad says as we hug. "She's already pushing."

"Seriously?" I look at mom for confirmation. She nods.

"She's early," mom says as she runs her hands through her hair. "I don't know if they tried to stop labor or what. She doesn't want anyone in there except for Ben."

"He made it then?"

"Yeah, I'm pretty sure he broke every speed limit in town to get here."

"Well, that's good." I pace for a second. "So, I guess we wait?"

"Yeah, unlike with you we knew how long it would take. With your sister, she could be hours," Mom says.

"That would suck."

I turn at the sound of my name and find Noah coming toward us. When he reaches us, I give him the update and ask him about the three.

"My parents are there. Everything will be okay. Besides . . ." He holds his phone up, showing me the video app of the kids' rooms. "We can spy on them."

Noah and I sit. My parents pace. It makes me wonder if they did the same while I was in here weeks ago or if they sat and watched television. Knowing my mother, she paced and the hospital has probably replaced the tiles already.

An hour goes by.

And then another.

I go to the window and look at the darkened sky and see that it's snowing. Christmas is in two days, and I don't know, there's something magical in the air.

"Ben."

My dad's voice has me moving from the window to the front of the waiting room.

Ben's smiling. "Elle's fantastic. She gave birth a little over an hour ago and we just needed some time to gather ourselves as a family before I came out to get you."

"Is my daughter, okay?"

Ben's smile widens. "She's damn perfect."

Noah pats Ben on the shoulder. "It's a whole other feeling, isn't it?"

Ben tries to hide the tears in his eyes but can't. "I love my wife, but damn, I've never felt my heart soar like this before. It's a whole other level."

"Not to be an ass," I say. "But can we go in? I need to see my sister."

"Oh, yes. Sorry." Ben leads us in and while I know what to expect, my parents and Noah don't.

"Oh, shit," Noah says when he sees Elle.

"Elle! Oh my God, twins?" Mom screeches as Elle beams. Elle's in her bed, holding a baby in each arm. Mom then looks at me. "You knew?"

I nod. "I keep my sister's secrets," I say with a shrug.

"Why didn't you tell us?" Dad asks.

"Honestly, once we found out Peyton was having triplets, Ben and I wanted to keep this to ourselves. I'm surprised no one figured it out with how big I was."

"Well, I was huge, so they probably thought you were normal." I step closer to inspect the babies. "Are you going to tell us their names?"

Elle looks down at the baby in her right arm. "This little guy is the oldest by eight minutes," she tells us. "Everyone, I'd like for you to meet Mason Jett Miller. We're going to call him Jett."

Our mom gasps and covers her mouth, while our dad fist pumps. "Jett is a kick ass drummer name."

"And this little guy—" Ben is interrupted when the door to Elle's room bursts open.

We all turn to find Quinn standing there, with wet hair and breathing heavily. "Liam called and said . . ." he comes closer and halts when his eyes land on Elle. "I missed it?"

"Actually, you're right on time," Elle says. "I'd like you to meet my youngest son, Sonny Quinn Miller."

Quinn isn't one to show emotion, except for now. He nods and his lips clench. "Wow, he has my name."

"Of course he does, Quinny," Elle says. "Did you really think your sisters would have five kids in the matter of weeks and not give one of them your name?"

He looks from Elle to me, with tears tipping the rim of his eyes, and then at our dad. "Thank you."

Dad chuckles. "For what?"

"For this," he says as he looks around. "For giving me

this life when you could've easily shut the door and never look back, and for giving me this family." Now he's looking at our mom. "Being your son, their brother, and now an uncle is literally the best part of my life."

Elle lets out a sob. "Well shit, Quinny. You can't say emo shit to a woman who just had a baby."

"Two," I point out.

"Right, what she said."

I move to one side of Elle and Quinn goes to the other. "No matter what, it's always us," Elle says and then looks down at her boys. "Whenever I mess up, don't you worry. Your auntie P and uncle Quinny will take care of you. Believe me, their phone numbers will be the first thing you memorize."

We visit for another half hour and then Noah and I head home, with Quinn in tow. Once we get back to the house, Noah and I head upstairs and find Liam sleeping in Juniper's room and Josie in the boys'. We give them the news and tell them we'll see them tomorrow.

Noah sees his parents out and then finds me leaning against the door jamb to the boys' room.

"What are you doing?"

"Waiting for the clock to strike midnight."

He looks at his phone and after a moment shows me the screen. "Now what?"

"Now, we wish our children a Merry Christmas Eve and then we go to bed."

"I like that idea."

We start with Maverick and then Jace, whispering to them to not wake them. I head toward Juniper's room but pause in the doorway when I hear Quinn. We stand there and listen to him read to her *A Visit from St. Nicholas.* Noah and I listen to the entire story and then slowly step into the room. Quinn's in the rocking chair, with Juniper on his chest. His eyes are closed. It's like they're snuggling.

"Do you want me to take her?"

Quinn shakes his head. "I'm good. We're just chilling."

"She'll be up to eat soon."

"I'll come get you when she starts fusing. If you don't mind. I'm going to stay here with her."

"I don't mind," I tell him. "Is everything okay?"

He doesn't say anything for a long beat and then nods.

"Merry Christmas Eve, Quinn."

"Merry Christmas Eve, Peyton."

I close the door behind me and look up at Noah. He brushes his knuckles against my cheeks and then leans down to kiss me. "I'm saying this now before I forget, but this was the best damn Christmas of my life."

I can't help but smile. "I didn't buy you anything this year."

"Nothing will ever compare to Maverick, Jace and Juniper. They're the best gift of all. Besides you, of course." He kisses me again, turning me into a soft pile of nothingness.

Noah takes my hand, and we head toward our room. Seconds after the door closes, Maverick's monitor lights up with a scream. Followed by Jace.

I'll sleep when they're eighteen.

EPILOGUE

As I enter the small media room, I try not to look at my parents and wife sitting in the front row. I sit down in a metal chair, which is centered between two tables pushed together to look like one. My knees hit the metal legs under the blue tablecloth. Even without seeing the front, I know the Portland Pioneers logo is facing the audience.

The audience consists of media personnel, my agent, the owner of the Pioneers, our coach, our general manager, and a handful of my teammates. I focus my attention on Peyton, who has a steady smile on her face. Right now, I wish she was sitting up here next to me, holding my hand. There are times when I need her strength and today is no exception.

I look toward the door and see Harrison, Katelyn, and Quinn striding toward my parents. Quinn stops in front of the table I'm sitting at on this makeshift stage and gives me a fist bump. The tour he's currently on just happens to be in Portland right now for three nights and instead of staying in a hotel, he's been crashing at our apartment.

Once everyone's seated, I glance at my watch and sigh. Instantly, the sound of cameras clicking fill the air and bright lights blind me. I squint and raise my hand to block one in particular and then adjust the way I'm sitting because there's no way the camera person is going to adjust.

After a deep inhale and an attempt to swallow the frog in my throat, I lean toward the microphone. "Is this thing on?"

I want to think most of the room laughs, but in reality, I think only one or two people do. I could tell them I'm practicing my lame dad jokes so I can embarrass my kids in the future, but the truth is, I'm nervous.

Scared, actually.

I'm about to make a life-altering decision. One which I'm not sure I'm ready for.

I clear my throat again and lean slightly closer to the microphone so no one blurts out that they can't hear me.

"I want to thank you for being here today." I pause, needing to swallow the lump in my throat. "And I want to thank my parents, my in-laws, and of course my beautiful wife for being here." I wink at Peyton. She winks back, sending my heart into a tailspin.

"Over the past season there has been a lot of speculation about my time with the Pioneers, and well . . ." I lean back and sigh. "Shit, I don't know. The year didn't go as planned, that's for sure. We were a win away from going back to the big game and you all know how I felt during the press conference. Some of you even called and asked me about the fine I received because of the comments I made toward the officials. The first fine of my career I might add."

I roll a piece of lint between my fingers. "You all know why you're here today," I say and then inhale while I search for the words. The tears come first, forcing me to squeeze my eyes shut.

"Shit," I mutter and then groan. Even if I wanted to look at my family right now, there is no way. One look and I'll be a blubbering mess.

"Here's the thing," I say. "Recently, my wife and I welcomed triplets. We also moved back to our hometown to be closer to family. Splitting my time between here and Beaumont means I've missed some things with my kids, and it's not a great feeling."

I clear my throat again. "My time as an NFL quarterback has come to an end. I've decided to retire and spend the rest of my days annoying my wife. I guess I should say don't be surprised if I return somewhere because she will probably force me to leave the house."

Everyone laughs.

"I want to thank the Pioneers organization, my coaches, teammates, and the staff, as well as my family. Mostly, my wife. If it wasn't for her and the guidance she's given me for too many years to count, I don't know where I'd be right now."

The questions start immediately.

"What are you going to do?" a reporter asks.

"I'm not sure," I tell them all. "Right now, hang with my kids and help my wife. My stepdad offered me a coaching spot on the high school team, and my stepbrother is quite the athlete and has asked me to train him and get him ready for college."

"Won't you miss football?" another asks.

"Of course, but it'll always be a part of my life. And hell . . ." I pause and shrug. "Maybe next year I'll come out of retirement." There isn't a doubt in my mind the Pioneers are in the corner seeing red. They're the ones who jerked me around on a new contract and brought in Kyle Zimmerman—which I'm still pissed about, given Peyton's history with him—as well as drafted a quarterback in the first-round draft. I'm not their future and when I didn't take any of the offers that came my way, they figured I'd sign a new contract for peanuts. The offer was insulting especially after I won them a championship.

Their one and only.

"Noah." A voice in the back catches my attention. "Why didn't you take any of the offers other teams made?"

I try to see who's asking but the lights are too bright.

"Honestly, I wanted to stay in Portland."

I hope that stings.

I take a deep breath. "I want to thank you for all the support over the years. It's been a pleasure playing for the people of Portland." I turn off the microphone and stand. More questions are asked but I ignore them and walk off stage and out the door, heading to the small room where I waited for the press conference to start.

Before I can even sit down, Peyton rushes in and pulls me into her arms. Somehow, I manage to shut the door. As soon as it clicks shut, I let the tears flow. I'm angry with the Pioneers, but also damn happy they thought they could screw me over. Now, I get to be home with Maverick, Jace, and Juniper. I can give back to Beaumont and help Mack's team thrive. Maybe even bring another championship to Beaumont High.

And if I have a change of heart, I'll come back. There's a team out there that wants me, even if it's for a year or two. That team just won't be my beloved Portland Pioneers.

❧

Signed Paperback √
Vote for Liam Swag √
Hot Dad's Club Swag √
Visit HeidiMclaughlin.com

The Beginning of Forever

THE PORTLAND PIONEERS:
A BEAUMONT SERIES NEXT GENERATION
SPIN-OFF
Fourth Down
Fair Catch
False Start

THE SEAPORT SERIES
The Lobster Trap
The Love in Sunsets

CAPE HARBOR SERIES
After All
Until Then

THE ARCHER BROTHERS
Here with Me
Choose Me
Save Me
Here with Us
Choose Us

The Archer Boxset

NASHVILLE NIGHTS

Sangria

LOST IN YOU SERIES

Lost in You

Lost in Us

THE BOYS OF SUMMER

Third Base

Home Run

Grand Slam

Hawk

NORTHPORT U SERIES

Line Change

THE REALITY DUET

Blind Reality

Twisted Reality

SOCIETY X

Dark Room

Viewing Room

Play Room

THE CLUTCH SERIES

Roman

STANDALONE NOVELS

Stripped Bare

Blow

Sexcation

Before I'm Gone

HOLIDAY NOVELS

Santa's Secret

It's a Wonderful Holiday

Stranded with the One

Love in Print

THE DATING SERIES

A Date for Midnight

A Date with an Admirer

A Date for Good Luck

A Date for the Hunt

A Date for the Derby

A Date to Play Fore

A Date with a Foodie

A Date for the Fair

A Date for the Regatta

A Date for the Masquerade

A Date with a Turkey

A Date with an Elf

ENJOY THIS SAMPLE OF SANGRIA

You're never prepared for *that* moment. It could be anything from finding out you're pregnant or learning that your band, the one you've been in since you were seventeen, has just been nominated for a *Grammy*. I wish my moment were one of those, but unfortunately, mine comes in the form of finding out my husband of ten years, Van Phillips, has been having an affair.

And how does one find this out? Well, if you're me, you walk into your publicist's office to find your husband banging her assistant. I mean I'm happy that it's not my publicist bent over her desk with my husband pounding into her because that would really ruin my day.

There is no recovery for something like this. Even as I stand here with my mouth open with tears streaming down my face, *nothing* fixes this. Not the look of regret that he gives me as he pulls out of her and quickly stuffs himself back into his pants. Not the "oh shit" look she flashes as she hurries to fix her skirt, making me wonder where the fuck her panties are.

You're not prepared when your publicist actually walks

into her office oblivious that two people were just fucking on her desk and she asks if you're ready to get to work on your next tour.

What the fuck does someone do in this situation? There isn't a handbook on how to handle your husband when he gets caught cheating, let alone when you find out he has been unfaithful, although there should be because it seems to happen more often than not in Los Angeles. It's clear that I should've taken some classes on how to handle my emotions by the death glare he's given me. It's as if I'm supposed to "man up" and pretend as if nothing has happened. Like I am somehow at fault here.

Unfortunately, that is exactly what I do because I'm moving on autopilot, still trying to decipher if what I saw was real or an optical illusion because I can't fathom why my husband would cheat on me. It's not like we don't have a healthy sex life. In fact, he had no qualms taking care of my needs this morning. Apparently, I didn't take care of his, though.

I take one of the two seats in front of Laura's desk, cringing when she sets a pile of folders in the spot where my husband had her assistant bent over, the same one who is now scurrying away to fetch coffee. Not that I would drink anything she hands me because for all I know, she's trying to kill me so she can have my cheating-ass bastard of a spouse all to herself. Newsflash, Trina. . . Trisha. . . Tanya, what-ever the fuck her name is. . . she can have him. As far as I'm concerned this is unforgivable, and the fact that he's sitting down next to me as if nothing has happened makes my skin crawl.

Oh God, he fucking smells like her cheap ass perfume too. I pretend to gag. Except I'm really gagging since my stomach is doing its own version of gymnastics and I have a feeling that I'm about to lose my breakfast all over Laura's desk any second now. I lean away and not so subtly move my chair farther from him. He reaches out to touch me, but I glare at him. I throw so many daggers that I'm imagining each one hitting him square in his chest. He must understand that I don't want to be fucked with right now because he pulls his hand away.

That is until the tart walks back in with two cups of coffee. Laura doesn't look up from the paper she's reading when her mug is set on her desk, but my husband, he fucking perks up like this bitch is his only means to feed his caffeine addiction. And because I am living in some alternative universe, she has no qualms about brushing up against his arm and making sure he can see her tits when she unnecessarily bends over to give him his coffee.

"That's it, I'm out of here," I say as I stand up.

Laura looks up quickly, she's confused, and rightly so.

"Sit down, Zara," Van has the nerve to say. I can't even be bothered to look at him so I look at Laura and smile as best I can because right now shit hurts inside and all I want to do is break down and cry.

"I walked in a few minutes early for our meeting and found Van and your assistant fucking on your desk. You might want to sterilize it and find a new assistant because if you don't, I'm walking."

I don't need Laura to say anything. The wide eyes and open mouth are enough for me to know that I've shocked her. Behind me, I can hear Van yelling my name, but he's not following me. No, he chose to stay back with the bimbo instead of getting up and chasing after his wife to tell her how sorry he is and that what he did was a mistake. But I know better. I could tell by the look on his face that he was only sorry that he didn't get to finish before he got caught.

Outside the sun is shining, and it's hot. So hot that I'm sweating and my breathing is labored because I'm on the verge of a meltdown. I decide to walk, to get lost in the crowd even though that is nearly impossible because people are calling my name. They're grabbing at me, asking for a picture, an autograph and I can't stop and give them what they want.

I slip inside a tourist store where I can buy a fake Hollywood star and use the attached stickers to make my name. That would've been easier than paying the ridiculous fee that my band, Reverend Sister, paid in order to get a legit star on the Walk of Fame. I keep my head down and pick up a T-shirt that reads "I Almost Got Famous in Hollywood" which is something I would never be caught dead in and snag a hat off the rack. Anything I can do to hide my platinum blonde and purple hair from the people on the street. I'm not expecting it to help much, but a little would be nice.

Thankfully I have enough cash to pay for my items, and luckily the clerk doesn't recognize me, or if he does, he's not a fan and couldn't care less that Zara Phillips is in his store buying ridiculous Hollywood propaganda. Either way, I'm grateful that he's not asking for a selfie because there's no doubt in my mind that I look like utter shit. The last thing I need is my face on Instagram with comments leading to speculation that I'm stoned and on my way to rehab.

On my way to divorce court is more like it. I can't imagine what those headlines will be like. Of course, no one will believe that Van Phillips would do such a horrible thing to his precious Zara, his high school sweetheart, the love of his life and soul mate. Yet he did and did so without giving me a second thought.

Thinking about Van and whatever the hell her name is, sends my heart and stomach in opposite directions. I thank the clerk and don my newly purchased disguise before stepping back out and into the foot traffic. My name is called less, and it's more of people questioning whether or not they're getting lucky and seeing me walking down the street. Any other day I'd be happy to stop and chat with them, but not today. Today I want to get home and figure out what I'm supposed to do, and where I'm supposed to go from here because any decision that I make, is not going to be an easy one.

Our lives, Van's and mine, are intertwined in so many ways. From the time he joined my silly little garage band to the day we took our friendship to the next level. Everything we did, we did as a team with people around us and now those people depend on us. Reverend Sister isn't Van's or mine, it's ours and only works together if we're in it together and right now I don't want to be anywhere near him.

By the time the tears start to fall, and I mean really fall, I'm halfway home, and my phone is ringing with Van calling. The alerts are going off like crazy because the paparazzi are relentless and insist on snapping pictures of people. And when they put them online they add the most ridiculous headlines, except these are spot on, and tell people about my impending breakdown. It's coming. I can feel the gut-wrenching ache, my heart being ripped out of my chest, and every muscle and bone in my body in pain. The takeover is slow and almost alien-like. I can feel it in my toes, moving its way up my legs. It'll take some time for my brain to really figure it out. For the light bulb to go off that my marriage is over.

And it is over. I can't forget what I saw and if I can't do that there is no way I could forgive him. There is no way that I'd let him touch me after what I witnessed. The thought has me doubled over, and someone is yelling from a passing car, asking if I'm okay. Mentally I flip them off because do I look okay? No, I don't. Nothing about my appearance screams that I am okay.

Van's car is in the driveway when I reach the gate to our house. I stand there, like a celebrity stalker, looking at the property. The half-circle driveway with its pristine concrete leads to two amazing French doors that I chose. Beyond those doors, the marble flooring that I had to have extends up the sweeping staircase and fills the hallway that leads to my bedroom with its balcony that overlooks my swimming pool. Everything about this house is what I wanted, complete with an empty room for a nursery because damn it, Van promised me we'd start trying for a baby.

What a liar he is. What a snake and a cheat. Why would he do this to me? The question is, do I even want to know? Do I want him to tell me that I nag him too much or that he doesn't love me anymore? Could I take those words from the man that I have given everything to? The one that I have been in love with since he walked into my garage and pulled a set of drumsticks out of his back pocket and went to town on the set of drums that were set up. Watching the muscles in his arms flex and the magic he created was an epic turn on.

No, I don't think I could because knowing that my husband thought it was okay to stick his dick into another woman while still married to me. . . really there's no excuse. I punch the code for the gate and step through, and when I enter the house, it's quiet except for the sound of my heavy footsteps.

There are two choices in front of me: One—go find him and confront him. Two—start packing his shit so he can get the fuck out. Option two is what I choose because it's the most raging action I can think of right now. Kicking him out